STRAIGHT OUTTA
CRONGTON

Also by Alex Wheatle

Liccle Bit

Crongton Knights

STRAIGHT OUTTA CRONGTON

ALEX WHEATLE

ATOM

ATOM

First published in Great Britain in 2017 by Atom

3 5 7 9 10 8 6 4 2

A CIP catalogue record for this book
is available from the British Library.

ISBN 978-0-349-00288-0

Typeset in Palatino by M Rules
Printed and bound in Great Britain by
Clays Ltd, St Ives plc

Papers used by Atom are from well-managed forests
and other responsible sources.

Atom
An imprint of
Little, Brown Book Group
Carmelite House
50 Victoria Embankment
London EC4Y 0DZ

An Hachette UK Company
www.hachette.co.uk

www.atombooks.co.uk

Dedicated to the women who marched all over the world on the 21st of January, 2017.

Contents

1

Three Meals a Day

'Mum! Why d'you let *him* take my dinner money?'

She was sitting on her bed, tying her dressing gown belt around her waist – it needed washing but I had used the last of the bio capsules to clean my PE kit the previous evening. Sleep clogged up the corners of her eyes. Her mascara now looked as if she'd applied it with a mop. Stupid woman couldn't even wash her freaking make-up off before she went to bed.

'Mum!' I repeated.

She stretched and yawned before she finally answered me. 'There are a couple of crusty rolls in the kitchen and I think there's a scrape of peanut butter in the cupboard.'

Her voice sounded rough, as if she had been eating bristled doormats.

'Let *him* eat the rolls,' I spat.

She covered her ears.

'Mum. I need some money for school!'

'Stop shouting, Mo. Can't hear myself bleeding think; I've got a ringing headache. Get off to school. Aren't you late?'

I took my mobile out of my back pocket. Eight-twenty. *Cell bells! Holman's gonna bruise my ears again.*

'I'm going back to bed,' Mum said. She scooped the gunk from her eye with a fingernail and wiped it on her dressing gown before flopping back on to the mattress. 'Take the rolls, Mo, and get off my case, will ya? We didn't get in till after three.'

Half of the quilt was on the floor. There was a dent in the mattress where *he'd* slept. The ashtray was full. The room stank of beer. The bin was full of cans. I swore I'd never drink alcohol. Mum pulled the bedding over her head, turned her back to me and curled up like an unborn baby.

Frustration crackled inside me. 'You're freaking *useless.*'

'So ya always say. Can I get some sleep now?'

I stood there, arms folded, staring at her, but she didn't move a muscle. I heard a noise from the kitchen. *He* was still here. I left Mum's room, slamming the door behind me, and turned into the hallway.

He was sitting down at the kitchen table, sipping a mug of tea. He threw me an oh-shit-Mo-hasn't-gone-to-school-yet look. I hoped he burned his lips. Name-brand trainers niced up his feet. (Where'd he got them? He was supposed to be skint.) He wore a too-tight Real Madrid football shirt, number seven on the back. The shape of his man boobs underneath almost made me spew. Jack Sparrow was inked on his fat right bicep. A pirate ship was tattooed on the other. His goatee beard scratched his neck. How could Mum smack tongues with him?

I looked at him dead on. 'That five pounds Mum gave you – that's my dinner money.'

'Those rolls in the kitchen are for you,' he said. His reasonable tone pissed me off big time.

'I don't want any freaking stale rolls for lunch; just give me the fiver and I'll be off your radar. You and Mum can go back to your drinking party.'

'You've got a dirty mouth for a fifteen year old,' he said. He stared at me as if he wanted me to smile at his miserable wit but I would *never* give that prick-head the satisfaction.

'If you don't give me that fiver it'll get dirtier,' I challenged.

'And you say you want to do media in college? With a mouth like that? They're not gonna let you read the *Six O'Clock News*.'

'*Photography* and media. And I'm not playing with you, Lloyd. Give me the freaking fiver!'

'I have to sign on today and go for a job interview in Ashburton – warehouse work. You should be wishing me luck.'

'Then use your welfare wheels – your *feet*. You could do with the exercise.'

He gave me a hard look but I didn't give a shit. He wasn't my dad.

'You shouldn't have killed all your money on beer,' I added. 'How much did that cost ya? Or cost *Mum*?'

Lloyd stood up. His chair scraped out behind him. His

glare intensified. He took two strides towards me but I didn't flake. I returned his stare like a shark.

'It was my birthday on Sunday—'

'So?' I cut him off. 'It's Tuesday now. I see them name-brands; you've been spoilt rotten. It was my birthday two months ago and I didn't even get the "n" of nothing!'

'I haven't seen your mum since Friday. Do we have to ask your permission to celebrate?'

'I don't give a freaking spare rib how you celebrate,' I ripped. 'Just gimme the fiver!'

'I'll be getting my money from the social on Friday,' Lloyd said. 'I'll give you back the fiver then. I'll even treat you to a pizza or take you out to the Cheesecake Lounge.'

Sit in the Cheesecake Lounge with him – is he nuts? He must've drunk more than I thought last night. *God!* If I ever got as liquor-happy as them, I hoped someone would put me out of my misery.

'You choose,' he offered. 'My treat.'

Again, his calmness sucked the patience out of me. I stepped up to him and made a grab for his back pocket. He caught my wrist and pushed me away. Lloyd was fat but strong. He picked up his tracksuit top from the back of the chair and pulled it on. Before making his way to the front door he seized me with another stare. 'Mo, you need to calm down. Chill out. What's this all about? Eh? You and Sam having problems?'

'How many times do I have to tell you? Sam *isn't* my boyfriend.'

'Could've fooled me. Have a good day at school.'

I could smell his pound-shop deodorant as he passed by me.

How could Mum sleep with that jailbird? He acted all calm and nice now, but he treated us like shit and got away with it. He was just using Mum but she was in denial. Didn't she ever learn from her past mistakes? When any man gave her attention she went all *I'll-do-whatever-you-want-My-Tonkness*. Stupid woman. *God!* It made me cringe when she called him 'My Tonkness'. It had to stop. We flexed so much better when he wasn't around. If she wouldn't stand up for us, I would.

I ran up behind Lloyd and booted the back of his left leg as hard as I could. He hopped as he turned around. First shock then anger filled his eyes. I tried to punch him in the ribs but my fist only found flab. I aimed to boot his balls. 'Gimme back my freaking fiver, you prick!'

He grabbed my arms tight and I felt his fingers crushing into me. He pulled me towards him. I got a blast of stale beer from his mouth. I kicked out again. I didn't quite get his coconuts but caught him somewhere near the groin. He closed his eyes and grimaced on contact. *Good!*

His nails were scoring my skin and his eyes narrowed into hateful slits. He released his grip and shoved me away. I lost my footing and crashed down on my butt.

'Enough, Mo!'

His fat cheeks were twitching. He made a crunched fist. He was simmering. Dread flooded through my arteries. He wouldn't dare.

'*Don't* push me, Mo! I don't wanna hurt you. Why can't you accept that me and your mum are tight now? *Deal* with it.'

'Is that what you do to Mum when you don't get what you want? Is it? When she can't give you the money you want?

Like pushing girls over, do you? Did you do time for that too? Why don't you take your bad-breed, fist-happy self back to prison where your lumpy ass belongs?'

Lloyd paused. I knew my last comment burned him. *Good!*

'Go to school, Mo.' He opened the door. 'Try to calm down.'

'Don't come back!' I screamed after him.

He slammed the door. I opened it and shouted down the stairs. 'Leave me and Mum alone!'

Lloyd didn't reply. I went back inside.

I stomped back into Mum's bedroom. 'Did you see that, Mum? *Your boyfriend* was about to hit me. *Your* jail-bird, saggy-ass, can't-get-a-job boyfriend. And it ain't the first time.'

Nothing.

'Mum?' She was fast asleep. I shook her awake. 'I said, he was about to smack me again, Mum!'

She rolled on to her back but she didn't open her eyes. 'He's promised not to lay a finger on you ever again. I made him say that to ya in front of ya face. And didn't he apologise? He's been trying to make it up to ya ever since, Mo, but you won't let him. Now go on with ya! I don't wanna get any more letters.'

With that she curled back into a ball. I glared at her shape.

I hated living here. Hated it!

I went back to my room to get my stuff. I caught a glimpse of myself in the mirror – my hair was like a bad 1980s pop video, but whatever. I grabbed my school rucksack and headed out.

I'd gotta find somewhere else to live. Maybe Elaine would have me.

2

Sam Bramwell

We lived at number thirteen on the second floor of Slipe House in South Crongton. It'd been home for as long as I could remember but Mum said when I was a baby we'd spent some time in a hostel for beat-down women. She didn't say much about those days.

I felt my shoulder throb and wondered if the council had a place for teenage girls who were being smacked-down by their mum's boyfriends.

I trudged down one flight of concrete steps. Sam's mum was standing outside her front door, wearing her bus-driver's uniform and a suspicious expression.

'What's with all the cussing and slamming going on upstairs? Are you and Clarrie-May all right?'

Lorna Bramwell was seven years older than my mum but she looked a world younger.

'We're good,' I replied. 'It's the same old. Had a slight dis-agreement with Mum's boyfriend.'

She approached and inspected me, running a finger over my cheek. Her dyed-amber dreadlocks fell across my shoulder. 'Did he do anything to you, Maureen?'

I wanted to answer 'Yes,' but something stopped me.

It wasn't the first time that Lloyd had had an issue with me. The previous Saturday morning, Sam had come round first thing and fried me some eggs, dumplings and plantain for breakfast. I saved the leftovers to eat later – we were out with Elaine all day – but when I got back home, hungry, and checked the fridge, there was diddly-scratch in there. Mum had given my food to Lloyd. I was steaming. Mum and I had a real ding-dong. I swore, she slapped me, and Lloyd made things worse by weighing in. 'You shouldn't use foul lan-guage against your mother,' he said, kinda grinning as if he was enjoying seeing us fight. It was all his fault.

I went to bed furious and famished. Later that night, I noticed Lloyd's Real Madrid shirt drying in the bathroom. I picked it up and pissed on it. The stain covered the number seven. I left it in a heap outside Mum's bedroom door. Lloyd clearly found it because the next morning he crashed into my room and backhanded me while I was still asleep. The force of the blow knocked me out of bed. My nose spilled blood for the longest time and I had to walk around most of that morning with bog paper stuffed up my nostrils while staring at the ceiling.

It was worth it, though. *Hate him!*

'No,' I finally replied to Lorna. 'If he put one fingernail on me you'd know about it. I'd holler about it from the top of the slab. Trust me on that.'

Lorna angled her head and narrowed her eyes. 'You sure?'

'Double sure.' I smiled. 'It's all minor. I'll be all right.'

'Hmmmm.'

I wanted to change the subject. 'Sam gone?'

'Yes, he left about an hour ago. He needed to finish some homework and wanted to get a book out of the school library.'

'I'll catch up with him,' I said. 'See you later, Ms Bramwell.'

'Try to have a good day, Mo.'

I burned my soles to school but I was still fifteen minutes late. The receptionist was writing my name down in the late-comers' dot com book when I saw Holman. He was wearing a black tie and black shoes so shiny I could see my face. He approached me with his hands behind his back. He was about to say something but he checked himself. He studied my face as if he was a plastic surgeon looking over an ageing A-lister.

'Everything all right, Maureen?' he asked.

'Yeah – why shouldn't it be?'

'You do realise you're late again?'

'Of course I realise! Why do you think I'm in a rush?'

'Do . . . you want to talk to me about anything?'

Does he wait for me every morning at reception in the hope that I'm gonna spill my issues? Dickhead.

'No! I don't wanna talk about anyting. So shift your shiny shoes and let me get to class.'

I didn't wait for Holman's response and felt a bit bad. I knew he meant well but sometimes he got on my case.

I joined Elaine in history. She was wearing enormous fake eyelashes. When she noticed me, she fluttered them. Ms Gorman didn't love my lateness – she didn't say anything but her eyes followed me into my seat. On a screen behind her was an old photograph, in grainy black and white. Something about the rise of the Nazi Party.

'Why are you late?' Elaine asked.

'It's a long one,' I replied.

'And what happened to your hair? More on point, what *didn't* happen to it?'

'I should ask you the same ting about your lashes. You look like you've got the Gates of Mordor stuck over your eyes.'

'Burn you!'

'Burn you back, bitch!'

'Elaine Jackson and Maureen Baker!' Ms Gorman broke our flow. 'If you really want to insult each other, can you at least try to put it on hold until my lesson is completed?'

Sarcastic cow. Gorman thought she was so witty. I swore I'd tell her about her armpits one of these days and point out that her tight trousers won't get her on *Crongton's Top Model*.

'So are you rolling to the movies with us after school?' Elaine whispered.

'I can't,' I replied.

'Why not?'

'Cos my funding's low. I haven't even got any dinner money.'

'Again? Don't fret. I'll get you someting from the Chicken Coop.'

I nodded. 'Wings and fries will go down neatly. They're only £1.99.'

'And we'll get you in to the movies.' Elaine grinned. 'We'll try the same skank we did last time. So stop bitching about your budget and step up.'

'Elaine Jackson!' Gorman shrieked again. 'I realise how difficult this is for you, but can you stop discussing your after-school plans until break? Could you do that?'

'But I've done all the work!' Elaine protested. She stood up, placed her hands on her hips and did that Turkish belly dancer head move – I practised it in my bedroom but could never get it right. 'The Nazis were led by this devious bruv with moustache issues called Hitler. He wanted to blame someone for Germany's issues after the First World War so he pointed a big nasty arrow at the Jews. Then he went all land-greedy cos he wanted *everyone* to do his mad salute. He blitzed the next-door neighbours, Poland, which England didn't love so they declared war and—'

'That's enough of your performance, Elaine,' Gorman cut her off. 'You can sit down. I'm just *asking* you not to interrupt the focus of others.'

Elaine sat down, turned to me and dropped her acting tone. 'So are you coming?'

'What are we gonna watch?'

'Not sure – dunno what's on.'

'I don't care,' I said, 'as long as I can get outta the house.'

Elaine tried to read me again. 'What's kicking off in your yard, Mo?'

'Nothing,' I lied.

We made it to break without Gorman moaning at us again. Elaine went off to see Ms Crawford, her drama teacher, while I looked for Sam – at morning break he was usually in the playground playing table tennis but he wasn't there. I tried the library and there she was, with her swimmer's legs and *Hollyoaks* face: Shevray Clarke, Sam's new squeeze. She was standing outside the entrance with two of her crew, blocking the way, and when she spotted me she cut her eyes as if I'd just eaten her cat and puked it out over her pillow. Peering through a window I could see Sam staring at a computer screen. I decided to be polite to Shevray.

'Can you get out of my way, please?'

Shevray glanced at her two friends before she gave me another eye-pass. 'Can't you leave him alone now?' she spat. 'We all know you're trying to make a play for him. Vacancy's taken, so stop haunting him.'

'Yeah!' One of the other girls glared at me. 'Step off!'

'Shevray, trust me,' I warned, 'it hasn't been a good week for me, so don't drop your insecurity issues on my bunions today. I haven't got time for your shit. Sam and I are just friends – always have been – so get your skinny ass out of my way before I smack your face into a rectangle.'

Shevray wasn't skinny. She had stroke-a-licious legs. It pissed me off no end.

She crossed her arms and tried to glare me out. *Stupid bitch.* As if that was gonna scare me. I returned her stare while almost pushing my face into hers. She backed away a step. 'She ain't worth it,' she said to her sistrens. 'Let's skip.'

Shevray and her crew rolled away. One of them looked

over her shoulder and gave me a bitch look. On another day I would've boxed that stare right into the biology lab but I couldn't be arsed right then. I just wanted to see Sam.

I found him inside at the computers. One half of his head was covered in afro and the other was styled in cornrow plaits. *Cute.* When he became aware of me, he stood up and gave me a warm hug. It was good to feel his arms around me, to sense his cheek against mine. It made me feel all tingly. It reeled me back to the time we dated. I closed my eyes. It lasted three weeks over the summer holidays. None of our friends knew. It was all niceness that way. No one blocking our flow. Stolen kisses in his room when his mum was at work. Me constantly telling him to take his hands off my butt and my chest – I wasn't ready.

Then he had to go to Jamaica with his mum to bury his grandmother. He was gone four weeks. When he came back things were just ... awkward. He wanted us to be friends again. I didn't love that decision. In fact I hated it, but I had to ride with it – I'd known him since I was dot years old and if it was a choice between being friends and losing him for good, well, there was no question. Still, it clawed me to see him linking with Shevray. *Why the skirts and blouses would he wanna go there?* I knew damn well why. Long legs, a decent curved bumper and an E4 series face. *Boil her!* I pulled away.

'Better not let Shevray see this,' I laughed. 'What you up to?'

'Oh, just doing my research for the Black History Month wall,' Sam replied. 'About Mary Seacole and her role as a nurse in the Crimean War. It's getting there.'

Sam's Black History Month project was impressive to the max – history was his thing – but I wanted to deal with the Shevray issue. It bugged the heartbeats outta me. 'Your new squeeze tried to block me from stepping into the library just now. You're gonna have to chat to her. Trust me, if she don't back off I'm gonna get coarse with her.'

'She's just upset cos she thinks we see too much of each other.'

'I've known you longer than her,' I protested. 'We grew up together, live in the same slab, went to the same nursery and primary school. We blew out each other's candles at birthday parties. Our mums took us shopping in buggies and—'

'That was then,' Sam cut me off. 'I can't spend as much time with you cos—'

'Cos she gives it up easy. Admit it! That's why you went for her. And in the little time we had ... I didn't.'

'It's not that.'

'Stop your lying. You're just like the rest of the brothers in our year – some new girl flashes a bit of flesh, pastes on some make-up, wears a Hollywood rom-com bra and all your blood rushes to one place.'

'She's got more to her than that,' argued Sam. 'She's the top swimmer in our school. She's bright.'

'She's bright at dropping her clothes nuff times a day!'

Sam shook his head. 'That's uncalled for.'

It was uncalled for but I wanted to rage at him. 'She gave you grief the other day cos you came around and cooked me brekkie. Admit it! Why d'you tell her?'

'Cos that was the truth.'

'She didn't have to know. That's *our* time.'

'She's my girlfriend, Mo. You want me to lie to her about my movements?'

'What have your movements with me got to do with her? We've been sharing shit for ever. When your mum was outta work I helped you out – brought you groceries – and didn't broadcast it to the whole damn world.'

Sam's face curled into a smile. 'Didn't you jack them from Dagthorn's?' He started laughing. *God! Wish he didn't do that. Fittest of the fittest! Can't believe he's slurping tongues with long-assed Shevray.* 'Do you realise what would've happened if my mum had found out?'

'So? It's the thought that matters.'

'Look, Mo, I appreciate—'

'No, *you* listen,' I cut him off. 'If your girl's gonna spit warts all because you come to my yard now and then, don't bother banging on my gates again. I *mean* it!'

I didn't mean it but I said it. *Shit!* He was the only good thing in my life. When we were kids he'd bring over his Connect Four and we'd play for ever. He'd make me birthday cards from the stuff his mum brought back from work. He calmed me down when me and Mum had a ding-dong. Whenever his mum bought him new garms he'd check with me to see if they were on point. Sam was the one who took me home and nursed my wounds if I got in a fight at school. But he was with *her*.

'It doesn't have to be this way, Mo. We could be good—'

'*Don't* say the F word. I've got all the friends I want. Yes, it *does* have to be this way. Keep yourself outta my radar. You're *hers* now.'

Sam looked at me hard, not quite believing what I laid down. But he had to hear it. *I just can't do this shit any more.*

'If that's how you want it, Mo, I got to respect that. Well . . . Thanks for helping me out with that research about Marcus Garvey,' he said. The tone of his face switched. 'That saved me nuff time.'

Damn! Why is he so reasonable?

'Gotta find Elaine,' I said. I could barely look at him. 'Enjoy your day.'

Before Sam muttered something I was out of there. I didn't look back. I skipped to the girls' toilets, found a cubicle and parked on the seat for the next twenty minutes. I held my face in my hands and cried. I had to let it out.

I managed to compose myself enough for my next lesson. Ms Riddlesworth knew maths was my thing so she never bitched about me being late for class – she just smiled at me as I took my seat.

3

Mission Impossible

Home time. I headed out. Elaine was standing outside the school gates with Naomi Brisset. Naomi lived in a children's home unit in South East Crongton and had tried some mad ways to escape it. Not much impressed Elaine and me, but the story of Naomi's latest great escape made us cry with laughter. She'd baked hash cookies for the care workers, so while she was packing her bags the staff were falling over each other in fits of giggles. They found Naomi two days later crashing with some Rasta dude above a Korean restaurant in Ashburton. Despite Naomi broadcasting to the world that they were engaged, social services storm-trooped her ass back to South Crong.

'Mo!' Naomi called. Her frizzed-up hair moved with the breeze. 'The next *Mission Impossible* is on! Please tell me you wanna see that rather than some sad comic-book film—'

'*Fantastic Four* is playing,' cut in Elaine. 'And the bruv who plays the fire guy – whatshisname? – is the living beefness. Anyway, we're *always* watching Tom Cruise films. He's *ancient*!'

'He's over fifty but I wouldn't say no,' I laughed. 'And he still does his own stunts.'

Elaine pulled a face. 'Mo, you're disgusting! Would you seriously give it up for an ash-head?'

'His hair's brown,' I argued.

'Are you living in my world, Mo? He's probably got a personal colourist living in his crib. Anyway you lot are taking liberties! I'm the only one who's got any funds so it's my choice.'

'You're the one who always wants to step to the movies,' I said. 'You could save your pennies and we could just chill out.'

'Chill out where?' Elaine wondered.

'The Shenk-I-Sheck,' Naomi suggested.

'Naomi,' Elaine said with disgust. 'Are you sick? It's full of old people. That's where my pops takes his girlfriend when he can find a babysitter.'

'And my uncle goes there too,' put in Naomi. 'He's on the level – he always used to visit me in the home on Sundays and give me little treats.'

'That sounds all wrong,' I said.

'I'm *talking* about lollipops and Starbursts!' replied Naomi. 'He'd give me cigarettes an' all.'

'Oh,' I said.

'Is that the uncle with the black fedora, smiley jacket and black plimsolls?' Elaine chuckled.

'Yeah,' replied Naomi. 'He's a performance poet – or

reckons he is. He's always down the Shenk-I-Sheck on a Friday night.'

'Picking up girls,' I added. 'He's the living perv. Whenever he looks at me I feel a button popping off and a zip coming down.'

'Another reason why I'm not going down the Shenk-I-Sheck,' said Elaine.

'He might ogle a bit but my Uncle Dan's harmless,' said Naomi.

'Say that to the judge,' I said. 'They're all after one ting – trying to get someting for nothing.'

'The guys don't come all empty-handed,' reasoned Naomi. 'They actually offer to buy you a drink. Last time I was down there this brother bought me a whisky and Coke and a straw-berry cupcake. His name was Stranger Kroll – he was wearing this cool hat I wanted to swipe. When he went to take a piss I sank my drink and bounced out. You see, we don't have to spend any funds, we can listen to some old school beats and some bruv will step up sooner or later to buy us shit. What's the big wrong in that?'

Elaine breathed in hard through her nose and shook her head. 'Naomi, I love you to the max but read my lipstick,' she said. 'I am *not* stepping down the Shenk-I-Sheck. Besides, we're still in school garms so we won't get through the border check. That's the final on that one. If you guys can't think of anyting better to do, let's roll to Movieworld.'

Movieworld was just off Crongton High Street. Naomi and I waited outside the emergency exit on a side street while

Elaine bought her ticket. By the time Naomi had blazed two cigarettes, I heard the door being pushed open. Elaine's head appeared. Her eyelashes fluttered like ravens doing synchronised sit-ups. *'Hurry up!'* she said.

'Where's my gummy bears?' asked Naomi. 'You know I love my gummy bears when I'm watching a movie.'

'Are you taking the piss? Step the frick in!'

We pulled the door closed and made our way up a dimly lit staircase. Elaine led the way. I always expected the alarm to scream out when we tried this skank but it never did. I'd do this even if I did have the funding to buy a ticket – it was an adrenalin rush and a half. We found ourselves in the corridor leading to screens one, two and three. Ads for all the upcoming features lined the walls.

'I need to take a piss,' said Naomi.

We bounced into the ladies'. While Naomi did her business I took a drink from the cold tap. Nerves always made me thirsty. We rolled into the screen all laid-back, as if Tom Cruise was a blood relation, and took three seats in the back row. I could've done with a bucket of popcorn or a box of Maltesers but skankers couldn't be choosers.

The screen was showing trailers but even though I loved trailers I couldn't help thinking back over the day – about my row with Lloyd over the fiver and about telling Sam I no longer wanted him knocking my gates. *Why did I say that? God! I'm gonna miss that half-afroed piece of henchness dropping by for a late-night chat.*

The film was a good distraction for me, otherwise I would've gone home, locked myself in my bedroom and cried like a nine-year-old One Direction fan. Then I'd have had to put my headphones on so not to suffer listening to Mum and Lloyd bumping the headboard and bruising the floorboards.

After the film we all stood round outside the cinema. 'It's not even seven yet,' said Naomi. 'We can still go home, change and chill at the Shenk-I-Sheck. What are you two saying?'

'I've got some English to do,' replied Elaine. 'And I'm peckish so need to get back to my yard.'

'What about you, Mo?'

I didn't want to go home, at least not until Mum and *he* were asleep. But the *Shenk-I-Sheck*?

'Nah,' I finally replied. 'I'm too tired. And I've got some homework to do too.'

'You two are boring, man,' Naomi protested. 'At least tell me you're gonna be up for shopping on Saturday?'

'Er . . . we'll let you know about that one,' said Elaine.

'You two are so grey,' said Naomi. 'But I don't wanna step back to my unit yet – you don't wanna know how boring my key worker is. "How are you feeling today? I know you miss Crumbs. Are you connecting better with your teachers? Are you beginning to feel positive about things?" *God!* She goes on for ever.'

'Then ask to see someone else,' I suggested.

'Nah – they're all the same. There's a bruv I know who's got a stash of dragon hip pills. We could—'

Elaine abruptly pulled Naomi's arm. She confronted her head on, almost jabbing her eye with her finger. 'No more going round guys' yards and sampling legal highs! Remember last time?'

'You have to admit, Elaine,' I said, 'last time was too funny.'

'Funny?' Elaine raged. 'The bruv sitting next to me tried to feel me up! I warned him about it and he did the same shit again! He only got my message when I fanged his thumb and scratched his face.'

'*That* was the funny part,' I chuckled. 'His thumb was bleeding. He ran to the toilet but there wasn't any batty paper. And on our way out, Naoms swiped his Grey Goose.'

'Did you take it home?' asked Elaine.

'Do I have ten fingers? Course I did,' replied Naomi. 'I hid it in my wardrobe and had it for a nightcap for the next three evenings. There was about half a bottle left but I sold it for five notes to this kid in Year 8.'

'Why d'you sell it?' I asked.

'Cos I wanted to buy this new orange lipstick to go with these orange trousers I jacked from a store in Ashburton. Waste of friggin' money it was – started to come off after two hours.'

We all fell about in giggles.

4

Fronting Up

'So if we're not gonna chill down the Shenk-I-Sheck then what else is there to do? Homework?' Naomi asked. 'You two are sad like a soggy day in Scaraton Ash.'

'Didn't I get you in to see Tom Cruise?' Elaine said.

Naomi thought about it. 'You're *still* grey.'

Elaine jumped on Naomi and we had a play-fight in the middle of the street. By the time we'd finished I had bruises on my wrists (Naomi loved giving Chinese burns), scratches on my neck and a dead arm. We brushed ourselves off, fixed our hair and walked Naomi back to the home. She lived on Waterhouse Street, near the flats of Wareika Way. It was a three-storey house with a neat front garden. If I had spilled all the shit about Mum and her boyfriends, I could've been living in a place like this. I thought about that a lot.

We waited outside while Naomi went to get us a drink. She

came out with three beakers of orange squash. 'Sorry it's not someting stronger. They watch me like one of them spy drone things when I'm in the kitchen.'

We drank thirstily while Naomi sparked a cigarette in clear view of whoever was watching us from a window. We'd known her for a few months but she had never invited us inside. We didn't ask why.

'Don't flop out on shopping on Saturday,' Naomi said before she went inside. 'I need to get some tops. All I want you to do is watch my back.'

'I think my mum's got an agenda for me,' excused Elaine.

'And I'm walking the hoover,' I said.

Naomi shook her head and sucked her teeth.

We said goodbye and I followed Elaine back to her slab. I didn't say much but she was yapping on about going to drama school and joining some amateur theatre group to gain acting experience. We stopped by at Dagthorn's to buy chocolate and shared a bar. As we neared her place she stopped and stared hard at me. 'What's going on, Mo?'

'What d'you mean?' I replied.

'You've hardly said Jack or Jill to me since we left the cinema,' she said. 'I can tell when you're stressing out about someting. What really happened this morning?'

'Woke up late.'

'And a pig screwed a duck on the moon!'

'I'm *not* lying, Elaine.'

'And Tom Cruise is waiting for me upstairs to take me out to dinner. Come on, Mo.'

I stared at the ground.

'*Mo!*'

Uncomfortable silence. I could feel her eyes fire-poking into me. Finally I looked up.

'It's Mum's boyfriend,' I admitted.

'What did he do?' Her eyes flashed with anger. She seemed just as mad at me for not spilling to her as she was vexed with *him*. 'Give me the full review,' Elaine demanded.

I hesitated. Elaine wasn't the type of friend who would hear my woes, pat me on the back and say, 'there, there.'

'*Mo!* Tell me the score.'

I sat down against the wall. She gave me another fierce look. I closed my eyes and I could feel my heartbeat licking my tonsils.

'We're not moving a fidget until you start leaking.'

I opened my eyes. I told her about Mum giving my food to Lloyd at the weekend, his Real Madrid football shirt, getting clapped out of bed and him raising a fist after I booted him in the leg. Then about this morning when I thought he was gonna do the same again over the fiver. She listened with nuff attention, sometimes placing a hand on my shoulder and brushing my hair out of my face. She gave me a tight hug when I finished. I couldn't stop the tears falling.

'I did wind him up a bit,' I said. 'I mean, pissing on his fave shirt. And you know my mouth when I'm ready to offload.'

'*He's* a grown man!' Elaine said. 'He has no bloody right to put his fat hand on you and fling you outta bed. You hearing me, Mo? No right at all. My pops don't live with me and we have some crazy ding-dongs when I see him but you think I'd let him smack the blusher out of my cheeks? *No freaking way!*'

'But he's your *real* dad,' I said.

'Don't matter,' Elaine replied. 'If you're seeing his lumpy chops across the brekkie table then he has to act like a proper dad.'

'What am I gonna do?' I asked. 'He's virtually moved in.'

'You're gonna tell the feds,' Elaine said.

'The feds? Ain't that drastic?'

'He raised a fist to you on Sunday, and then almost again this morning, right? Who knows what he might do when all sense skips away from his porridge ass?'

Different scenarios crashed into my head. Lloyd had only been out of prison for a few months. Mum hadn't told me why he went inside. If he had to sink oats for his brekkie again, Mum would never forgive me.

'I'm ... I'm not sure if I can tell the feds,' I said. 'Can you trust 'em? They might not believe me.'

'You have to, Mo,' said Elaine, placing an arm around my shoulder.

'Mum will go all T-Rex on me. Lloyd just got out from doing time.'

'Mo, listen to me. You're her number one priority, you hearing me? Or you're meant to be anyway. So I don't give a shit how vex she gets – Lloyd *has* to be reported. He's twice your size! One day he'll do more damage than dropping you outta your bed. He shouldn't even be gatecrashing your room!'

'But—'

'*No* buts. I'll tell you what we're gonna do. We're gonna go upstairs, get someting to eat – hopefully Gran's cooked today – and after that we're gonna march to the fed station.'

*

26

I had to keep sitting for another five minutes to download all this. Maybe one of those dragon hip pills could help me through this shit.

I followed Elaine into her yard. Before we got there, Elaine took off her false eyelashes and put them in a little purse. Her mum wasn't home but her gran was sitting on a stool in the kitchen with a tea towel draped over her shoulder. A Jamaican-flag-coloured headscarf blessed her head. She was sipping rum and Coke from a glass – the smell of it tickled my nostrils. Some old school Jamaican rock-steady was blaring out from a small ghetto blaster. 'Maureen!' she greeted. 'Long time me nuh see you! You forget where me live? You tink me dead?'

'No, no, Ms Jackson!' I replied. 'Just been proper busy. You know how it goes. Been revising, doing homework and whatnot.'

'None of this Ms Jackson foolishness, Maureen! Just call me Gran ... how is Clarrie-May?'

'She's all right,' I said. 'Still working part-time in the launderette.'

'That's good that she finally find someting to do.' She switched her attention to Elaine. 'And what time do you call this?'

'Gran, I told you I was going to the movies after school.'

'You never tell me a damn ting.'

'I told you and Mum this morning.'

Gran tried to remember. I thought it was kinda sweet. Mum never cared what time I breezed in after school.

'Aren't you forgetting someting?' Gran said.

Elaine smiled. She gave Gran a warm hug and a kiss on the cheek. *I wish Mum and me could be like that.* 'Mind you knock me drink over! You know how expensive that rum is? *Don't tell your mother.*'

'I won't.'

'You want your dinner now? Meatballs in my own home-made sauce and rice. You want to try me cooking too, Maureen? No matter what me grandchildren say, it won't murder you.'

'Yes, please.'

'Give me five minutes to warm it up.'

Elaine led me to her room. Denzel Washington stood guard on a wall overlooking her bed. Terence Howard looked all things hench on the back of her door. Piles of DVDs in plastic see-through covers wrestled for space on her dressing table. I sat on her bed. Elaine closed the door. 'I hope you're peckish, Mo. Gran always gives big portions and she hates it when you leave someting on the plate.'

'Trust me, I'm well hungry,' I said. 'Those wings and fries I had for lunch couldn't fill a skinny grasshopper.'

'Are you OK?' Elaine asked, probably sensing the dread I felt inside.

'I could do with a drink.'

'I'll get you some blackcurrant squash.'

As soon as Elaine opened the door her little bro, Lemar, burst into the room. He jumped on the bed and sat beside me.

'Get out!' Elaine barked. 'Mo hasn't got any time for you today.'

Lemar threw his arms around my neck and gave me the biggest smile in the world. *So cute.* Wished I had a liccle bruv.

'It's all right, Elaine.'

'Behave yourself!' Elaine instructed Lemar. 'And *don't* touch anyting in my room.' She went to fetch my drink.

'So how's your first year going at South Crong High?' I asked.

'Too much walking around,' Lemar complained. 'Why can't we have all our lessons in one room? The teachers should move to us! It'd make things easier.'

He bounced off the bed and started to go through Elaine's DVD collection. 'Art's my fave lesson but I wanna draw people rather than apples and oranges,' Lemar continued.

Lemar was a sweet distraction. I laughed when he told me which teachers he liked and hated. I tried to show compassion when he explained why he didn't want to change into his PE kit.

'Some drop-lip girl called me Liccle Bit,' he said.

'Don't worry about it,' I said. 'You'll soon spurt up. Trust me on that.'

'Will I?'

'Of course. Before you know it you'll be playing b-ball for the Crongton Crewnecks.'

'Really?'

'For real!'

Elaine returned five minutes later with a tray of hot food in her hands. She glared at Lemar. 'Out!'

'But I was chatting to Mo.'

'Move your backside before I boot you out.'

Lemar left in a sulk. I wanted him to stay. *Now I'll have to think about stepping and spilling to the feds.*

'This will fill you proper,' Elaine said. 'But it's a bit spicy –
Gran puts Jamaican jerk in everyting.'

By the time I'd finished my meal, my nose was running
and my chest felt like a furnace. Elaine had to get me another
drink. I sank it in one go.

'You ready?' Elaine asked.

I wasn't ready.

I nodded.

Gran was watching TV in the lounge. 'Are you going out
again?'

'Yes, Gran,' Elaine replied.

'Where? You just got here. You can't rest up your foot for
two minutes?'

'I'm helping Mo with someting.'

'And what is that?'

Elaine's open mouth stuck on pause. I had to think quickly.

'We're going to the internet cafe to do some research – for
history.'

Gran nodded. 'Take care out there, girls, and head home
as soon as you finish.'

'We will,' we chorused.

Gran didn't know it but we wouldn't be seen dead at the
Well Charged internet cafe on Bushmaster Lane. It was in the
basement of an off-licence and it stank of weed, alcohol and
bad BO. Gs sold dragon hip pills and other mad chemicals in
there and the long-bearded owner, Johnny Osbourne, who sat
on a wonky stool behind a high counter, didn't care as long
as everybody paid their tax to log on.

It took us twenty-five minutes to reach Crong fed station.

Truth was I was kinda dragging my soles. I wasn't looking forward to leaking my personal biz to the feds.

We went inside and sat down in the foyer to wait while a mum complained loudly about some gulley-rat jacking a phone from her eight-year-old son. *Stupid woman!* I thought. *Why's she buying a mobile for a kid that young?*

The longer we waited the more nervous I became. Finally, the woman finished ranting. Elaine stood up. I remained seated.

'Mo. Get up.'

We approached the desk. A male fed was standing behind the counter in a short-sleeved white shirt and tie. His chin was so smooth I thought of the Action Man Elaine had bought Lemar for his birthday a few years ago. He was filling in a form.

'I don't wanna chat to a man,' I whispered.

'We'll ask for a woman,' said Elaine.

The officer looked up and smiled. 'How can I help you?'

I can't believe I'm doing this. Mum's gonna erupt. My legs felt all funny. My heart boomed like Nelson's cannons. I had to place my hands on the counter for support.

'My friend would like to report someting serious but she doesn't wanna chat to a man,' Elaine said. 'You downloading this?'

The fed nodded. He didn't seem to be offended. 'Yes, I understand,' he said. 'Please wait here while I get someone appropriate to hear your complaint.'

I was well happy Elaine was with me.

Fifteen minutes later a female fed appeared with some lady

31

in a grey trouser suit who told us she was a family liaison something or other. She led us through the station to a quiet room furnished with a settee, plain chairs and a table, on top of which stood a plain vase with plastic flowers. *What's the freaking point of that?* White blinds covered the windows. Elaine and I chose to park on the sofa. I wondered how many victims of violence and other woes had sat on these same cushions.

'Can we get you anything?' the officer asked.

'Water,' I replied.

'I'm all right,' said Elaine.

I could feel the beads of sweat multiplying on my forehead. The vein on my left temple started to throb. *God! I'm actually doing this.* Elaine held my hand. I clenched the other. I could hear a printer coughing out paper outside. Air conditioning was whirring somewhere above. The lady who went to fetch the water was taking for ever. She finally returned. I took a sip of water. I sank another. I wondered if it would be better if I tipped it over my head.

'Are we all comfortable?' the officer asked.

I wasn't comfortable but I nodded.

'How can we help you?' the fed asked.

The liaison officer flipped over the first page of her notepad and held her pen poised for action. 'My name is Ms Sharon Hunt,' she said. 'I'm here to support in any way I can.'

God! She sounds like Naomi's key worker – are all these people related?

Everyone looked at me.

'Tell them, Mo!' Elaine urged. 'Go on! Look at her face!'

Something locked down my tongue.

Awkward silence.

'Maybe we can start with your name and address?' suggested the fed. 'Perhaps tell us what school you go to?'

I took a mega breath and managed a quiet reply. 'South Crong High. My name's Maureen Baker. I'm fifteen years old and I live with my mum.'

The fed and Ms Hunt tried to show off their best oh-my-god-I-care-so-much expressions. Elaine was willing me on.

'It's my mum's boyfriend,' I resumed.

'And he crashed into her bedroom and smacks her out of her own bed!' Elaine blurted out, pointing at me.

I took in another gulp of air and described all my dramas with Lloyd. Ms Hunt could write shit down really fast – her fingers were a blur. Elaine stroked my back as I spoke – I wanted to tell her not to rub so hard cos I felt like puking.

The feds wanted an official statement. I had to go through the whole story again.

They asked if I needed to see a doctor. No.

Then they started on something that properly made me freak.

'You're only fifteen,' said Ms Hunt. 'We have to inform the social services. Do you understand that you're at risk and we may have to take appropriate action? Or at the very least alert other institutions so they're aware of the—'

'The social are *not* taking me anywhere!' I spat. 'I just want Lloyd outta my flat. That's all. I just wanna live with my mum!'

I thought of Naomi living in her children's home unit and

never inviting us inside. What the freaking bricks went on in those places?

'No one is going to separate you from your mum,' said Ms Hunt. 'But she may need help or advice in giving you more protection from . . .'

Suddenly, I felt too hot. The pressure inside my head was too intense. Sweat leaked from my armpits. I could feel it around my belly button too. I sank the rest of my water and stood up. 'Elaine – I can't do this.'

'But you was doing brilliant, Mo,' Elaine said. 'You're nearly finished.' She looked to the fed and queried, 'Isn't she nearly finished?'

The fed nodded. 'If you like, Maureen, you can take a break – maybe go out for a bit of fresh air or even come back tomorrow to finish and sign the statement?'

'There's no rush,' Ms Hunt said. 'We'll be happy with whatever works best with you. If you like we can make a call to the child protection officer at the council and make sure you're staying somewhere safe tonight?'

'*NOOOO!* I'm not staying with peeps I don't know!'

I could feel their stares burning through my skull. My brain felt as if it was gonna explode. 'I WANNA GET OUT OF HERE!'

Elaine stood up and held me. 'Open the door,' she said. 'Let me take her out.'

Before I was led out, Ms Hunt poured me another cup of water. The fed opened the door. Other officers looked up from their desks and PC screens. I couldn't bear them gawping at me so I buried my face into Elaine's shoulder and let her guide me. When I opened my eyes again, I found myself in the car park with Elaine, the fed and Ms Hunt. We all sat down on a bench. My hands were shaking. I searched for a tissue in my school bag but couldn't find any. Guessing what I was looking for, Ms Hunt offered me a hankie. 'Can I get you anything else?' she asked. 'Cuppa tea? Biscuits?'

I shook my head.

'Can you leave us for a sec?' asked Elaine.

The fed and Ms Hunt glanced at each other before nodding. 'Of course. Take all the time you need.'

They clip-clopped back inside. The evening air cooled my forehead. Traffic whooshed by beyond a high brick wall. I held the cup to my lips and drank.

'It's a brave ting you're trying to do, Mo,' Elaine said. 'Maybe we'll come back tomorrow and finish off the statement.'

I was glad to hear Elaine say that. I breathed easier and mopped the sweat from my face.

'We'll ask the feds to drop us home,' said Elaine. 'That's the least they can do.'

'Not all the way,' I said. 'I don't want Mum or Lloyd to see them dropping me off.'

'I hear that,' said Elaine as she hugged me again.

5

Mummy Dearest

Before we left the station the fed asked me, 'Maureen, are you sure you wouldn't like to sign the evidence you have given us so far?'

The word 'evidence' shocked me. In my inner vision I couldn't help seeing white-wigged peeps in Professor Snape cloaks. I shook my head. 'I'll ... I'll come back tomorrow. Or maybe by the end of the week.'

'Please do,' said the fed. She forced a sympathetic smile but I could see disappointment in her eyes.

In the squad car I asked to be ejected two blocks from my slab. Elaine climbed out with me. *Freak my days!* Sam would never believe I had taken a ride in a fed car.

'You want me to step in with you?' Elaine offered.

I checked the time on my mobile. 'It's after nine,' I said. 'Won't your mum be cussing out on your balcony?'

'Yeah, she will be, but I wanna see you're all good.'

'It's all right, Elaine. If he tries anyting you'll be the first one I'll call.'

Elaine gave me a long embrace. 'Look after yourself, Mo, and if that fat prick even looks at you like he wants to try someting, then skip quick-time to my yard. Promise?'

'Promise.'

I rolled towards my block. Elaine stood there watching me till I was right inside. Tiredness pounced on me as I climbed the stairs. I felt heavier with each step. For a moment I stood outside Sam's gates. I wanted to tell him about my day. I wanted to see his face, his half afro, half plaited cornrow hair. His smile. But he was with *her* now. They could be curling tongues on his sofa. I didn't think Shevray would say no if Sam wanted to feel up her chest and go down south.

I tried to delete the image of *them two* from my mind. I ran up the next flight of stairs and entered my flat. I was immediately hit by a smell of disinfectant and lavender. In the kitchen, the radio was blasting out Abba's 'Chiquitita'. I headed there and found Mum on her knees with a scarf on her head, yellow rubber gloves on her hands, scrubbing the inside of the oven. A bowl of soapy water was beside her. I turned the volume down on the radio.

'Mum!'

She turned around and smiled. Grime kissed her chin. 'Ahhhh! My baby's home. Where've you been?'

'Went to the movies.'

'With Elaine?' she asked.

'Yeah.'

'Such a nice girl – good family. Saw her mum the other day in the supermarket – she's always in a rush. I said hi to her and she was off like a shot – on her way to work.'

I looked at the puddle that was rippling around her feet. 'Mum, it's nearly ten – what are you doing cleaning the oven at this time of night?'

She stood up and pulled her rubber gloves off. She dried her forearms with a tea towel before flaming a cigarette. 'The place was a mess,' she said. 'So I decided to clean it up – ain't that what you've been telling me? To do my share of the cleaning?'

'Don't smoke near that oven,' I said. 'Where's Lloyd?'

She ignored my warning, pulling hard on her cancer stick. 'He thought it best . . . he thought it best that me and you have some quality time together, you know? A mum and daughter ting. And he's really sorry, you know, about what happened this morning, and at the weekend. He's trying really hard with you.'

'He thought it *best*, Mum?' I repeated. '*He* thought it *best*?'

'I don't get your meaning, babes?'

'What do *you* think is best, Mum?'

She gave me a hard look and killed the smoke of her cigarette with her fingernails. Then she turned her back on me and started to wash a few things in the sink. 'I'm trying too, Mo. I took a sickie from work today. I waited for you. I was gonna wash your hair and plait it today, you know, in the style how Elaine does it. I bought your fave chocolate mousse – it's in the fridge.'

She went over to the fridge, opened it, reached inside. She

held out the treat. I refused to take it. She put it back in the fridge.

'Mum . . . we have to talk.'

'About what, babes?'

'Lloyd.'

'Didn't I tell you he's sorry for what happened Sunday? He called about six and asked how you were.'

'Why doesn't he tell me sorry himself?'

'He will, Mo. Next time you see him he will. He just wanted us to have this time together. He's considerate like that.'

'Considerate? Why didn't *you* want to spend *quality* time with me, Mum? You couldn't wait to get me out of the damn flat this morning.'

Mum turned her back on me again and washed her hands in the sink. I sat down at the kitchen table and couldn't help being impressed by Mum's cleaning – even the cobweb that had been expanding in a corner of the ceiling was gone.

'If you want,' she said, 'I can still wash your hair. I bought some conditioner.'

'I can wash my own hair, Mum – I'm not a kid.'

'We wanna take you out for something to eat on Friday. How does the Cheesecake Lounge sound?'

Her tone was becoming more desperate – like a Crongton market trader trying to sell bruised apples.

'*We?*' I repeated. 'I ain't going nowhere with *him*. I wouldn't even skip down the steps of our block with *him* or chill in the same park.'

She turned off the taps and stood still for a while, staring out of the window – apart from the slab next to ours, there wasn't much to see. Then she grabbed the tea towel and dried her hands. She finally turned around to face me. 'He didn't get the job he went for today. He's been trying so hard. They always hold his criminal record against him.'

'Boo-freaking-hoo. Do you want to play your violin? I'll get my harp.'

'*Don't* let your mouth run away with you, Mo. I'll smack that sarcasm right out of your cheeks. I'm *still* your mother!'

'*Mother?* Who gave you that description?'

For a short second she seized me with a brutal stare. Then she forced a smile, slapped the rubber gloves back on and, like a *Simpsons* character with bright yellow fingers, sparked another cigarette and sucked on it. I was gonna have to do something about her smoking one day, but not then.

'As I said, he's very sorry for what happened,' she said. 'He wants you both to get along. Don't you want that, Mo? It'll be better for everybody.`

'It's hard to get along with someone who beats you down,' I spat. I couldn't help my sarcasm but if she was seriously sorry she would outlaw his fat arse from ever stepping on our tiles again. Why couldn't she see he had red alert puffing from every breath? He was frigging lucky I hadn't finished my statement to the feds. I'd only done that so I could save her skin from embarrassment. If he put a fingernail on me again I swore I'd chant to the blue bloods like Beyoncé at the Super Bowl.

Her eyes filled with guilt. She threw the cigarette in the sink, dropped to her knees and resumed cleaning the oven.

'Lloyd's the only happiness I've had for a very long time,'

she said after a while. 'I haven't had anyone show me any real affection since ... you know. And I've dated some real bastards.'

She wasn't wrong.

'You can do better than Lloyd, Mum.'

'I want us to be a family,' she said. 'Lloyd's got a little boy – four years old. Jason's his name. If you want you can meet him.'

I didn't reply.

'Babes, what do you say? Do you wanna meet Jason? Loads of energy he's got, cute as anything, and really clever – knows how to spell his own name. You wanna see how high he builds his building blocks!'

Ain't that all sweet for Jason. Woo-frucking hoo. He's probably a spoilt brat. They'll probably get me to babysit him while they're knocking pillows and scraping the mattress.

'He'd love to meet you – you could be his big sis! Lloyd dotes on him and so do I when I get the chance to see him.'

'Does Lloyd smack him outta bed an' all?' I snapped.

She muttered something under her breath that I didn't quite hear. Her cleaning became more frenetic, as if she was trying to scrub away the bad vibes between us. I knew she was hurting but she kept putting Lloyd before me. I stood up and made for my bedroom, leaving her scouring that black oven and cursing my existence.

I crashed on my bed. Mum turned up the volume of the radio. Lionel Ritchie was singing 'Hello'. I got a powerful urge to speak to Sam again but I resisted. Instead, I got up, kicked my door closed and took out my fave photo album from the bottom of my wardrobe. *God! When's the last time I bought someting new?* I opened the first page. Mum and me on a beach in Bournemouth. I must've been five or six. I was wearing a pink vest, white shorts that were too long for me and flip-flops. I was building sandcastles. She was in the background, sinking in the wet sand, the froth of the sea drowning her butt, a floppy straw hat on her head and a cigarette in her gob. She was laughing. I had no idea who took the pic.

6

Naomi's Not So Secret Admirer

Mum didn't speak to me the next morning. She didn't even try. When I was up and dressed I went into her room. The whiff of tobacco tunnelled up my nostrils.

'Mum.' I gave her a big shove. 'Mum!' No movement. I knew she was faking sleep. Whatever. I'd let her play Little Miss Stropanora.

I went into the kitchen. The bowl of water and scouring pad was still on the floor from the previous night. The cornflakes box was empty and so was the bread bin. I only found crumbs in the biscuit tin. There were no eggs in the fridge. I decided on the chocolate mousse for brekkie. Damn, it was good. Chased it down with water. In the bathroom I had to use all my strength to squeeze out a slither of toothpaste to scrub my molars. I stared at myself in the mirror. Shevray was prettier than me – she definitely had bigger tits and more strokeable thighs.

I left for school. Again, I paused outside Sam's gates but thought better of it.

For once I was on time but as I bounced through reception Mr Holman spotted me. He smiled at me so I thought it would be kinda rude to moon-slide away as he approached.

'Maureen,' he said. 'Good to see you on time today.'

'Are you trying to be sarky? Don't even try it – it don't suit you.'

'I just want to give you some information.'

'What information? Hurry up cos I've got IT.'

'The school's decided to employ a full-time counsellor for the students.'

'So?'

'We teachers are not trained to deal with some of the issues that students are struggling with. We'll be sending out letters by the end of the week.'

'So you think I need a counsellor?'

'I . . . I didn't say that.'

Holman looked flustered, his mouth the half of a full cuckoo. I left him catching nits and went to my first lesson of the day.

Considering the drama of the day before, I had to give myself ratings for my work at school. My French was coming along sweetly – *Mon francais est tres bon!* – and Elaine and I helped each other on an IT task.

Mum had texted me five times telling me to come straight home after school but I blanked her – if she could go into strop status and give me the mute treatment then I could do the same shit to her.

44

Elaine had to research something online for her English revision so she, Naomi and I stepped to South Crong library. The foyer was full of posters hollering SAVE OUR LIBRARY. Leaflets protesting the same thing covered the counter. We all booked to go online but on our way to the computer room we bucked into Linval Thompson. I had seen him around the ends, peacocking his look-at-me-I'm-bad strut, sinking shots of Grey Goose and getting charged on rockets. He used to go to our school. What I thought *was* weird was him carrying a book. A start-up business book.

'Naoms!' he called out. 'How comes you don't ding me yet? Don't you tune into your voicemail? Man's been waiting patiently for your summons!'

Linval was wearing name-brand tracksuit bottoms, trainers and a massive puffy anorak that could've floated the *Titanic*. Half-covering his bald head was a blue sweat-rag.

Naomi blushed while Elaine crossed her arms and kissed her teeth. 'She's not interested,' she said. 'So can you step off and take your BO to a different zone – we're studying.'

'Now, Elaine,' Linval replied, 'what have I ever done to you to turn you into the biggest cock-block in Crong Town?'

'It's who you trod with,' Elaine countered.

I couldn't stop myself from giggling and Naomi joined in. Linval's expression switched to serious.

'Why you always dissing the bros I step with?' he challenged. 'They're my bona fide fam. They've got my spine. You know one of my bredrens got carved the other day?'

'Yeah, I heard someting about it,' said Elaine. 'It's tragic but I diss most of the bruvs you step with cos I bet they're all into hustling, intimidation and all kinda crookery. If you're in that game bad things are gonna go down.'

I could sense Linval's temper brewing. 'One of these days someone's gonna box your renkness straight outta your gums!' he threatened.

'So your crew smack down girls too?' Elaine replied. 'Do you all wanna get a medal for that?'

'Elaine! Elaine!' Naomi cut in. 'I've got this.'

Elaine full-stopped her dislike of Linval by kissing her teeth once more.

'As you can see, I'm still at school,' said Naomi, pointing to her blazer. 'Do you believe me now? How old are you? Twenty? Twenty-two?' You're too old for—'

'Nineteen,' cut in Linval. 'Johnny Depp is linking with a chick twenty-five years younger than him so it's *still all fabulous* – me and you can bounce arm in arm on the boardwalk.'

'But you're never gonna open the gates of a chocolate factory,' I laughed. 'Or sail with ghosts in the Caribbean.'

I couldn't help spitting my jokes to kill the tension but Elaine and Linval didn't love the interruption.

'Naoms!' Linval pleaded. 'Forget about your cock-block sistrens. We could start off on the level, step to the movies, smack down some pins, sample the Strawberry Delight in the Cheesecake Lounge, take a ride to the roller park in Ashburton – can you skate? What say you, Naoms? Anything you wanna do I'll turn up all correct and proper and be the perfect gentleman. On the most respectable level!'

Elaine and I burst out laughing.

Linval ignored us. 'What are you doing Saturday?' he asked.

'She's going shopping,' I said.

'And she don't need an escort,' added Elaine.

Linval searched his anorak pocket and pulled out a wad of money held together by a gold clip. Naomi's eyes widened. Elaine shook her head while I tried to count the cash. He must've been holding up about £300.

Linval grinned. 'I'll take you shopping. We'll go to the name-brand shops in Ashburton. I'll buy you some garms and we can step to the Steak Palace and munch some well-done buffalo ribs with fries. What say you, Naoms? We'll take a cab there and back – don't want you carrying your name-brands on a dutty bus!'

Naomi was still ogling the notes. 'May ... maybe another time,' she said. 'But I prefer shopping on my own or with my sistrens.'

Elaine started walking away. 'Come, Naomi, we have to study – the hour's already ticking.'

Linval put the money back in his pocket. 'Give me a ding!' he said to Naomi. 'We can flex *good*. Your sistrens are putting up resistance to me cos no man is summoning them. They're *jealous*.'

'OF WHAT?' Elaine exploded. She turned around, skipped up to Linval and almost dug out his eyes with her forefinger. 'You think I need a man to spoil up my life and tell me what to do? *Move* your cruffy self from my eyesight and your armpits from my nose-zone!'

'You're mad if you think I wanna be summoned by the rogue-hounds living in these ends,' I put in.

Linval laughed a mocking laugh. Before he left he pointed

his fore and little fingers to his ear. 'Ding me, Naoms. Or text me if your credit ain't too sweet. I know you're feeling me. Let's go all Marvin Gaye and get it *on!*'

'Who's Marvin Gaye?' I wondered.

Linval wrapped his arms around himself and started to whine and grind with his eyes closed. '"Let's get it onnn." YouTube it.'

Naomi and I burst out laughing but Elaine gave Linval an eye-pass that must've scared his ancestors.

As we made our way to the computer room, Elaine was still shaking her head. 'Naomi, *don't* let him sway your head with the funds he's bragging off.'

'Did you see it though?' Naomi said. 'He must've been holding up over three hundred notes!'

'But where does he get his notes from?' I said. 'The only brothers I know who carry funds like that are Gs.'

'Exactly!' Elaine nodded.

We sat down at the computer bank but research and homework had dropped from our agenda.

'But I like his swagger,' said Naomi. 'I'm tired of bruvs at school just admiring the goods on show but they don't wanna step up and say anyting. Look at Kingsley Golding. A bruv in the sixth form. He just stares me out. Prime, solid chonk of henchness but he's quieter than a monk's fart!'

'You're not *goods*, Naomi,' I said. 'I want a bruv who's stepping up to me to see more than that.'

'And Linval's bad news – trust me on that,' said Elaine. 'He's on a G trip.'

'You're overreacting,' said Naomi. 'He just smokes a bit,

that's all. And who doesn't fire up rockets around here? Everyone's on it. Just the other day I caught my key worker doing it in her car before she came to see me.'

'If I was your key worker I'd be taking someting a liccle stronger than a rocket,' laughed Elaine.

'That's not even funny!' said Naomi. 'Anyways, she came to see me and wants to get all up in my biz. Am I interested in seeing my pops, she asks. *Shit, no!* He hasn't got anyting to bring me apart from his drunk-up bruk-ass self.'

'If that was my pops I wouldn't give him the time it takes to have a hot piss,' remarked Elaine.

I thought of Lloyd. I wanted to change the subject.

'Can one of you give me the score on this Linval?' I asked. 'Who does he step with? What kinda crookery and evilry is he into?'

Elaine and Naomi looked at one another.

'Elaine!' I raised my voice. 'Naomi! *Don't* blank me.'

'Keep your blasted voice down,' said Naomi. She pulled her chair closer to mine and checked over her shoulder. 'He rolls with Folly Ranking and his crew – one of them got gored the other day outside the Four Aces bar in central Crong – some bruv called Marshall Lee.'

'Marshall Lee?' I repeated. 'Never heard of him. Folly Ranking? That name's clanging someting – isn't he the top G in our ends?'

Naomi nodded. Excitement lit up her face. 'I met him once down the Shenk-I-Sheck,' she revealed. 'He wears these enormous white trainers and he's got this belt with a solid gold buckle. And—'

'Sam said someting about him,' I cut in.

'Folly Ranking defends the ends,' interrupted Naomi. 'He robs brothers he doesn't recognise and sells his shit from internet cafes, off-licences and Ruskin Green where the council put up all those blue exercise bikes. He collects protection money from two barber saloons that I know of too.'

'Whenever he steps up to you,' said Elaine, 'you should be giving him the coldest blank. You don't wanna get cocktailed with a dangerous bruv like him or Linval.'

Cold saliva trickled down my throat.

Naomi smiled. 'Linval won't treat *me* like shit.' I wasn't too sure if she had a thought for the brother who got stabbed. I had the vibe that no matter what Elaine was gonna lay down about Linval, Naomi was ready to link with him.

'Them Gs are all the same,' Elaine said. 'Do you really think you're the only girl he's smacking on right now?'

Naomi thought about it. 'Maybe . . . but he's got funds though.'

'Take your tits out of his wallet,' I said. 'It's not all about the notes.'

'Yes it is!' argued Naomi. 'I'm not gonna link with some sad college bruv who has austerity issues about buying me an extra-large milkshake. What are we gonna do with our time? Go for a walk in the boring park and feed the ducks with stale bread?'

'Get to know him,' I suggested. 'Find out what he's all about. Encourage his dreams. Support him when he's going through shit. Be there for each other.'

As Sam's image crashed into my head, Elaine and Naomi stared at me as if I was reciting Mongolian poetry.

'I don't think she wants to be his priest,' said Elaine.

'Mo,' laughed Naomi. 'Last time I looked I was fifteen – you know, the age when you're supposed to have some fun? I'm not thinking about giving it all up for some guy with a nine-to-five, stepping up the aisle and then wiping the butts of his screaming kids. Screw that! *Jeez!*'

'But be careful,' put in Elaine. 'If he trods road with Folly Ranking, he's polluted with jeopardy. Look what happened to Marshall Lee.'

'They're not so bad,' said Naomi. 'So what if they sell a few goods here and there. If they didn't do it, someone else would. You know that. And around these ends it doesn't matter if you trod with a crew or not, you can still get jacked, cracked and whacked. Remember, I lost Crumbs. He was like a proper bruv to me. He never was a G – just curious.'

I spied the grief in Naomi's eyes. She wasn't wrong. As long as I could remember, somebody was always hustling something in the ends. One of Mum's ex-boyfriends, Nicodemus, used to sell weed and allsorts from our front door. A trail of peeps would perch on the wobbly stool in the kitchen night after night. They would hand over notes to Nico while test-sampling his merchandise. I used to get as high as Thunderbird Five making my night-time cocoa. He bought Mum garms, gold rings, necklaces and one of them steam mop things. He took me to the Ashburton Park funfair when I was nine years old – he even hustled his shit there. Then one day he disappeared. Mum couldn't fit into those name-brands any more and she long ago pawned off her gold. That was how it went down in South Crong.

'Just don't get in too deep with him,' warned Elaine, placing her hand on Naomi's shoulder. 'You're still vulnerable after you lost Crumbs.'

'Elaine's not wrong,' I added.

We group-hugged.

'Shall we do our homework now?' I said. 'That's why we come here.'

'When we're done can we go to the Shenk-I-Sheck?' asked Naomi.

'NOOOO!'

While we were helping Elaine with her revision, I received a further two texts from Mum.

MAUREEN, WHERE R U???

MAUREEN, COME HOME!!!

God! She must be really stropping out to call me Maureen. If she thinks I'm gonna change my mind about going somewhere with Lloyd, she's seriously mistaken.

Elaine and I walked Naomi home and yet again she spent the entire way trying to persuade us to go on this mission or that adventure. Before she went through her front door she said, 'I'm gonna link with Linval. See what he's saying. Underneath all that swagger I think he's on the level. And *that* bod is ripped in all the right places. He's proper funny too.'

Elaine was about to say something but changed her mind. Instead she shook her head.

'Don't give it up just because he's flashing notes in your zone,' I said.

Naomi grinned. 'You think I'm gonna allow any bruv to get me on a discount?'

'Just be careful,' Elaine said. 'If one of his bredrens can get shanked then the same shit could repeat on him . . . or anyone who rolls street with him.'

Naomi quarter-smiled. I guessed she loved being close to that danger. We embraced again before she entered her gates. When she pulled the door shut, Elaine said, 'We're gonna have to go all guardian-angel on her.'

'Yep,' I agreed. 'Definitely no *shopping* missions.'

'Maybe we *should* step with her on Saturday – make sure she don't try someting off-key?' Elaine suggested.

I thought about it. 'She's gonna have to learn not to do crazy shit when she's on her lonesome.'

'Good point.' Elaine nodded. 'Are you ready?'

'Ready for what?' I replied.

'To finish and sign your statement, Mo.'

I started walking away. Elaine caught up with me. 'Same as last night, I'll roll up with you.'

I didn't answer.

'Mo?'

I stared at the ground.

'Mo!' Elaine pressed again. 'Are we gonna do this?'

I stopped in my tracks and slowly shook my head.

'Mo! Please don't tell me you're gonna let that fat prick get away with it. He could've done you serious damage.'

'Do you think I like it this way?' I raised my voice. 'He

53

won't do it again. Mum made him promise. I wanna move on.'

'Nah! It can't go down like that,' Elaine argued. 'If I have to heave your bones to the fed station myself then I will. Watch me! You can't allow any man to get away with shit like—'

'Elaine! *Shut up!* Jeez and peas. When you start hollering like that I can't think.'

'So you're not coming?'

'NOOOOO!'

Silence.

We glared at each other.

After a while, we walked on.

'Why?' Elaine wanted to know.

'I think . . . I think Lloyd knows he done a major wrong,' I said. 'He wasn't there last night. Mum said he was sorry – she wants me to meet his four-year-old son. I think Mum wants to build a proper fam. I was reviewing the situation today and maybe it'll be best if I—'

'Mo? What're you telling me, sis? Believe me, you can't trust a man like that. He's done bird and you don't know a nish what he's done it for. It might've been for banging up his ex-girlfriend or showing his bits to ash-heads in Crong park. I cry for his son being raised by an off-key hooligan like that.'

'I don't think it's any of that,' I said. 'And at least that boy's gotta dad. I wouldn't love being the one who jacked that away from him.'

'What is it with my two sistrens today? One of them wants to link with a G from Folly Ranking's crew and you want to play happy fams with a man who clapped you out of your own bed. You can't allow it!'

'I don't wanna go to the feds,' I said. 'I felt sick in there. It's one ting telling you what went down, but telling the feds? Wasn't it you who told me they beat down half the people they arrest? I haven't even told Naomi.'

Elaine pulled my arm and fronted up to me. She didn't say anything for a few seconds but when she did, she said it slow. 'Mo, *don't* give him another chance. If my mum had a boyfriend and he put his hands on me, my dad would search for someting heavy and sharp in his toolbox, *trust* me on that.'

I brushed off Elaine's hand. 'Lucky for you you've got daddy backup,' I said. 'My dad's not around. And no one knows where his waste-self is!'

I carried on walking. Quicker now. I fought back the tears that were stinging my eyes.

My dad this and my dad that! Shut the freak up about your dad. At least you got one!

I glanced over my shoulder. I wanted to see her running towards me. I wanted her to catch up with me and give me another one of her long hugs. But she didn't. Elaine was still standing in the street exactly where I left her. I felt awful. It wasn't her fault my dad went AWOL.

'Are you coming to my yard for dinner?' she called. 'Gran's roasting some fish.'

'Fish?' I shouted back. 'Elaine, you know I can't stand fish. The smell of it mangles my stomach.' I remembered the last time I followed Naomi to the fish and chip shop – I puked up all shades of beige all over the newsagent's window next door. 'Anyway, Mum's been texting me, wondering where I am.'

'Hold on.'

As Elaine approached me I felt a tear in my left eye. I didn't want to wipe it away and make it so obvious. Then she hugged me and I wrapped my arms around her neck and clung there. I could smell the coconut oil in her hair and in that moment it was the most comforting thing in the whole world. 'Same as yesterday,' she whispered. 'If he even gives you an off-key look, then skip to my yard quick-time. Promise?'

'Promise.'

'At least follow me home,' Elaine insisted.

7

Pressure Drop

I walked Elaine back to her slab and again she insisted that I come up for a sandwich or something. I declined. I needed some thinking time. I headed to the park. Three bruvs were slouching on the climbing frame sharing a rocket. Young fams were loving the early evening sun. Mums rocked kids on the swings. Dads were playing ball with their sons. I envied them. Maybe I could agree to meet Lloyd's son, Jason – not his fault he had a jailbird for a pops. It might not have been the standard fam I'd always dreamed of but it was the best I could hope for. After all, *this* was South Crong. Mum was seriously into Lloyd and there wasn't a damn thing I could do about it. I didn't have to swing along with him – just keep out of his XXL-sized way. It'd just be a good-morning, good-evening, how-did-your-last-job-interview-go thing then I'd step to my room. But if he laid one paw on me again I'd do something darker than reporting him to the feds. I swore I would.

Heading back to my block I was willing to give Lloyd one last chance.

I pushed the key into the lock. I checked my mobile – it was just after six. I walked along the hallway. The floor was dust-free. Mum must've got her ass up and her Mrs Sheen on. The radio wasn't blaring so I guessed Mum was at work. Then I caught a whiff of tobacco from the kitchen and I headed there. Lloyd and Mum were sitting at the table, holding each other's hands. Lip stains marked two coffee mugs. Bourbon crumbs were sprinkled on a saucer. The skin surrounding Mum's eyes was two tones darker than the rest of her face. The ashtray was full. Four unopened beer cans were sitting next to it. They both looked at me like I had crapped on their Valentine's Day cards.

'Cristiano Ronaldo broke his big toe?' I asked.

Lloyd shook his head. Mum stroked his forearms as if she was trying to revive a dead squirrel. It took her a few seconds to look at me. Her gaze hardened like a gone-wrong hypnotist.

'Why?' she asked.

'Why what?' I replied.

She stood up. In-out, in-out, she breathed, veins throbbing, lips trembling, waiting for that moment to launch her cuss attack. Then it hit me, hard, like the tallest slab in Crongton had come down on my forehead – *the feds had called.* Her hand groped for Lloyd's shoulder before the eruption. In-out, in-out. Her arteries danced like trapped worms in her neck.

Lloyd stared at the floor, doing his best to keep his mouth sealed – Mum must've talked him into a promise of silence. Good call.

'Can't I have any fricking happiness?' Mum screamed. 'Don't I deserve that after all these years? Lord help me I've put up with enough low lives treating me like shit. Do you know that when I had you I could've put you in a home? My life would've been so much fricking easier! But I didn't. I kept you! And this is how you fricking thank me?'

'Your boyfriend boxed me out of bed, Mum! What was I supposed to do?'

I glared at Lloyd, challenged him with my eyes. I'd much rather go to war with him than Mum. He looked away and chomped his lip.

'I *told* you he said he was sorry!' Mum spat back. '*You* wound him up yesterday. *You* kicked him!'

'THAT'S NO EXCUSE!' I raged. 'When he clapped me out of bed *I* didn't boot him first! How can you allow that in our own flat? You're *meant* to protect me.'

'Mo, I'm really sorry for that,' Lloyd interrupted. 'But I didn't retaliate when you kicked me yesterday, did I?'

Elaine's voice was in my head. She wouldn't tolerate this.

'If you're so sorry then get your droopy behind out of our flat!' I raged at him. 'I'm not living with anybody who puts their claw on me.'

'Did Elaine put you up to this?' Mum asked. 'Did she? Tell her to mind her own fricking business. I've always said that girl's mouth is too large – just like her mum! Giving their opinions when no one wants to hear them. Tell her to stop poking her nose into other people's business – she should worry about her old man carrying on with that rent-a-crotch from Crongton Green.'

'Elaine's got nothing to do with it. And *don't* bring her fam into it!'

'Then why did you go to the police? You know what they're like – framing and beating up people – especially the people you like to go around with. They've been around here today, looking for Lloyd. That's all he fricking needs! He's been out there every day looking for work. He's trying to make a new start. They've been asking all sorts of questions. I was so worried I didn't go to work.'

'I *bet* you were worried. Who else is gonna buy you your beer? You've never fretted so much about *me*.'

'Do you know what could happen to him? Do you? You *know* he's out on licence.'

'No, I don't freaking know, but I couldn't give one Quaker oat what happens to him.'

'*That's* not called for, Mo,' Lloyd protested, standing up. 'I *am* and will be your mum's man. We can all make a go of this but you're making it very difficult.'

'You think this is difficult? You haven't seen shit yet. And you're *not* gonna raise your fat hand to me again. I swear if you do I'll do someting much worse than squealing to the feds.'

'If he goes back inside it'll be on *your* conscience,' Mum ranted. 'There's Jason to think of. He needs his dad. Did you think about that before you snitched to the police? *Did you?* Depriving that poor boy of his dad!'

'Mum, you don't get it, do you? He *hit* me! Did *you* think of that? Doesn't that clang your alarm bell?'

'And he said *sorry*! He swore to me he'll never do it again. It was dealt with. What more do you want? Do you want him to ask for an audience with the fricking pope and promise him too?'

'He'd probably lie to the pope's ass too and jack his wine,' I fired.

'If Lloyd goes back inside, I swear, I'll *never* forgive you. *Never!* I'm entitled to be *happy*. Didn't you say to me last year that I need someone in my life? "Go out more, Mum." "Meet someone, Mum." "Have a life, Mum." Didn't you say that?'

'Yeah I did. But not *him*!'

'Can we just take this down a notch and—' Lloyd said.

'I'll calm down when *you* go missing from my world and end up as a cold case,' I yelled. 'A very cold case.'

Mum marched up to me, arms swinging by her side and her face drenched in tears. I didn't back off. She grabbed my shoulders and started shaking me. 'I'm *not* putting up with it, Mo. You're talking back to me as if I'm a piece of shit. *I'M YOUR MOTHER FOR GOD'S SAKE! I KEPT YA AND I COULD'VE LET THE SOCIAL HAVE YA!* You can't tell me who I can and can't see; I have a right to choose who I want in my life!'

'Get your hands off me!' I screamed. *'Get offff!'*

Mum's tears free-falled down her cheeks. My lyrics had cut deep. *Good!* Her head shook wildly. She closed her eyes. She lashed out blindly, clawing my face. She even scraped at the skin behind my ear. It stung me like a wasp. I tried to hold on

61

to her arms but she went all leopard on me, so I crunched my fingers into a strong fist, levered it behind me and let it loose.

Mum didn't see it coming. She dropped to the floor like a builder's rubbish bag. *Budoof!* I stared at her, prostrate on the ground. The pain from my hand shot right up my arm through to my shoulder. Before I could do anything to relieve the agony, Lloyd was after me, both fists clenched. He snarled like a bad-breed dog. His eyes narrowed. His cheeks reddened. *God, I've gone too far this time.* I swallowed pure undiluted fear. *Shit! He's gonna merk me.* I froze.

I could hear someone banging down our gates. *Saved!* I could feel my legs again. I ran to the hallway.

'*You freaking bitch!*' Lloyd ranted. 'I try to be nice to you but you just give me lip! I even offer to take ya out and you throw it back in my face. I'm gonna shut that mouth of yours!'

I screamed as loud as I could. It seemed to unnerve Lloyd. Someone was trying to bulldoze our front door. Lloyd backed away, unsure of what to do. Mum emerged into the hallway. *Bllaanngg, bllaanngg, bllaanngg!* She and Lloyd swapped frantic glances. In their hesitation, I opened the door.

Standing there brandishing a bread knife in her hand was Sam's mum, Lorna. *Relief!* It was a weird sight. She was in her bus driver's uniform. Grey trousers pressed sharp. White blouse. Green and black striped tie. Badge number 23182. She walked slowly but purposefully towards Lloyd. I heard Mum gasp, frozen to the spot. Lloyd backed away. He held up his palms. Lorna backed Lloyd up against Mum's bedroom door. Deadly intent was in her eyes. I'd never seen anyone go without blinking for so long. A film of sweat covered my face.

'I swear on my last breath that if you ever – *ever* – trouble Mo again,' Lorna warned in a voice of pure granite, 'I'll gladly serve whatever bitch time I get for the organs I'll carve out of your rotten self!'

Mum covered her mouth. The blade wobbled in Lorna's firm grip. It glinted under the naked hallway bulb. Lloyd's body stiffened, his gaze hypnotised by the jagged steel in front of him. I could feel a draught from the open front door. Something tiny crawled along the floor.

'It . . . it was just a disagreement,' Lloyd managed.

'You take me for a fricking idiot?' Lorna replied. 'From what I was hearing you were trying to kill her.'

'It wasn't like that.'

'Mo!' Lorna suddenly called out. 'Grab a few of your tings. You're gonna be staying with me for a while.'

I ran into my bedroom. I found my sports bag and began stuffing it with clothes. I chucked my deodorant in there too and my brushes and combs. I frantically looked for my school rucksack until I realised it was still strapped to my back. I crossed the hallway. Lorna was still holding up Lloyd with the knife. Mum was in mad shock, tears dripping down her cheeks.

I rushed into the bathroom, picking up my soap and shampoo. I returned to the hallway. 'Ready,' I said.

Lorna backed away.

I forgot something. I hot-toed into my room again, opened my wardrobe and grabbed my photo album. *I can't believe I'm doing this. Shit! Should I really leave Mum with him? He might take it out on her. No, what am I saying. Gotta skip quick-time. She set up her dinner table. Now she's gonna have to sit her ass down and sink her meal.*

Before I left I searched Mum's eyes. She was staring vacantly over my shoulder. Her arms were folded. Her back was sliding down the wall. I had to get away.

I skipped down three steps at a time. I almost tripped over. Sam was waiting outside his front door. 'I heard the shouting,' he said. 'Mum wouldn't let me go up with her. You all right, Mo?'

'Not really,' I replied.

I wasn't all right. My head blazed. I sort of half-collapsed into his arms. I dropped my photo album. Sam picked it up. I heard a door being slammed. Feet rushed down concrete steps. The same door was kicked open again.

'You can freaking keep her – she only got in our way anyway! Stay at your boyfriend's, Mo. Take his psycho mum! Let them feed ya! Let them pay your bills! Let them put a roof over ya head!'

Lorna and Sam helped me into the flat. My right hand still zinged from the punch I'd thrown. Lorna was breathing heavy. Relief marked her eyes. They carried me into their lounge. Sky News was reporting something about refugees. A small green Buddha sat on a coffee table. A poster of Nina Simone overlooked the three-seater sofa where they placed me gently down. Tenderly, Sam nestled a cushion under my head. There was a rubber plant in a corner that almost kissed the ceiling. It made me remember *Jack and the Beanstalk*. Mum read me the fairy tale as a bedtime story when I was little. *Fee fi fo fum!* Sadness surged within me. I could smell incense.

'Is Mum all right?' I managed.

'She's being a bit dramatic but she'll live,' Lorna said. I noticed a joss stick burning in a mug on the coffee table.

Sam sat beside me and tapped my shoulder. 'You're safe now,' he said.

'Chubb lock the door,' Lorna ordered.

Sam got up and pulled his keys from his pocket. Lorna dropped into an armchair. She let out the mother of all sighs and gazed up at the ceiling. 'That,' she said, 'was a dumb thing to do. He's three times my size. But we heard shouts and screams.'

'We was gonna call the feds,' said Sam.

'Call the *police*,' Lorna corrected. 'But there wasn't enough time. It sounded as if they were killing you up there! So I just grabbed a knife.'

I rubbed my right hand and closed my eyes. *God! Elaine's gonna be mad with me.* I didn't want to spill to the feds again but I should've followed her back to her flat.

'This *has* to stop!' insisted Lorna. 'I'll call the police now.'

'NOOOO!' I protested. I surprised myself with my loudness. 'Please leave it ... I'm *not* going back ... never. They deserve each other. Let *her* be happy with *him* if she wants. Let them rot.'

Sam and Lorna exchanged worried glances. I shut my eyes again. In my head I could see Mum lashing out at me. *She should be on my side! Why isn't she on my side?*

'Why does she *hate* me?' I blurted out. 'Why does she put *him* before me? If she didn't want me she should've had an abortion. It would've been better for everyone. She wanted to beat me down. What could I do? She's freaking evil. EVIL! What did I do to get a mum like that?'

I squeezed my fists as hard as I could. My knuckles cracked. My right hand felt hot and raw and I could feel a world of emotion fuming through my chest. All my agonies, my life-time of pains, gathered inside my head. I was ram-jammed full of it all. I didn't cry – I screamed. I screamed till it hurt my throat. I screamed so it cracked the corners of my mouth. I screamed till snot came out of my nose. I screamed till all I could do was croak. I wanted her to hear me. I wanted her to feel some of my pain. They probably heard me on Crongton Heath.

Sam and Lorna tried their best but I didn't want them to touch me. I rocked back and forward, my arms pressing against my stomach. When my vocal chords pleaded for mercy, I stopped. I wiped my eyes. Tried to focus. *God!* I was exhausted. *What have I done?*

8

The Shattered Mirror

Lorna parked next to me. She swabbed away the tears from my cheeks. She took out a tissue and wiped my nose. She examined my right hand. She tried to smile. 'Oh, Mo,' she said. 'Mo, you'd better get your hand checked over. It's badly swollen. Sam will take you to the hospital.'

Sam nodded. She cuddled me and kissed me on my forehead.

'I'm not perfect,' I said. 'But I *don't* deserve a mum like *her.*'

I locked Sam into my gaze. 'You're so lucky,' I told him. 'You've got a mum who'll do anyting for you ... my mum doesn't give a shit about me any more.'

'That's not true,' Lorna said.

'*Yes it is!*' I insisted.

I could hear Lorna drawing in a long breath. She placed her palms around my cheeks and held my gaze until I felt uncomfortable. 'Listen me good, Mo,' she started. 'Your mum is *not* evil . . . just shattered.'

'Shattered?' I repeated.

'When you have lived a traumatic life such as she has, it breaks you down. The glass front of your soul begins to fall apart.'

I shook my head. 'I dunno what you mean, Ms Bramwell.'

'Hear me good, Mo. When you're cracked and broken, you lose the ability to deflect the badness that is around you – you can't push it away so it penetrates and makes you lose all reason. Before long, you think bad is good. You even think harm is love.'

Before she stood up she stroked my forehead and hair. That was where Sam got his affectionate side from. She smiled. 'I have to go to work,' she said. 'Don't let badness crack you. Take care of your soul mirror.'

'What cracked and broke my mum?' I wanted to know.

Lorna paused. She glanced at Sam and then switched her gaze to me. 'One day, Maureen, I hope she tells you.'

'Can't you tell me?'

'No. It has to come from her,' Lorna replied.

'But—'

Before I finished, Lorna left the room. What did Mum have to tell me? Stabbing pain stopped me from trying to figure out an answer. I drifted into that space between ache, semi-slumber and sleep.

'I'll call a cab,' said Sam, nudging me gently. 'Mum's gone to work.'

'Thanks,' I said.

He gazed at me and touched my cheek gently with a finger. He ran it down to the corner of my mouth. He used to do that right before he kissed me. 'You'll be all right, Mo,' he said. 'You always bounce back – no matter what happens to you.'

I no longer wanted to go to hospital. I just needed Sam to look after me. He could nurse my hand. I would recover in his arms.

'It's feeling all good now,' I lied. 'Maybe if I just run cold water over it?'

'Don't even try it,' he said. 'When you crunched up your fist your face creased like a *Game of Thrones* victim.'

He wasn't wrong. I didn't argue.

'I finished the Black History Month poster today,' he said. 'Thanks and praises for your help in it – researching all that stuff about Jackie Robinson and Muhammad Ali.'

'We . . . we always were on point working as a team,' I said. 'You helped me with all that First World War stuff.'

He looked away. 'Yeah,' he agreed. 'I've missed all that.'

'Me too,' I quickly added.

'Let me call the cab,' he said. 'You need to get your hand seen to.'

He stood up and made the call. As we waited for the car to arrive I noticed him pressing his hands together and scratching the back of his head. I giggled at his nerves and awkwardness.

'Stop your stressing,' I said. 'I'm not gonna ask you to carry me to the cab.'

'No, it's not that.' He grinned. 'It's your turn to make brekkie next and with your bruk-up hand you won't be able to roll fried dumplings or flip an egg. And you know I like my brekkie on point.'

I picked up a cushion with my good hand and swatted him with it. 'You feisty wretch!'

'Do you know how many times you have licked me with cushions and other things? I should report *you* to the feds.'

I hit him again and chased him around the sofa. He eventually hid behind an armchair. My hand throbbed like a slamming boom box.

'*Mouth like a fishwife, temper like a banshee,*' Sam teased. '*Mo wants to lick me like Apollo Creed's son in* Rocky Twenty-Three!'

'Say that to my face and see I don't fly-kick your balls!'

'Why do chicks always wanna boot a man's balls?' Sam shook his head.

I couldn't help but laugh.

For a few minutes before the cab arrived, it was like summer again. Busting jokes, nuff laughter, teasing. The text from the cab company put a full stop to my joy overload. Sam helped me into the cab. I cursed the uneven ramps in our estate as the bumps caused me more agonies.

We were greeted in A & E by two drunks. One of them had blood seeping from his hand. Another had cracked his head. One bruv about my age was sitting in a corner pressing half a toilet roll against a shoulder wound. Blood stained his fingers.

I had no idea how long I had to wait for a doctor. I snuggled up to Sam. He stroked my hair just like Lorna did and it felt good. When they called my name I was proper disappointed – I wanted to stay with Sam. I wanted to hear him breathe, feel his chest rise up and down. *Kiss me photo album!* I had it bad.

9

Don't Tell Her No Lightweight Stuff

I was fretting more about spilling the score to Elaine than about whatever damage I had sustained. She had told me to go back to the feds about Lloyd.

I had two X-rays. My right hand was swollen and bruised but not broken. They gave me a tiny tablet for the pain and it hardly seemed possible something so small could make a world of difference. They asked how I hurt my hand and I spun some shit about playing b-ball. Maybe they could have given me a little something for my heart too. Because truth was, every time I thought about Mum, I felt sadder than sad. How could she attack me like that? Once upon a time she'd have stood up for me. She used to maul her boyfriends if they so much as jacked a dose of milk before I'd had my Shreddies.

I glanced at my reflection in the mirror once more. *If Mum doesn't want me, Sam definitely doesn't want this. Why should he? He's got Shevray. She's got smooth skin and her tits look good in clingy tops and swimming costumes. And she's never gonna roll to school in a baggy blouse. Girls like her should be forced to wear burkinis and saggy garms so the rest of us have a chance.*

Sam was still waiting for me in reception. I walked slowly towards him, and as I did I felt tears streaming down my cheeks. *Mo! You gotta learn to control your emotions!* He stood up as I reached him. He helped me sit down.

'Anything broken?' he asked.

I shook my head. 'Just heavy bruising.'

'You're tough like old tree bark.'

'I hope you're not dropping lyrics about my complexion.'

Sam chuckled. 'Are you ready to go?' he asked. 'Shall I call a cab?'

'Not yet,' I replied.

We sat down. I nestled up to him again, placing my cheek against his collarbone. He put his arm around my shoulders. I closed my eyes. It was sweeter than sugar in a mug of cocoa.

'We heard the shouting,' he said softly. 'I was gonna go up myself but Mum told me to keep my butt downstairs. How long has this been going on, Mo? You need to report it. If you want, I'll be a witness. Whenever you want me to give my statement to the—'

I placed a finger on Sam's lips. 'Ssssshhhh.'

We said nothing for ten minutes. It was pure bliss. Sam and I together. I imagined us curling up on a sofa in the dark. Rain licking the windows. Humming along to *The Wire*'s intro. The Baltimore ghetto ends. Stringer Bell doing his shit. Gs in white T-shirts. The feds swearing more than the crims. Sam's gentle breath upon my neck.

He broke the silence. 'I've been thinking,' he said.

'Don't bruise your brain,' I joked.

'Seriously, Mo. Been thinking even before tonight's drama.'

'About what?'

'Me and you.'

'There is no me and you. There's you and Shevray.'

'I'm gonna clang the bell on that one,' Sam said.

I sat up and gripped Sam with one of my coldest glares. 'So my mum tries to maul me and then her boyfriend threatens me and that makes you wanna sack Shevray and talk about me and you? It don't go so.'

Sam couldn't find an answer. He stared over my head. Of course I wanted to flex with him again. But I didn't want him to think I was easy.

'I got scared,' he said after a while. 'I mean, you're my best bredren—'

'I don't wanna be your best bredren!' I snapped. 'I'll leave that to Crabulous, Onions or ... whatshisname?'

'Turtle Leg,' Sam corrected.

'Let one of them be your best bredren!' I raised my voice. 'I wanna be your ...'

I tailed off. I didn't want to say it.

'I hear you,' he said quietly. 'It still scares me. Say we become an item and it goes all wrong. We'd lose everything. I've known you all my days.'

'Since we had our ting this summer, I haven't had a personality transplant and last time I checked myself in the mirror

I looked about the same – apart from the stresses around my eye corners. I haven't put on a Scream face and I haven't grown horns.'

'It felt ... weird,' Sam said after an awkward silence. 'We grew up together. Like a brother and sister. We even went on holiday together.'

'You call that a holiday? It pissed down all week and the caravan toilet wouldn't flush.'

We were seven years old. Sam had just learned how to play chess and he spent most of our holiday trying to teach me. For his troubles he got a rook, a bishop and nuff pawns flung in his face. I only wanted to play knock down ginger on caravan doors – even if it was raining. On the last night Mum won some money on the bingo. She spent it on a bottle of Appleton's rum, two cowboy hats for her and Lorna, a water pistol for Sam and a big cuddly leopard for me. I didn't know what she expected me to do with that big furry thing – I wasn't a cuddly toy kinda girl. When we returned to our caravan, Sam and I booted that poor leopard all over the place. We pulled out its whiskers, soaked it with the water pistol and put its head down the broken toilet. Mum confiscated it and sent me and Sam to bed. The drink started to flow. While they sang and danced to Beyoncé's 'Baby Boy' blaring out from Lorna's boom box, Sam and I sneaked out. We rat-a-tatted nuff doors. We had big fun, until the campsite supervisor caught us. He looked at us as if we were something a pig wouldn't eat. Our pyjamas were wet and grimy after slipping and sliding in the mud. He called us trash kids so I gave him the full Crongton ghettonictionary. He was shocked. Sam wanted to fly to his dad rather than face up to Lorna – his mum went all Professor Snape when it came to discipline. I said I'd run away with him but he didn't know where to start. He didn't have a clue where his dad was. It started raining. Sam cried. I might've been only seven years old but I fell for him on that day.

'Why did you go for Shevray?' I asked.

He looked away. Suddenly his fingernails were much more interesting than me.

'She's . . .'

'Go on,' I urged. 'Say it! She's got a curve-a-licious bod rather than a flat-pack one and she gave you the travelcard to her crotches. That's what went down, innit?'

Sam hesitated. 'One of her friends told me she liked me,' he said after a while. 'I guess I went with the flow. I can't lie – bredrens were giving me nuff ratings – but it isn't all that. Sometimes she's too loud. Too brag-a-dacious for me.'

'They wouldn't give you ticks if they knew you were linking with me right?'

'I . . . I . . .'

'Admit it!'

He lifted his head and gazed at me. Damn! I wished he wouldn't do that. 'I don't care about what they think any more, Mo. Yeah, I'm not gonna lie, I'm still kinda terrified of what might happen to us but it's always been you. It won't feel weird this time – not any more.'

'You're just saying that cos of all the drama tonight. Your emotions are broadbanding all over the place.'

'It's not cos of tonight.'

'Then why did you blank me when you came back from your holiday?'

'It wasn't a holiday, Mo. My mum was proper devastated. When we came back she started burning again for a few days. I didn't want you to sniff that.'

'I could've helped. You know me, Sam. What happens with our parents is between us and no one else. You deleted me from your radar!'

He stared at the floor and interlocked his fingers. 'I'm not gonna blank you any more, Mo. On the level.'

'Aren't you forgetting someting?'

'What?' Sam replied.

'Shevray,' I said. 'Before I even think about you and me you're gonna have to drop two lyrics on her.'

Sam nodded. 'I'll chat to her tomorrow.'

'Talk to her proper,' I insisted. 'And don't tell her no lightweight shit. She deserves to know the full score. She's bound to hate on me but, hey-de-lardy-ho, I'll deal with it.'

'I will,' Sam said.

I felt a smile rippling from my lips but I killed it. I didn't wanna look triumphant. 'You can order a cab now,' I said. 'Back to your place. I've gotta ding Elaine and tell her what went down. Maybe it'll be best if I stay with her.'

'But Mum said you could stay with—'

'Call the cab, Sam.'

'You can stay in my room. I'll change the sheets. I'll crash on our couch.'

How could I stay in his room? It'd be like inviting a choc addict for a sleepover at the Cadbury's factory.

'It's better that I stay at Elaine's,' I said.

He shook his head as he pulled out his phone. I closed my eyes and inhaled a few deep breaths before I dinged Elaine. She picked up immediately but it took me another three seconds before I could say anything. I was shaking.

'Mo? Are you gonna say something or are you gonna start heavy breathing on a sister?'

I told her everything that had played out. She downloaded it and then invented a world of new cusses and curses for Lloyd and my mum and in spite of it all I couldn't help but chuckle when she let rip with, 'You wanna report that kick-a-licous, frog-jawed, lord of the bishop chokers to the feds!'

'Go back to Sam's flat, pick up your tings and come to my yard,' she urged. 'Don't even think about staying in the same block as them. That could lead to episode two of the same drama.'

'What . . . what about your mum?' I asked.

'I'll chat to her and swing her around.'

'You really don't mind?'

'As long as you don't fart in the bed, sleep with the TV on or try on my eyelashes.'

I laughed at that but a shock of pain from my hand reminded me I was still at the hospital. 'OK,' I said, finishing the call. 'I'll see you in about half an hour.'

The cab arrived fifteen minutes later. Sam opened the door for me. 'When you get to South Crong, take the scenic route over the ramps,' I said to the driver.

I snuggled up to Sam once more. He placed an arm around me and peered through the window.

'Remember the time that social worker came around to interview Mum?' Sam said after a while.

'Yeah,' I replied. 'What were we? Eight? Nine years old?'

'Eight,' Sam recalled. 'Mum was babysitting you. Your mum went out shopping. You booted up a fuss and didn't wanna roll with her. The social worker was sitting in our lounge waiting for Mum to make her a coffee. She was all stoosh-like with her *Apprentice* trouser suit and her murder trial briefcase—'

'And we pretended to be twins,' I laughed.

'It was during Mum's depression,' Sam recalled. 'The social worker was doing an assessment – to see if she could still look after me.'

'And it was your idea to pretend we were twins,' I said.

'No it wasn't, it was *your* idea,' Sam argued.

He laughed a little. I placed my hand on his neck. He glanced at the oncoming traffic. I sensed his awkwardness.

'I told her I was born five minutes after you,' I said.

'And I said Mum wasn't told that she was about to have twins. Then you said we were in the papers and on morning TV – the first black and white twins born in the country!'

'Oh my gosh, the look on her face!'

'Your mum came back into the room with her coffee and couldn't work out what was going on.'

'Then you burst out laughing.'

It was true. I was always the first one to giggle. Sam was the key to my best memories.

*

The cab arrived outside our slab ten minutes later.

'Stay in the car,' Sam ordered. 'Lloyd might still be King Konging around the block. I'll get your stuff.'

'Don't forget my photo album,' I said.

'Do you want me to go with you to Elaine's?'

'Just see me to the B of the block,' I replied. 'Thanks, Sam.'

Once Sam was back, the rest of the journey was completed in silence. I flicked through my photo album: Sam and me on the swings in the park at four years old; standing outside our holiday caravan licking ice lollies in the rain; posing outside our slab in our school uniform on our first day of secondary school; riding the dodgems at the Crongton Heath funfair; me pretending to cut his fro with a giant pair of garden shears on sports day.

We pulled up outside Elaine's slab – the B of the block. I paused before opening the door. Sam glanced at me, pulled me towards him and kissed me on the corner of my mouth. I tasted something minty on his lips. Some sort of love current fizzed through my veins. My heart went into hyperdrive. I pulled back. I had to take a couple of seconds to compose myself. I glanced at the driver's reflection in the rear mirror – he was trying to murder his grin.

'Make ... make sure you chat to Shevray,' I said.

I picked up my belongings and climbed out of the cab. 'Stay inside the car,' I said to Sam. 'I'll be all right. Thanks and praises for taking me to the hospital.'

I gazed into his chestnut eyes. Sweet Disney Bambis! I had to get out of there.

'Will I see you at school tomorrow?' he asked.

'I don't think so,' I replied. 'I won't be able to write.'

'I'll call you then – I might have to use Mum's phone cos my credit needs some juice.'

'Tell your mum thanks,' I said. 'You never told me she had an inner warrior queen going on.'

Sam laughed. 'You ain't seen shit. You wanna see her if I forget to sweep up my toenail clippings from the lounge!'

'Uggghhh!'

10

Love It, Don't Crush It!

Climbing the stairs to Elaine's flat was more painful than I had expected. I arrived at her front door rubbing my hand. I clapped the letter box. Elaine answered it. 'Mo! Come in, sistren!'

She hugged me like the last scene in a Hollywood rom-com. 'Love it. *Don't* crush it,' I said.

She led me along the hallway. I had to cover my nose and mouth as I passed the kitchen – some evil fish pong was trying to pollute me. I bustled to the lounge. Elaine's Mum, Yvonne, was goggle-boxing on a sofa watching some US feds show. Elaine's grandma was falling asleep in an armchair with a mug of coffee in her hands. I could smell rum.

'Do you want anything to eat?' asked Yvonne.

God no.

'No thank you, Yvonne. I've already had someting.'

'Something to drink?' Yvonne offered.

'I'm good,' I answered.

'So . . . ' Yvonne resumed.

There was a long pause. I just wanted to sit my ass down after trekking up so many damn steps.

'So how long do you think you'll be staying with us?' Yvonne asked.

'Why the interrogation?' cut in Elaine. 'Mo's day hasn't been blessed. Her hand's seriously bruised up and she just wants to rest her bones for the night.'

Yvonne turned to me. 'Treat our place as your own,' she said. 'Don't even ask if you want something from the kitchen – just take it.'

'Thanks, Yvonne.'

I heard a door opening. Lemar emerged into the hallway. He was still in his school uniform minus his tie. On seeing me he skipped up and threw his arms around my neck. This family held the gold medal for hugs. My bruises didn't love it but my soul did. 'Mo! Mo! Are you staying with us, Mo? How long for? You can help me with my homework! When Elaine helps me she's worse than the teachers! Do you like Frosties? Can you try to swing Mum into buying Frosties for our breakfast? We're gonna love having you here. Can I draw you?'

'Lemar! Don't even try it,' said Yvonne. 'You are not getting any Frosties. Too much sugar. Deal with it. And I'm sure Mo hasn't got the time for you to sketch her.'

I smiled and nodded. It was nice to be wanted.

'Maybe you can take me to get my fro cut,' suggested

Lemar to me. 'Or do you think a flat top and a side fade would top me off all neatly?'

'Not now!' Elaine barked at him.

Before I had a chance to respond to Lemar's welcome, Elaine pulled me into her room. 'Excuse me, Mum, Gran.'

I placed my stuff on her bed. Elaine pushed the door closed. Terrence Howard stared down from the wall. 'Make yourself comfortable. This is *our* room now. You got someting to sleep in?'

'No,' I replied. 'Didn't I tell you? I sleep butt naked.'

'Not in my bed you won't.'

'I'm joking!'

'You better be! You're pretty, Mo, but you're not FKA Twigs.'

'So you wouldn't mind her snoogling up to you in just her skin?'

Elaine thought about it. 'I love a man with nuff detail in the abs section and kind eyes but if I had to choose between sharing my bed with you or Twigs, you're flying through the window, bitch!'

I laughed at that one.

She pulled open a drawer and threw me a plain white T-shirt and tracksuit bottoms.

'I still think you should go to the feds,' she said. 'You shouldn't let that flabulous dickhead get away with it.'

'Elaine, can we do a *Frozen* and let it go?' I asked. 'I don't wanna brew and stew on anyting. Just wanna rest and chill tonight.'

'Have you got your toothbrush and stuff?'

'Er, no. In the rush to get out I forgot it.'

'No worries,' Elaine said. 'I'll get a spare one from Mum.'

She left the room. I sat down on the bed. I checked my phone but there were no messages. I wondered if Mum was thinking about me. Was she sorry? Maybe in the morning she'd beg me to come home. I wanted to understand and forgive her – and I wanted to know that secret Lorna was on about, if it would help. But one thing I knew for sure: I wasn't stepping anywhere near my towers again until Lloyd hit the kerb. Mum had to give me a tick on that one.

I pulled on the tracksuit bottoms and T-shirt. I thought about dinging Sam to tell him I was settling in but I had zero credit. I heard voices outside. I crept to the door and pulled it ajar. I peered through the crack. Gran was still in her armchair. Her eyes were closed but her mouth was open. The TV was still playing – on the screen, some weird-looking chick with diversity hair was investigating something in a feds lab. Raised whispers were coming from the kitchen. I tuned in my lobes.

'Our flat is already too crowded,' Yvonne said. 'Me and your grandmother have to share a room and you *know* how hard she snores. Sometimes I have to sleep on the sofa just so I can get a little peace. And there's already a road block for the bathroom in the—'

'It's only for a few days,' Elaine cut in. 'We can't fling her out. She's got nowhere else to go. Her mum's boyfriend banged her up bad the other day. Her hand's all bruised and swollen up from mauling with her mum.'

'I know all that, Elaine. You don't have to keep telling me.'

'She came straight from the hospital.'

'Then why doesn't she go to the police?'

'She doesn't wanna go to the feds,' Elaine said. 'Look, Mum, when Mo's mum wakes up in her yard and she realises Mo's not there, she's gonna see sense, fling the gut baggage to the drain and beg Mo to come home.'

'And say she doesn't? What then? She can't stay with us for ever.'

'It won't come to that,' Elaine said.

'You can't be sure of that. I'm just saying, Elaine. It's not right and if she doesn't say anything, we'll have to call social services and get them involved.'

'No, Mum. You know what they're like with their million questions and zillion forms. Mo's not on that. She doesn't trust them.'

'Elaine! Listen to me. I understand she's one of your best friends but Mo's not our responsibility. Of course I feel for her but sooner or later the social *have* to know what's going on. And another thing. When her mum finds out she's staying with me she is gonna give me untold grief. You know what her mouth is like and I swear, I am not having her coming here and—'

'Mum, can she just stay for the next few days and then we'll review the situation?'

'OK,' Yvonne agreed. 'But let's not make a few days turn into a week and then a month and before I know it I'm seeing someone else wearing a paper hat around my Christmas table.'

'Thanks, Mum.'

'Oh and one more thing.'

'What?'

'I think Lemar's got a thing for Mo.'

'Mum, Lemar's got a ting for any girl in my year who says hi to him. He'd have a ting for a meerkat if it could dress up in a school PE skirt. What do you expect? He's an eleven-year-old boy.'

'All the same, we need to keep an eye on that situation. Did you see him with her?'

'He's just playing, that's all.'

'I have to dye my fringe now,' Yvonne said. 'But I still know when a boy gets the heat in the cheeks for a girl. And he's got it bad.'

Lemar! He's only eleven. That's all I need.

I closed the door and sat on the bed. I took my photo album out of my bag and flipped through the pages. Elaine came in a moment later. She gave me a glass of blackcurrant squash. I took a sip.

'You sure your mum doesn't mind me staying over?' I asked.

'Course not,' Elaine replied. 'She wants you to stay for as long as you want. She really feels for you. We all do.'

She parked beside me and studied the photographs in my album.

'Is that Sam Bramwell?' she asked, pointing out a pic of Sam and me playing soccer in Crongton Park.

'Yeah,' I replied. 'I think we were nine years old.'

'I dunno what he's doing with Shevray,' Elaine said. 'The biggest mouth in the south.'

'Not for much longer,' I said.

Elaine threw me a stare. 'What are you saying, Mo? You know someting I don't? Is he sampling someone else?'

I paused. *Should I tell her? I can't lie. I've wanted to spill to her for months.*

'Promise you won't offload on me,' I said.

'Offload for what?'

'And promise you won't laugh.'

'Why would I laugh?' Elaine replied. 'You better tell me now, Mo Baker, cos if you don't I'm gonna stomp on your hand.'

I sucked in a long breath. 'You remember the summer holidays?' I said.

'Of course,' Elaine replied. 'Naoms and me didn't see you much. You were on a low-profile tip. Either that or you was on one of your long sulks.'

'It wasn't a sulk. I was ... linking with somebody.'

'Linking with somebody?' Elaine repeated. 'Who? And you never told me? Why didn't you spill? That's dark, Mo. Aren't we sistrens? Who?'

'Isn't it obvious?'

'Andre Thuram!' Elaine guessed. 'That French bruv's always checking out your rear package – especially on sports day when you were running the hurdles.'

'I fell over,' I recalled.

'Exactly!' Elaine giggled. 'All your business was showing. Praise the Lord that your knickers were clean that day!'

'They're clean every freaking day!'

'Andre's all right but he's a bit too short,' said Elaine. 'He needs to do someting about his monobrow situation. You should tell him he can get one of those nose-hair trimmers in Boots. That'll do it.'

'It's not Andre Thuram!'

'Gregory Lato,' Elaine guessed again. 'That Polish bruv in my drama class. He can always make you laugh. Remember he asked you for a dance at David Worrell's party? He's not too bad but he's a liccle skinny for my liking. He needs some of Gran's dumplings. You know me, Mo, I prefer my furniture to be padded out – don't want no weak wicker someting – Gregory needs to discover toothpaste too and—'

'It's *not* Gregory Lato.'

'Then who?'

I drew in a long breath . . .

'Sam.'

Elaine's face morphed into a query. 'Sam? But . . . but ain't he like a brother to you? Ain't that incest?'

'How can it be incest? He's black and I'm white!'

'Your mum told me that when you were liccle she bathed you both in the same bath. If my mum had tried that with me and Lemar, I would've drowned the liccle brat so he could never leak the tale. *Know* that.'

'Yep, the bath ting is all true,' I said. 'We kinda got closer this summer.'

Her mouth opened wide. Her astonishment was even broader. Then she hit me with a pillow. *Boooofff!*

'What was that for?'

'Cos you never told me!'

Boooofff!

'Will you stop that? I'm spilling now!'

'But ... how ... when, what happened?'

'His mum started working twilight zone shifts,' I explained. 'We linked up, chilled, watched TV, box sets. He put his arm around my shoulder—'

'And got it on! Did you—'

'No I didn't,' I stopped her flow.

'You're lying to me, Mo Baker!'

'I'm not lying to you, Elaine Jackson – on the level.'

'You mean horizontal on the couch – so you lost the big V? Did you tell him to smack on a condom? Did it hurt? *Don't* let him go all rough rider on you and *don't* get yourself pregnant, Mo Baker!'

'No, I didn't lose the big V. And I'm not dumb enough to get myself pregnant, Elaine Jackson. Jeez and peas! Take your hype down a notch. Just because we were linking doesn't mean I gave it up.'

Elaine shook her head. 'You're a secretive, devious bitch with a capital B,' she said. '"I'm busy; Mum won't let me out; I haven't got any funds for the cinema; I'm well tired." And all the time you were sampling Sam Bramwell's As, Bs and Cs!'

'As, Bs and Cs? What are you on about, Elaine?'

'Abs and butt cheeks – Naoms came up with it.'

'I've always liked him,' I admitted. 'From when I was about seven.'

'You had a crush on him when you were *seven*? You're a freak, Mo Baker. But isn't he licking lobes with Shevray?'

'Seriously, do you have to put it that way? Gross.'

'Mo, what do you think they do when they've got one-on-one time? Fill in *Harry Potter* colouring books?'

I had to pause as I tried to delete the image of Sam licking Shevray's ears from my mind.

'He's ... he's gonna sack her. She's too brag-a-dacious for him – his words.'

'He's not wrong. That deep space probe can pick her up on its radar when she gets in a flow."

'So before Sam and me link up again, he's gotta spit her out like she's a Bolivian chilli.'

Elaine puffed out her cheeks. 'Mo, you are one dark, conniving mare! You and Sam Bramwell ... *God!* Can't wait till Naoms hears.'

'No, you can't—'

'She's our sistren, Mo,' said Elaine. 'Please let me tell her – can't wait to see the look on her face. Didn't she go on about how bruvs weren't stepping up and chirping you? And she told you to wear Z-list celebrity tops and shorter skirts to showcase your legs.'

'Yeah, that did piss me off big time.'

'Are you sure you haven't lost the big V, Mo? If you did I'm not gonna judge. Just be safe and—'

'No!'

I couldn't convince Elaine that I was still a virgin – I kept on trying until we fell fast asleep. I did miss my own bed and my selection of DVDs. Maybe I'd ask Sam to get more of my stuff. Who knew how long I'd stay with Elaine? Shit! Maybe I'd end up in a home. If I did I hoped it'd be with Naomi or at least somewhere close to the ends. Hopefully, it wouldn't come to that. Mum would see sense and fling that fat prick out of our flat.

11

Granny Jackson

I woke up to find Elaine's side of the bed empty. I checked my phone. Nothing. Indexing the digits hurt my hand. Couldn't believe that Mum and Lloyd both rushed me. Why hadn't Mum phoned, or even texted to see how I was? Not even a where the bleep are you. She must have been so loved-up with Lloyd that she'd prefer to share the flat with him rather than me. I couldn't go back. *God!*

My future was wrapped in dread. I shook my head to try to stop thinking about it. My mouth felt dry. I took a few sharp breaths. I climbed out of bed, smacked the pillows and smoothed out the duvet. I made my way to the kitchen. Something funky was in the air. I found Granny Jackson sat on a stool reading a Jamaican cookbook. She was wearing a black cardigan and a nightdress that tickled her toes. A stubbed-out rocket was burning its last in an ashtray beside her. She was holding a mug of coffee. 'Morning, Gran,' I greeted, trying to ignore the stench of weed.

'Oh, Mo! Me forget you was here. You finally get up. Everybody gone.'

I glanced up at the clock on the kitchen wall – 9.45 a.m. 'Gosh! Didn't realise I slept so late.'

'Do you eat fried dumplings, Mo? And I could stir up some scrambled eggs with it.'

'That would be great, Gran. Thanks.'

'You just sit down at the table and I'll bring it to you.'

I returned to the lounge and tried to remember the last time Mum cooked me a hot breakfast. I could hear Granny Jackson spraying air freshener. The whiff of it almost made me sneeze. It felt strange being inside Elaine's flat while she wasn't there. I parked at the table and tried to imagine what would go down when Sam gave the Wellington boot to Shevray. Maybe he wouldn't drop the bomb at school. That wasn't his way. It'd have to be a one-on-one situation. She would totally flip out. She'd probably want to hunt me down and recolour my face a different shade of bruise but I reckoned I could handle her if none of her sistrens jumped in. At least by the end of it I'd have Sam to myself. We could get back to watching box sets on his TV while Lorna was working the moon shift. I allowed myself a little grin.

Granny Jackson brought in my breakfast and gave me a knowing smile. 'Who is he?' she asked.

'Who is who?' I replied innocently.

'The young man you're dreaming about?'

'But I'm not thinking about anybody—'

'Mo, you don't tink I was fifteen once? You have a glow about you.'

I took a chunk out of my fried dumpling. It was good. Filling.

'Yes . . . yes, there is someone,' I admitted.

Granny Jackson sat down beside me. She patted my back as I sank my scrambled eggs.

'I had someone too when I was your age,' she said. 'The pastor's son.'

'Pastor?' I repeated. 'What's a pastor? Someone who stirs someting in a jam factory?'

'No, no, girl! He was the son of the church minister in our village. Lord forgive me! He was the best ting me ever see on two legs. There were tings I wanted to do with him that are *not* in the Bible. Yes, sah!'

I giggled. Somehow, I didn't think she'd told this story to Elaine.

'His name was Ezekiel,' continued Gran. Her eyes came alive. 'All the girls called him Easy. And he was the only reason I went to church. Yes, sah! Tall and broad he was with skin smooth like chocolate spread. He always wore his hat tipped to the left. And he was . . . what does Elaine say? *Firm* in all the right places.'

I had to chuckle again.

'Wash your mind, Mo, becah me *know* what you thinking!'

I almost choked on my breakfast. It took me a few seconds to compose myself. 'Did . . . did you go out with him?' I asked.

Granny Jackson shook her head. 'Me used to get so nervous me could hardly say two words to him. He welcomed people into the church and it's a wonder me never drop every time me see him. Me had the love bug bad!'

'Did he know how you felt?'

'No he didn't,' Gran replied. Sadness swam in her eyes. 'We were preparing to move to England and me was getting very distressed. Me tell my mother about my feelings for Easy but she just laugh.'

'Your mum laughed at you?' I said, outraged.

Granny Jackson nodded. 'Yes, sah. She called it puppy love. "You're only fifteen," she say. "By next week you won't even remember there was an Ezekiel." For me it was like big whale love. Yes, sah! Me cry all the way to England. But me can't complain too much. Me married ah good man – Kenroy – not as striking but hard working and devoted – God rest his soul. But even now me still tink about Easy's smile and the way him walk. So handsome. Me guess people don't forget their first love.'

'Is he still alive?' I asked.

'Yes, sah!'

'Why don't you go and see him?'

Gran playfully slapped my shoulder. My back rippled in pain but I tried hard not to show it. 'Oh, Mo. No, that would not be a good idea. He married some highty-tighty woman who loved to wear a wide hat and white gloves. They tell me she still paste on her redder than red lipstick and squeeze her big self into her Sunday best just to go to the push-cart vendor for a box juice.'

I chuckled again.

'It's *good* to hear you laughing,' Granny Jackson said.

'When you come in yesterday, you looked as miserable as a soggy puss that couldn't catch the rat.'

'Your stories are tooooo funny,' I replied.

'But let me tell you someting, Mo,' Granny Jackson stressed. She pointed at me. '*Never* let anybody downgrade your love for this ...'

'His name is Sam,' I said.

'For Sam,' Gran repeated. 'If you're fifteen or ninety-five, it's still real. There's no such ting as puppy love. No, sah! It can hurt just as much. They fill up your head just as much. Your heart pumps just as hard, yes, sah! So no matter what time you have with him, treasure it.'

'I will, Gran.'

'And in time,' she said with a cheeky smile, 'if you can make it last, invite me to the wedding. Me might even make you ah big rum cake!'

'Wedding? To be honest I'll be more than happy just going to the movies with him.'

12

North Crongbangers

I dozed off again after breakfast and I woke up to hear Granny Jackson singing a Dennis Brown song.

I didn't understand the lyrics but her chanting warmed my soul. I thought of Mum. I checked my phone once more but still nothing. I thought Gran sensed my grief cos she came over and gave me a long hug. I didn't have to say anything. I cried in her arms for the longest time.

'No worry about nothing, Mo. Tings will turn out all right. Just you wait and see. Sweet chile, after darkness there must come light.'

That afternoon I helped Gran bake a carrot cake. While mixing the ingredients with my left hand, she entertained me with tales of Caribbean ghosts, headless chickens, strange Obeah men who lived in the hills and runaway donkeys. It was much later when my phone buzzed. The cake was out of the oven, baked golden, the flat was funky with the sweet smell of cinnamon and I was enjoying my slice. I looked at the phone, thinking it might be Mum . . . but it was Elaine.

'Mo, me and Naomi are in the diner on the Broadway. Can you make it down? Got someting to tell you.'

'Can't you tell me now?' I said.

'It's about Lloyd,' she said. 'He's well dangerous – toxic to the max.'

'Lloyd? My mum's boyfriend?'

'Yes!'

'Dangerous? How dangerous?'

'Linval was waiting for Naomi when school finished. He leaked some info – come down to the diner and I'll give you the full flow. I haven't got much credit.'

She killed the call. I told Granny Jackson I was linking with Elaine and Naomi down the diner. She smiled, gave me five pounds to buy myself a treat and hugged me before I left. 'By the way,' she said to me at the front door, 'me take it becah it helps soothe the painful arthritis in my hands.'

She brought her forefinger to her lips. 'Sssshhhh!'

I didn't feel like stepping all the way to Crongton Broadway so I took a bus. Barrington's Hollywood Diner was a few doors away from Lovindeer's Lounge Bar. I rolled in. The jukebox was playing 'Heigh-Ho' from *Snow White and the Seven Dwarves.* Hanging above the jukebox was a black and white film poster of James Cagney in *White Heat.* The staff behind the counter were dressed in black aprons and white baseball hats and they all wore their stupid-o'clock-on-a-Monday faces. Framed photographs of movie stars blessed the walls. Elaine and Naomi were sitting at a table at the back sucking milkshakes and munching fries with a well serious Al Pacino staring down over them.

'Mo! Over here!' Naomi hailed. 'Over here.'

As soon as I parked myself, Naomi almost leaned into my face and blurted out, 'Sam Bramwell!'

'Keep it under lock,' I said. 'It's no big deal. It's not even on yet cos he's linking with Shevray at the moment and he's gotta—'

'No big deal?' Naomi cut me off. 'He's one of the fittest bruvs in the school.'

She wasn't wrong. I flashed Elaine a glare that said 'Why'd you have to leak to her?'

'You wanna nibble on anyting?' Elaine offered.

'Yeah,' I replied. 'Fries and a strawberry milkshake. I've got funds—'

'It's all right, I'll pay for it.'

Elaine went off to get my munch. Naomi tilted even closer to me. 'So what happened? You two split up in the summer and now you're linking again? Has he dropped the grand piano on Shevray yet? She's *not* gonna love you but I feel one on one you can take her out. Mind you, her shoulders are kinda broad with all that swimming and shit. She's probably got a bitch of a punch on her.'

'I think I know that, Naoms. I don't wanna maul with her.'

'So when's he gonna click the ejector seat on her?'

'That's up to him,' I said. 'For me and him to link *that's* what he's gotta do.'

'And you *stick* to that, Mo! I linked up with a guy earlier this year. He told me he had some baggage – an ex who wouldn't let him go. He said he had to be gentle with her. Some weeks later he's *still* with the same floozy, telling me he doesn't know how to drop her cos she's bawling lakes and shit. So you know what I did, Mo? I sacked *him*! Man ain't taking no liberties with me and that's what I told Linval.'

'And no man's gonna take libs with me either,' I said.

'Good for you, Mo,' Naomi said, patting me on my shoulder.

'Now, what's the lowdown on Lloyd?' I asked. 'You said he's toxic?'

Elaine returned with my snack.

'Thanks,' I said. My eyes didn't leave Naomi. 'What else is dodgy about him apart from giving me a double flab of grief?'

Naomi swapped looks with Elaine. Celine Dion's 'My Heart Will Go On' boomed out from the jukebox. Some blonde chick behind the counter was singing along to it.

'*Tell* her!' Elaine urged.

'He's a top G in North Crong,' Naomi said.

'A top ranking G?' I repeated. 'Semolina-butt Lloyd?'

'No jokes,' Naomi revealed. 'Sean O'Shea, Major Worries, Jim Kelly and Remington Moses – all of them hard core crims. Sean O'Shea's the Crongfather. They say he's the mad one.'

'Sean's the mad one?' I said. 'Lloyd should ask him for a play-off to challenge that.'

'Lloyd did five years' bird for aiding and abetting,' Naomi revealed. 'They gored a bruv outside Louis' Italian restaurant on the Crong circular. Hacked out his throat. Blood flowing like ketchup in a Mac Ds. Lloyd was the driver. His face was caught on CCTV mid-getaway.'

'Funny ting was though,' Elaine added, 'most peeps say that Sean did the carving but he got off – not enough evidence. Plus some North Crong bitch gave him an alibi. Word on the road says Sean was in the back seat of Lloyd's car but the CCTV couldn't quite make him out. Lloyd did the full five years cos he wouldn't snitch on the Crongfather.'

This was crazy talk. Louis'? Mum's ex, Nico D, had taken her there a couple of times. Blood and getaways and mad Sean O'Shea ... Lloyd a top ranking G? A chill scratched down my neck. I had guessed he'd probably done bird for burglary but now I thought about it, I couldn't imagine him leaping his lardy bones over backyard fences, hot-toeing away from hounds. Still. A North Crong G? He wasn't garmed like one. Why was he always broke?

'Linval thinks Sean O'Shea merked Marshall Lee,' Naomi continued. 'Shanked him nine times outside the Four Aces. His kidneys were showing. Linval says Sean's got a custom-built blade, you know the one with the grooves and notches on one edge – eight centimetres wide and twenty long, and sharp as a pimp's toothpick. When he's dissecting a bruv he twists it. He's the living psycho. Nuff witnesses saw it but no one's spilling to the feds. Don't blame them.'

'Er ... who's Marshall Lee?'

'The South Crong G who trod with Folly Ranking and Linval,' Elaine explained.

'You sure you've got the right Lloyd?' I wanted confirmation.

'Beer gut, right?' Naomi asked.

'Yeah.'

'Real Madrid football shirts?' Elaine said. 'The number seven on his back?'

I nodded.

'Has he got a birth mark on his neck?'

'Yeah he has,' I remembered. 'It goes round to his back.'

Jeez and peas. Lloyd.

'But he's never got any funds,' I said. 'When he's on a liquor rush he's always dipping his paws into Mum's purse. He even jacked my dinner money the other day.'

'Apparently, since he finished his bird he wants to go straight,' Naomi said. 'The G life got too much for him. He doesn't talk with Sean O'Shea or the rest of them North Crongbangers.'

'Whether he links with them or not, stay out of his radar,' warned Elaine. 'He's well toxic.'

'But what about my mum?' I said. 'She must know about it.'

We all glanced at each other. Say she didn't know that Lloyd was waist deep with the North Crong crew? He might've told her some twirl about him doing a sentence for something else.

'I want to get more of my stuff,' I said. 'You know – my DVDs, my headphones, more of my clothes.'

'We'll roll with you,' offered Elaine. 'You're not stepping back to your slab on your lonesome.'

'That's all right,' I said. 'I'll ask Sam.'

'Make sure you do,' said Naomi. 'In fact, and this is for your lobes only, Folly Ranking and his crew are planning to take Sean O'Shea out.'

'Take him out?' I repeated.

'Merk him,' Naomi said. '"Rip him open till his blood paints the road ramps," is what Linval told me.'

My back sort of went into a cold spasm as I imagined the belly of this Sean O'Shea being carved from north-east to south-west.

Elaine gave Naomi a hard look. 'She didn't have to know that!'

'Doesn't matter to me,' I said. 'They can waste each other all they like – as long as none of them are troubling me. I am not going back to live in my flat while Lloyd's still there. G or no G.'

I sank my strawberry milkshake too fast. Elaine and Naomi chatted on but I was still trying to get my head around the Lloyd situation. Sean O'Shea might've been in my flat.

'Mo! What's a matter with you?' Elaine slapped me out of my daydreaming.

'Oh, sorry, was just thinking,' I said.

'Are you up for Saturday?' Naomi wanted to know.

'Saturday?' I replied.

'I'm heeling up to Ashburton,' said Naomi. 'I need to feed my wardrobe. I'm tired of the Crongton market shit I get from the home – it's embarrassing.'

'But my hand is mash up,' I said.

'Naoms.' Elaine shook her head. 'Don't do this, sis.'

'I'm not asking you to do any running,' Naomi stressed. 'All you gotta do is bounce into the store and look well suspicious. I'll do the rest.'

'But you've got more garms than me,' I said. 'You don't need more.'

'Let me put an exclamation on that one,' cut in Elaine. 'Naoms, it has to be said – you're too brand-licious!'

'Can't believe my two sistrens are letting me down, man,' Naomi moaned.

'Hold on a sec,' I said. 'Have they ever caught your ass when you've been on a shoplifting spree?'

Naomi pointed to herself. 'Me? Been caught? Are you taking the piss, Mo? I'm too smart for them. Why do you think I plan my missions? You're my diversion.'

I shook my head. 'Hey, I need to borrow a phone – have to chat with Sam.'

'Planning your next link.' Naomi grinned as she passed on her mobile. 'I can't lie. I wouldn't say no.'

'You two been joined at the lips again?' Elaine wanted to know.

'They'll be joined at the hips before too long,' laughed Naomi.

I felt heat in my cheeks so I decided to ding Sam outside – Naoms and Elaine were bound to tease me.

'Sam. What's up?'

'I was gonna call you later, Mo. You keeping good? How's your hand?'

'A bit better,' I replied. 'Hurts when I grip someting.'

'My mum's got some Epsom Salt – it soothes muscle pain. You put it in your bath and you soak in it. I'll bring it around if you want.'

'No, Sam. Elaine's mum is just about tolerating my bones staying there – but I mean only just. I don't wanna gas mark nine the situation with you coming around.'

'I hear that.'

'How was school today?' I asked.

'Same old – different supply teachers. I presented my Black History Month display at lunchtime. It's looking sweet now. Ms De Bois gave me good ratings but she told me to slow down a bit next time.'

'Congrats, man! I know you worked proper hard on that.'

'Thanks.'

'Sam ... did you ... chat to Shevray?'

'She wasn't at school today. She texted me. She's sick – got flu.'

'Oh ... '

'I could ding her and lay it down—'

'*No.* Don't do that. Best to have a one on one.'

'You're right. Are you coming to school tomorrow?'

'No,' I answered. 'Hand's still giving me a little grief. Gonna rest my skin tomorrow. What's the day today?'

'Thursday.'

'I'll be back at school on Monday ... Sam, have you seen my mum? Has she knocked on your gates asking for me?'

'Er ... no, Mo. Haven't even heard a soft cuss out of her.'

'You reckon she's spoken to your mum?'

'Not that I know of.'

'Oh.'

There was a long pause. I guessed Sam could sense I was fretting.

'Mo,' he said softly, 'why ... why don't you give her a ding, just to tell her you're all right ... or even text her. It's not good for a mum and daughter to—'

'No! Why should I? She should be the one who's dinging or texting me. But she won't cos she doesn't give a freaking shit!'

'Yeah . . . I hear you, Mo. She should be looking out for you. The situation's still not good though.'

Tears streamed down my face again. I wiped them away.

'Mo? Mo? You still there?'

I tried to compose myself. 'Yeah, I'm still here.'

'Are . . . are you all right, Mo?'

'I'm surviving,' I replied. 'Listen up, Sam. On Sunday I'm gonna get some more of my stuff – you know, more clothes, DVDs and whatnot. Can you come and get me? Wait for me on the B of the block?'

'Of course.'

'Until then, Sam, and if you see Lloyd, don't even say two lyrics to him, OK. Blank him completely.'

'I'm not scared of him and he can't terrorise me. What kinda man is he for beating chicks outta their snooze?'

'Sam, just keep outta his radar, right. Promise me.'

'OK, I will.'

'Come around about two on Sunday,' I asked. 'When I drop off my stuff maybe we can step somewhere to chill. Just me and you. If the sun blesses the day we can roll to the park or maybe take an expedition up the Heath. In the meantime you have to lay it down to Shevray.'

'I'm gonna drop by her gates on Saturday,' Sam said.

'Good.'

I killed the call. A sweet surge of goodness swelled inside me. My fam life might have been gurgling down the ghetto drain but at least Sam and I were gonna be on point. Shevray might soon think I'd done a major wrong but we were together first. Ancient movie peeps were singing something about a good morning as I returned to the diner. Elaine and Naomi were blowing kisses at me but I didn't care. There was a bounce in my step.

13

Breakfast at Manjaro's

Elaine and I spent Saturday evening in her room watching a DVD. We had tried all day to ding Naoms but she wasn't picking up. It wasn't like her. The film was called *Hanna*, starring Saorsie Ronan, about a girl whose pops teaches her survival skills and how to boot grown men's balls to the max. I wished someone had taught me how to crunch a guy's ribs – then I'd just kung-fu Lloyd's jubbly butt out of our flat.

After the film finished, Elaine decided to plait my hair. As she tugged and twisted my locks I dreamed of having any kinda dad – just someone there to protect and hug me when I'm on the down-low. Why can't Mum find a man on the level? A man who'd give me a fiver for washing his car on a Sunday afternoon. A guy who wouldn't mind stepping to Dagthorn's to buy the batty paper when he'd used it up. A bruv who could at least simmer some pasta and wok-fry a few veggies. A knock at the door interrupted my thoughts.

'Come in, Gran,' said Elaine.

But it wasn't Granny Jackson. Yvonne poked her head around the door. 'Can I come in?' she asked. Her tone was soft.

Elaine shared a glance with me. 'Yeah, of course,' she replied.

'I was just about to crash but I received a disturbing call,' Yvonne said.

'What, Mum?'

'It's your good friend, Naomi.'

'What about her?' I wanted to know.

Yvonne drew in a long breath. 'The call was from the home. Mr Cummings – not sure how he got my number. He told me . . . He said that Naomi's run off.'

'Run off?' I repeated.

'She was caught shoplifting,' Yvonne explained. 'They collected her from the police station. She was quiet but OK. She seemed to accept that she'd been charged with theft and would have to appear in court. She made herself a cheese and pickle sandwich. Half an hour later, a member of staff checked her room and she had disappeared – went out of the window. She's not answering her phone and she's been missing for seven hours.'

Elaine and I stared open-mouthed at each other. Guilt stomped me in the gut. We should've stepped with her and made sure she didn't do anything cradazy.

'Now, Elaine, Mo.' Yvonne looked at us gravely in turn. 'Mr Cummings has told me she has done it before but this is not a game. This is serious. And it's not about snitching so don't even go into that foolishness of covering up for her. We all want the best for her. Has she called you? Texted you? If you know where she might be then please tell us.'

I shook my head. Elaine stared at the carpet. Yvonne took her daughter's hands within her own. 'If you have any idea where she could be, let us know. Even if it's a wild guess. I think you know that Naomi is ... vulnerable ... impression-able. Mr Cummings told me a bit about her past. I'm sure you girls know her dad was an alcoholic. She was basically looking after him from the age of nine, doing the shopping and all sorts. Her childhood was very traumatic.'

'It was.' Elaine nodded. 'To the max.'

'Tell me about it,' I said.

'I don't know where she is, Mum,' Elaine said. 'And she hasn't dinged us – we've been calling but no dice. Yeah, we're sistrens but she doesn't tell us everyting. She keeps that stuff on a zero profile. And me and Mo have only known her for a few months.'

Yvonne turned to me. She spied my eyes. My heartbeat ramped up to rapid. 'Mo? Any places that you can think of? Hangouts? Any other friends? Boyfriends? Exes?'

Naomi didn't have many friends. As far as I knew, just Elaine and me. I thought of the South Crongbanger Linval Thompson but pressed my lips together. I found it hard to look directly at Yvonne.

'Are you sure?' Yvonne urged. 'If she doesn't turn up soon they'll have to get the police involved – they probably have already.'

'I *won't* be talking to *them*!' snapped Elaine. 'Don't trust them. Nobody around here does.'

Yvonne crossed her arms and diverted her gaze. For a moment I thought another round of mum versus daughter would boot off again.

An awkward silence filled the room.

After a while, Yvonne tried once more. 'So you're not gonna tell me anything?' Her hands were now on her hips. 'The home's number one priority is finding Naomi. She won't be in trouble when she returns. That's Mr Cumming's promise.'

'Nothing to tell,' I said. 'Honestly, Ms Jackson.'

There was a long pause. Yvonne kept glaring. It felt too intense – like standing in the middle of the school hall on your lonesome with all the teachers closing in around you, staring and accusing.

She left the room. I blew out a long breath. Elaine got up and pushed the door to. She sat back down on the bed. 'I think I know where she is,' she whispered.

'Then why didn't you spill?' I said.

Elaine watched the door, as if she was expecting Yvonne to crash back at any second. 'She's probably with Linval.'

'Where?'

'Remington House – ground floor. It's where all the South Crong Gs hang out. Can't remember the number.'

'You should've told your mum,' I repeated. 'They're not playing. The feds will be hunting for her.'

'Cos it's not Linval's yard,' Elaine explained. 'Naoms told me he just crashes there. It belongs to one of his crew – probably Folly Ranking. If social workers and feds bash on their gates, Naoms will be up to her gills in all kinds of trouble and madness with some psycho Gs. You know she will. Linval, too.'

'So what are we gonna do?' I asked. 'She's still not picking up her freaking phone.'

We thought about it.

'I could go to her,' I offered. 'And chat some sense into her dense head.'

Elaine had her serious face on.

'No, Mo. Linval doesn't know you as well as me. If that's the plan then it's best that I roll with you.'

I gave Elaine the fierce eyeball. 'Do you need a dose of Day Nurse?' I said. 'Your mum won't give you an oyster to leave your flat tonight. If we both go missing right now she'll bang us down worse than what Folly Ranking could do. But if I went on my lonesome you could tell your mum I had to drop home and pick up a few tings?'

'Mo, hear me. We go together or we don't go at all. We'll step out when Gran and Mum are asleep.'

'Can I rewind on that one?' I protested. 'I don't think I'm gonna risk your mum *Hunger Gaming* me if I try to sneak out.'

'My mum's *not* gonna maul you. We *have* to satnav Naoms.'

'I don't wanna disrespect your fam, Elaine, but your mum's *military* . . . and she's on to us.'

'Trust me, Mo, Mum's not gonna put a knuckle on you – she might mince *me* though.'

'Even more reason not to step out all cloak and dagger tonight.'

Elaine flopped back on to her bed. 'OK,' she said after a while. 'We'll find Naoms in the morning after my mum's gone to work.'

I hardly slept a snore all night. Elaine got up about three times. On the third occasion she brought back corned beef sandwiches, custard creams and blackcurrant squash. I hadn't had a twilight zone feast since the time one of Mum's exes got the serious munchies – he bought us barbeque ribs from the Hot Rooster.

I checked the time – 5.15 a.m.

'What time does your mum leave for work?' I asked.

'Seven-thirty.'

The minutes dragged their asses. At six-thirty we heard a light being turned on in the lounge. Someone switched on the TV. Sky News was reviewing the morning newspapers. The toilet flushed.

'While you're getting ready for work do you want me to make you some scrambled eggs, Yvonne? With some fried plantain and hard dough bread?'

It was Granny Jackson's voice.

'No thanks, Mum. No time to eat. We have a delivery this morning.'

'I'll make it for the girls and Lemar when they get up.'

'Make sure the girls help you with the housework today – that oven needs cleaning. I'm sure they've got homework and revising to do too.'

'Yvonne, you tell me already. Me not going *senile* yet.'

We heard Yvonne leave just after seven.

'Gran always takes her shower around eight-thirty,' Elaine

said. 'We'll go missing then. I don't want her interrogating us on our way out. She will sniff it's got someting to do with Naoms.'

'Say she doesn't take her shower,' I said. 'She might decide to watch TV all morning. What are we gonna do then?'

'Mo! Don't mouse out on me. Man! Do you need to watch another *Mission Impossible* film so you can get in the spirit of our mission? Think of what Tom Cruise would do.'

'I just don't wanna upset your gran.'

'She's a Christian. You wanna hear her sing her hymns. She'll forgive you!'

'What about her lecture yesterday about learning goodness from badness?'

'Getting Naoms back to her home is all about goodness,' Elaine reasoned. 'Badness isn't on my programme.'

She had a good point.

Gran went to have her shower at 8.33 a.m. exactly. 'After me put on me clothes me will stir up some scrambled eggs and plantain,' she said on her way to the bathroom. 'You ever had fried plantain before, Mo?'

'Er . . . no, Gran, that'll be lovely.'

'It goes so nice with hard dough bread! And me think me can hustle up some bacon too. You will love it!'

The bathroom door closed. Gran started singing a Bob Marley song. God, I felt guilty. We crept towards the front door. Lemar suddenly emerged from his room. 'Where are you—'

Before he could drop another word Elaine grabbed hold of him and smothered his mouth with her hand. Lemar squirmed and wriggled free. 'Take your hands off me! Are you trying to suffocate me?'

'Keep your voice down,' said Elaine. 'We have to go somewhere. An urgent mission.'

'You gonna find Naomi?'

'What do you know about that?' I asked.

Lemar smiled. 'I listen when I'm not supposed to listen.'

'You're too fricking nosy!' Elaine snapped.

'Mum's gonna smack the vessels outta your blood cells . . . Can I come?'

Elaine pressed her forefinger against Lemar's lips. She gave him such a fierce glare that even his future grandchildren flinched. 'You didn't see us,' she said.

'If I didn't see you then I want paying without any delaying!'

'Get your bribing ass back in your room before I hammer-throw your liccle self into the next postcode!' Elaine warned.

We left Lemar fretting in the hallway – I hoped Elaine hadn't traumatised him too much. We closed the front door gently behind us. Not until we reached ground level did my heartbeat return to normal.

'Your mum's gonna roast us,' I said. 'Your gran too! And when we make it to the spirit world we'll be grounded there for all eternity.'

'Mo, stop going on so negative – hopefully we'll be back before Mum gets home.'

'Where's Remington House?' I asked.

'It's about a ten minute clop to the east side of the estate,' Elaine replied.

With our nerves rushing our steps, we arrived there eight minutes later, hearts banging hard.

Remington House was a four storey slab fronted by black railings and a concrete walkway. We climbed three steps and walked slowly along the ground floor balcony. There were ten flats on the level, the windows covered by blinds and net curtains. Someone was frying fish. *Oh no!* My insides squiggled and triggled like a breakdancing worm. I tried to ignore the pong. I glanced up. Some flats had bigger satellite dishes than others. A man was delivering flyers on the third floor. On the second floor, an old woman in an even older dressing gown was dragging a black rubbish bag. There were no telltale signs like bass-thumping tunes to indicate where Folly Ranking's crew resided.

'Which one?' I asked.

Elaine thought about it. 'Number eight or nine.'

The doors of eight and nine were identical – polished panelled brown wood.

'Number nine,' Elaine decided.

We skipped up to the door. Elaine rat-a-tatted the letter box as if she was special forces hunting for the world's most wanted – the earthworms under Crongton Heath probably heard it. She stood firm and cleared her throat. I stepped back. I was still trying to wave away the fishy pong polluting my nose. No one came. Elaine smacked the letter box again – even the man posting flyers paused and looked down. Footsteps. We heard a key crunching in the mortise lock. I retreated another metre. I nearly retched. Elaine didn't move an inch. The door opened. Linval appeared. He was wearing a white vest and black tracksuit bottoms. White fluff polluted his misshapen afro. Sleep matter clogged up his eye corners. Holey socks exposed his dirty toenails.

'Where's Naomi?' asked Elaine.

'Why are you banging down our gates so early on a Sunday morning, man?' Linval snapped. 'Don't you observe the freaking Sabbath?'

'Sabbath!' Elaine repeated. 'What do you know about Sabbath? You probably think its goths taking a communal bath.'

'If all you're gonna do is cuss me then *remove* your dirty armpits from our gates!'

'Don't even go there with my armpits,' Elaine retaliated. 'Especially when you come out here with your landfill toenails!'

Linval didn't have a reply for that one. I had to check myself from laughing.

'Where's Naomi?' I asked.

'She's not here!' Linval spat, still fuming about the toenail joke. 'Why don't you go and sabotage somebody else's morning!'

Linval went to shut the door. Elaine plonked her right foot inside. *'Don't freaking lie to me, Linval!'*

'What're you doing, Elaine? Step off from our gates! I'm not playing!'

'I swear if you don't tell me where Naoms is I'm gonna make the biggest piece of noise in these ends since Norma Taylor couldn't find her lottery ticket. Now *where is she*?'

'How do I know? I don't know her movements

twenty-four-seven. Remove yourself from our gates, girl, before I slap your feisty lips into the park. *Disappear!*'

'I'M HUNTING FOR MY SISTREN, NAOMI BRISSET,' Elaine yelled. 'DOES ANYONE KNOW WHERE SHE IS? SHE'S BEEN KIDNAPPED! CAN SOMEONE PLEASE HELP ME? SHE'S MY BEST FRIEND!'

Panic spread over Linval's face. His eyes ping-ponged from one corner to the other. I didn't know whether to laugh, vomit or hot-foot it out of there. 'All right! All right! I'll get her! Drop your tones, girl, I beg you! Just hold on tight. I'll get her.'

Footsteps. Linval turned his head. He switched back to us. 'I beg you, Elaine, just keep the vocals down, all right?'

A bald-headed man appeared. He was tall enough to jack light bulbs from lamp posts. A beard grizzled up his cheeks and what looked like a diamond stud niced up his left ear. His sweat-stained, name-brand T-shirt clung tight to his chest like a balloon stretched over a beer barrel. He had Rihanna's-bodyguard biceps. Black tracksuit bottoms wrapped his snooker-table-strong legs. His backside was as solid as a wrecking ball. Elaine took a step back. So did I. Who in mad Crongton was this?

'Linval!' he called. His voice was nuclear submarine deep. 'What's all the fuss, bruv? We're supposed to be on a low profile in this yard. Didn't Ranks and me tell you that?'

'Yes you did. These chicks have come for Naomi,' Linval replied.

'Then be a gentleman and let them in,' said the walking slab.

Elaine and I swapped rapid glances. Linval pulled the door

open for us. We stepped inside. I was proper relieved – any more exposure to the fishy smell and I would've decorated the front door a very different shade. A framed photo of the film cast of *Bugsy Malone* hung in the hallway. A tune rang in my head.

Neat wooden tiles covered the floor. Linval and his brick-house bredren led us along a hallway to the kitchen. It was cleaner than my own. Something was frying on the stove. Alphabet magnets coloured up the fridge. An incense stick was burning in a small flowerpot on a windowsill.

'Where's Naoms?' I asked.

'She's still sleeping,' said the heavyweight.

'In *my* bed,' added Linval.

'You better not have troubled her!' Elaine warned. 'I *swear* if you have—'

'Settle your rage, girl,' said Muscle Dot Com. 'No one's troubled anybody. We live decently in this yard, and it's the way Ranks wants it – a low-profile tip.'

'I slept on the couch,' said Linval. 'Naoms came here yesterday afternoon on the down-low – well upset.'

Fried eggs and tomatoes were spitting in the frying pan. Toast had already popped out from the toaster. One of those NutriBullet juicing extracting things stood on a counter. Cassandra Wilson was singing over jazzy funky beats from a boom box up on a shelf. We sat down around a small table. Knives, forks and paper towels substituting napkins were already laid out. A jam jar and a knob of butter in a saucer were in the middle. It was civilised to the max but it all felt weirdly off-key.

'Who are you?' Elaine asked the big man.

He washed his Hulk hands in the sink and dried them on a paper towel. I imagined them round the scrawny neck of some poor skinny bruv. 'Manjaro,' he finally replied. 'Some bruvs call me Big M. Do you ladies want some brekkie?'

No one in South Crong had ever called me a lady. I guessed Elaine was thinking the same thing cos she studied Manjaro as if he was a new species of mankind. The toast, eggs and tomatoes were teasing the living cravings out of me. I wanted to say a big yes.

'No thanks,' said Elaine. 'Just tell me where Naoms is.'

'Second door on the left,' said Linval. 'She's sleeping.'

Elaine couldn't wait any longer. I followed her to the door. She pushed it open. There she was, sprawled on a double bed, still in her jeans and a black hoodie. Her trainers and socks were on the floor. Standing on the bedside cabinet was a full glass of something green. The ashtray next to it was full. Posters of celeb chicks including Rihanna and Azealia Banks covered the walls. A flat-screen TV was fixed over the dressing table. Elaine snapped the blinds open. Sunlight rushed in. 'Naoms. Naoms! Come on, girl. Get your ass up!'

Naomi opened one eye, scrunched up her face and closed it again.

'Naomi! Get your freaking ass up! Do you know how much tribulation me and Mo are gonna be in cos we bounced down here?'

Squinting at the sun, Naomi yawned a big yawn before focusing on us. 'Why are you sistrens stalking me? I'm all right. Safe. No need to ring the alarm.'

'Why are we stalking you?' I repeated. 'Are you taking the piss? One of your carers dinged Elaine's mum last night and said your skin's missing. The feds are hunting your tail!'

'*Good!* Let them hunt. Let them sweat and fret. *Bastards!*'

Elaine yanked Naomi's arm until she dropped on the floor. *Budoof!* 'Get your butt out of this bed and outta this yard!' raged Elaine.

'All right! All right! I'm coming. I'm gonna have someting to eat first though – I'm starving.'

'Why did you go missing?' I asked.

'Cos they're getting on my tits,' replied Naomi. 'Man. Anybody would think I'd stolen the queen's knickers! "Do you understand how much trouble you're in? You've been banned from every high street store in Ashburton! You'll have to face a magistrate! You could be sent to a secure unit. It'll interrupt your education. This could ruin your life! The way you're going you'll end up in prison. *Blah blah freaking blah!*'

'Maybe they wouldn't get on your tits if you stopped going on shoplifting sprees,' said Elaine.

'I had some bitch bad luck, that's all. Didn't have you helping my ass out, did I? Could have used my sistrens *then*, couldn't I? I needed more eyes,' Naomi replied. 'I made it past one security guard but bumped into the other. Elaine, I had this top-ranking baby blue top for you and, Mo, I jacked this—'

'Naomi!' shouted Elaine. 'They caught you. Deal with it!'

'Naoms,' I said. 'You gotta stop doing this shit.'

We heard a knock on the door. Manjaro poked his head inside. 'Are you ladies OK?' he asked. 'You sure you don't want any brekkie? There's enough for everyone. Naomi, didn't you drink that juice I made for you last night? It's good for you – cleans you out.'

'Er . . . no, I fell asleep,' replied Naomi.

'So you ladies want something to yam or not?' Manjaro asked again.

'No, we're stepping,' said Elaine.

'No, we're not,' cut in Naomi. 'I'll have someting.'

'Er . . . me too,' I said. 'But I don't want that green stuff. You got anyting else to drink?'

Manjaro looked offended. 'Yeah, we have some orange juice and a few bags of herbal tea.'

Elaine kissed her teeth.

We followed Manjaro back into the kitchen. Linval was already munching fried eggs and tomatoes on toast. We joined him at the table. Elaine was the last to take her seat.

'Do you realise the feds are hunting for her?' Elaine said to Manjaro.

'Yeah,' Manjaro replied. 'But you didn't spill that she might be here, did you?'

'No,' I said. 'We don't spill . . . but we could've—'

'What did I say?' cut in Naomi. 'I *told* you my sistrens wouldn't snitch.'

'Good!' said Manjaro. 'You can't trust the feds . . . you can't trust anybody. You have to rely on yourself and your close Gs.'

I looked at Elaine. She was nodding.

'We're just helping a sister out,' said Linval, crocodiling half a slice of toast with one bite. 'We'll always help South Crong peeps. *That's* what we're representing.'

'To the max,' added Manjaro.

'She's coming back home with us,' I said.

'Only cos *he* won't let me coch here for a few days,' Naomi said, pointing at Manjaro. 'That would really stress out Mr Prick-head Cummings and his staff. I get a pleasure overload just thinking about it.'

'When I said *one* night I meant *one* night,' Manjaro confirmed.

14

Folly Ranking and Early B

A few minutes later I was sinking eggs on toast. I washed it down with lemon and ginger tea – the Gs had no coffee or hot chocolate. Naomi ravaged her brekkie and asked for extra toast. Even Elaine accepted a glass of orange juice, poured by Manjaro. For himself he used the NutriBullet thing to make this green, minty-smelling juice. The buzz of the thing bounced on my nerves. He offered it to all of us but no one accepted.

While Naoms was scrubbing her molars in the bathroom, Manjaro filled her chair and started to build a rocket with extra-large Rizla papers. Elaine and I watched his saveloy fingers rolling his joint in silence. Linval lit another incense stick but it couldn't breeze out the sweet smell of high-grade weed.

'You don't mind me burning, do you, ladies?' Manjaro said. 'I like to blaze a rocket while I'm sinking my juice. It sets me up neatly for the day – helps me think.'

'Do what you wanna do,' said Elaine. 'It's your yard.'

'It's not my yard,' replied Manjaro. 'The owner will be touching down soon.'

'Folly Ranking?' I guessed.

'Yep,' said Linval. 'He'll be landing soon with Early B.'

'Who's Early B?' I asked.

'Our wordologist,' replied Manjaro. 'He's dropping in to chant some rhymes about the Marshall. You ladies know what happened to the Marshall right? Those hoodslugs who merked him will soon find out which way the blood flows on a pumpkin belly. *Trust* me on that one.'

I wasn't completely sure what Manjaro was talking about but guessed it had something to do with pure, X-rated savagery. The reality of what these Gs did for a living conked me in the brain. My nerves stiffened like a wire brush in a freezer.

'What's a wordologist?' Elaine asked.

'An MC,' Linval explained. 'A mic rider, lyrical spitter.'

'And our Minister of Information,' laughed Manjaro.

'We get it,' I said.

'Early B's gonna spout some conscious lyrics about the Marshall's life,' said Manjaro. 'We're gonna make a mixtape so warriors in these ends have something to salute him by. Trust me. North Crong Gs are all on a red alert. *They* know they gotta pay. A hard, sharp shank is gonna fall.'

Suddenly, I didn't feel hungry any more. I pushed my plate to the middle of the table. Elaine picked up a piece of my toast. 'Don't want it to go to waste,' she said.

Naomi reappeared as Elaine finished her slice. While she went to her room to collect her jacket, the letter box spoke.

Linval went to answer it. The lemon and ginger tea I'd drunk turned icy in my chest. 'Naoms!' I called. 'Hurry up!'

Two bruvs strutted along the hallway followed by Linval. The first of them was neatly dressed in blue jeans, blue Adidas trainers, a light blue T-shirt and a denim jacket. He had a number one trim and what looked like a ruby tooth in his front row. He wasn't as hench as Manjaro but I wouldn't have liked to have been the punchbag behind his fists. He entered the kitchen scoping me up and down. His eyes lingered too long on my chest. He grinned at me, his red fang glinting under the kitchen light. My heart changed gear. I wanted to get up and hot-toe it outta there. Something told me to keep my butt still. I could hear myself breathing through my nose.

The other guy was as tall as Manjaro but as skinny as a size zero model. His cheekbones were so sharp they could've shaved all the beards in *The Hobbit*. He was wearing a sky-blue tracksuit, identical Adidas trainers and a furry-looking deerstalker hat. I glanced at Elaine but she was admiring Manjaro's abs. 'Naoms!' I called again.

'We have guests,' the bruv with the red molar said. 'Let me introduce myself. They call me Folly Ranks.'

'If you mess with Folly Ranking, you're bound to get a spanking,' rapped the bruv in the deerstalker.

A dose of cold dread slid down my throat. My brain was urging me to step but curiosity beat the shit out of my common sense.

'You come to hear Early B chant the Marshall's eulogy?' Folly Ranks wanted to know.

I wanted to sip my tea but nothing was left. Elaine ummed and aahed – maybe she was just as fascinated as I was. The crew banged shoulders and bumped fists while I scrambled my brain for a reply.

'My name's Mo,' I managed. I pointed at Elaine. 'She's Elaine.'

'And how old are you ladies?' Folly Ranks wanted to know.

'Fif . . . fifteen,' I hesitated.

Folly Ranks' grin sunk like a cannonball in a well.

Naomi finally emerged from her room. 'You got here early,' she said to the guy in the blue tracksuit.

'That's why they call me Early B,' he replied.

'Can we stay and listen?' asked Naomi. 'Then I promise to step home after. No delays. No scenic routes. *Straight* home.'

Elaine's mouth flapped open but still nothing came out. I shrugged. I couldn't lie, there was something compelling about the South Crongbangers. I looked at Manjaro. He passed on his rocket to Folly Ranks. He sucked on the spliff long and hard. His cheeks hollowed. The smoke filled the kitchen. Even the way he held his rocket was menacing.

'OK.' Elaine nodded. 'We'll see what lyrics and rhymes this Early B's got.'

Early B raised his eyebrows and showboated his fangs like he had been promised sex. He poured himself a glass of water, gurgled and spat out into the sink. Linval led the way to the lounge. I followed closely behind Elaine and Naomi. Fear and excitement dragon-puffed through my veins.

'This is gonna be the bomb,' Folly Ranks said. 'You got everything set up?'

'Of course,' replied Manjaro. 'Schedule's on gloss for the boss.'

'Good,' said Folly Ranks. 'I want keys going out of this mix from South Crong, Ashburton to Notre Dame. Even if you find grass-munching bruvs in the wilderness, make sure they have a copy too.'

Linval nodded. 'Thy will be done.'

There was an open laptop resting on a dinner table. A music mix programme was booting up on the screen. Two small speakers and a microphone were plugged into it. Linval picked up a blanket and a pillow from a beige settee and dumped them on an armchair. Elaine, Naomi and myself dropped down on to the sofa. A red wooden coffee table in front of us had all the pieces of a chess set standing on it. The TV screen was massive – it could have been missing from Crongton Movieworld. DVDs and games consoles were piled in stacks below it. Karate statuettes and football trophies filled a glass cabinet. A *Django Unchained* film poster hung from a wall and beside it was a framed black and white portrait of Little Simz looking all serious in her black fedora.

Manjaro pressed a couple of keys on the laptop and a laid-back beat pumped out from the speakers. Early B picked up the mic. 'Testing microphone; testing microphone. One, two; testing microphone.'

Manjaro adjusted the sound levels.

'He's sicker than the bubonic,' Naomi said. 'He's got more flow than the Nile, more rhymes than a world of nursery schools and an on point delivery that FedEx can't match.'

'What are you – his PR?' Elaine joked.

'Baddest MC I've heard in the ends,' Naomi continued. 'Even better than the grime doctor, Jack Riddler.'

'Who the fruck is Jack Riddler?' I wanted to know.

'You need to flex out of your flat a bit more, Mo,' Naomi replied.

The groove was seductive. I couldn't help nodding my head in time to the beat. Elaine and Naoms jammed with me. Fingers started to click. Manjaro passed on his rocket to Folly Ranks. He tugged on it till it burned bright orange. I felt slightly charged and I wasn't even burning. Early B closed his eyes, flexed his shoulders and cleared his throat. Manjaro spanked up the bass.

> *'Marshall Lee was the second son in his family,*
> *He has a smart younger sis but she's too damn feisty,*
> *His mother serves school dinners for everybody,*
> *But his father died from an accident in the biscuit*
> > *factory.*
>
> *So money was tight,*
> *Gas, electric meters crashing at night,*
> *Marshall step to school in a shirt not so bright,*
> *To look upon his shoes was a terrible fright,*
> *Almost every day the Marshall catch up in a fight.*
> *Marshall didn't love geography nor history,*
> *Algebra mash up his brain, science was a mystery,*
> *He was a liccle bit better at wordology,*
> *But he could never escape other students' cruelty.*
> *They call him rough-foot, no-brand,*
> > *no-pocket-money,*

Marshall couldn't take any more liberty.
He beat down Nicky Batsford, stamp on his belly,
Mash up his eyes till Nicky couldn't see,
Crush Batsford's nose like he was in Apollo Creed
  Three.'

The Gs raised their fists in the air. 'BO! BO! BO!' they hollered.

We nodded and shoulder-juggled to the beat. Early B continued.

'Him get expelled and excluded,
His form tutor even said he was retarded.
The feds take him to a cell and keep him isolated,
Prosecutor press charges, his fam was devastated.
His mother cuss Marshall till her tongue get sore,
Marshall plead his case but his mother just ignore,
She smack-down his face, great pain on every pore,
Marshall shake his head and step outta door,
He start leak tears, call his mother a whore.
He roamed the streets of Crongton, sleep on the cold,
      dirty floor,
North Crong G attack him but Marshall broke his jaw.
He had no choice but to go into hiding,
He needed protecting, he came to Folly Ranking,
The Marshall tell his tale and we bring him in,
A South Crong G was in the making,
South Crong was the ends he loved representing.
Long haired, freaky people need not apply,

We don't want any mud priest, cleric or rabbi,
We don't want no religion or no snitcher that lie,
Being a South Crong G is a natural high.
Like the musketeers we're protecting every South
    Crong body,
Trouble one of us you trouble all of we,
Nuff necks will be carved in North Crong vicinity,
Our shanks and long blades will chop every artery,
Doctors better stock up on their blood capacity,
Vengeance will be taken for the great Marshall Lee,
Says the South Crong wordologist, the one Early B.
So please, South Crong soldiers, help me sing this
    song,
I don't need any promotion or radio station,
Or any X-Factor *or* Voice *audition,*
Or any music company or corporation,
It's me, Early B, at the microphone stand,
And a South Crong land is where my heart belong.'

'BO! BO! BO!' the Gs roared again.

Naomi clapped and pumped her fists but Elaine nudged me in my side. 'Mo, let's bounce,' she whispered. 'I'm not loving this revenge vibe.'

'Me too,' I said.

I stood up. I felt Folly Ranks' eyes hawking me again. Hadn't he heard that I was only fifteen? 'You're fleeing already, Mo?' he said to me. 'You're not gonna stay till we finish the mix? You could give it out at your school. We'll give you funds for that.'

I grabbed Elaine's arm and pulled her up. 'We have to make sure Naomi jets back to her yard,' I said.

'Without any delay,' added Elaine. 'The feds are hunting for her.'

Folly Ranks pulled on his rocket again. He tilted his head back and blew the smoke out of his nose. 'Don't be shy to fly back,' he said. 'We're all about making South Crong strong and that means defending the chicks and the junior cadets.'

'We've ... we've all got nuff tings to do,' I said. 'You know, revising, coursework, walking the hoover, shopping.'

'I feel that,' said Folly Ranks. 'A good education is a crucial thing. And defending your ends is *just* as important. Sometimes even more so. *Know* that.'

'Let's ... let's step,' I said to Elaine who was watching Manjaro download Early B's vocals on to a key. I had to elbow her to get her attention. 'Thanks for the brekkie.'

'Anything for a South Crong lady,' Manjaro replied.

15

Let's Talk About Sex

As we hot-stepped out of the lounge, Folly Ranks asked Manjaro, 'Have you heard from Junior Banks? Has he finished that mural on the side of Paul Bogle House yet?'

'I'll check with him later on,' replied Manjaro.

'I *want* it *done* by Monday night full stop,' Folly Ranks demanded. 'South Crong soldiers need to see it. I want them to start talking about it. When he's done make sure you take a pic and send that image online. I *want* that shit to be as viral as Hong Kong flu.'

'Thy will be done,' said Linval as he opened the front door for us. 'I gave him some notes to buy more spray cans just the other day.'

Ignoring the chill of the morning in his white vest, Linval stepped outside with us. He bear-hugged Naomi, squeezed a portion of her butt and kissed her as if he was munching a second brekkie. Naomi wasn't resisting. Elaine rolled her eyes. I thought of Sam. 'When are you gonna touch down again?' he asked her.

'Don't know,' Naomi replied. 'I'm gonna be on lockdown for ever cos of what happened yesterday. I'll probably have to see my key worker tomorrow and she'll lecture my ass till my menopause. My pops wants to see me too but he's got about as much chance of that as me sharing a plate of poppadoms with the queen.'

'Your ass doesn't need lecturing.' Linval grinned. 'It needs to feel appreciated . . . stroking.'

Naomi blushed. They swapped saliva again. Sam crashed into my head once more.

'*Naoms!*' called out Elaine. 'For frig's sake. Get your butt out of his claws and into motion!'

'I think that's what he wants,' I joked.

After another minute of squelchiness, they managed to separate from each other. Naomi waved to him as he returned to his flat. Once the front door was closed, Elaine offered Naomi one of her *Hateful Eight* stares.

'*What?*' Naomi protested as we set off.

'He's *too* old for you,' said Elaine. '*And* too toxic. Didn't you hear what Early B was rhyming about? They're on the revenge tip.'

'I'm not gonna look for vengeance with them,' said Naomi. 'Besides, what would you do if some North Crong hoodslug merked me or Mo? Would you let it drop?'

Elaine hesitated.

'If it was Sam or one of you two I'm not sure if I'd let it go,' I admitted.

'And Linval's *not* too old for me,' argued Naomi. 'He's not even nineteen yet.'

'When are you sixteen?' I asked Naomi.

'Next March,' she replied. 'The third. You sistrens better not go cheap on me. Why?'

'Legally, he *is* too old for you,' I said. 'If someone snitched you both to the feds, Linval could do bird as a paedophile.'

Naomi burst out laughing. Elaine wasn't impressed.

'Wait a minute,' Naomi checked herself. 'It'd be kinda cool visiting someone in prison. Kinda romantic. I could pass on weed by kissing him. Linval loves his herb.'

'They check for any illegal goods you might be carrying at the gate,' I said.

'Sometimes they give you the ultimate body search,' added Elaine. 'You know, every nostril, crack and hole. Trust me, they go through untold pairs of surgical gloves.'

'I've always wanted to know what it's like on the inside,' replied Naomi, not bothered by Elaine's description. 'I wonder if all the bruvs get tempted to turn to the gay side? You know what guys are like – they need sex on the regs. They can't help thinking about it.'

'There's no hope for you.' I shook my head.

'It's the blatant truth,' Naomi argued. 'No matter how nice and sweet they pretend to be, the end game is sex. Always will be. Even my pops, who's pissed three-six-five days of the year, will still take his side-stepping, red-eyed, unshaven, skinny ass to a bar and try to hit on a chick. The thought of having sex keeps him upright.'

It was all wrong but Elaine and I burst out laughing.

We rolled on for another fifty metres or so before Naomi spoke again. 'Why are you so negative on Linval?' she asked. 'You sistrens are just jealous cos I got a man.'

'*Jealous?*' Elaine repeated. '*Jealous*, she says ... and Linval a *man*? All cos he steps out with Folly Ranking, Manjaro and that twig Early B now? It doesn't make him a *man*. Besides, I don't need that kinda man polluting my life with no hyper-macho drama! All they do is bring stress to a girl's situation and beg you to lie down and open your legs.'

'You would lie down for Manjaro though,' Naomi giggled. 'You don't think I saw you scoping him? I'm not blind.'

'I was *not* scoping Manjaro!' Elaine protested. 'I'd never link or flex with any G! I wouldn't wanna get caught up in their North–South Crong war madness. I'm not on that. Give me a fit bruv who plays soccer or someting, gives his medals to his mum, takes me to the movies, allows me to fantasise about Tom Cruise and buys me the biggest bag of Maltesers.'

'Er ... yes, you were hawking him strong,' I said. 'Naomi's not wrong. Your eyes were on him like a lion tracking one of them deer things. If we stayed in that flat past lunch you'd probably end up pregnant with a future Mr or Mrs Universe.'

Naomi collapsed in hysterics again. Elaine smacked the back of my head but even she had a smile creeping on her lips.

'To be honest I was checking out his goods myself,' I admitted. 'It's hard not to when a bruv's got a bod as ripped as his. Does he crush bricks and put them in his pumpkin juice?'

'He's got weights in his room,' Naomi revealed. 'Linval told me he does a zillion sit-ups before he has brekkie. He's got this core ting that he works out on. Even his farts do circuit training. And he makes these health drinks that are freaking disgusting.'

'So what if he's got a pack of cut abs,' said Elaine. She pointed to her head. 'To impress me the bruv's gotta have someting whirring up here.'

'Sam's got all of that.' I smiled. 'He's a stepping Wikipedia – he knows nuff tings about everyting, especially history.'

'Will you stop going on about Sam this and Sam that,' Elaine moaned. 'Anybody would think he chats about black holes, quantum physics and the meaning of life with Stephen Hawking.'

'And Sam's got manners too,' I put in, not wanting Elaine to shut me down.

'This might sound like science fiction but Manjaro's got manners as well,' Naomi said. 'No jokes. When I washed up last night he knocked on my bedroom door just to say thanks.'

'No!' I said.

'Not lying,' Naomi confirmed. 'How many Crongton bruvs are like that?'

'*None*,' replied Elaine. She laughed. 'Zero! In fact, put a minus on that.'

'*Sam's* polite,' I said, in a raised voice.

Elaine stopped in her tracks, killed her chuckles and gave me a long glare. 'You need to be careful of that bruv,' she said. 'He was so freaking polite to you, he sacked you after your summer fling and started giving it to Shevray.'

I tried to rid the image from my mind. 'I . . . I don't think they got that far,' I said.

'Of *course* they did!' cut in Naomi. 'Every morning she bounces into school with her dick-a-licious smile that's wider than a clown's who's just won the lottery. She's not fronting her gums like that cos Sam Bramwell pecked her on the cheek after a game of Connect Four. No way! He got his grimy way with Shevray.'

'He-he won't be sampling anyting from her again,' I stuttered.

'That depends on whether you give it up to him,' Naomi said. 'Trust me on this, Mo. Bruvs are all the same – if they're not getting it from their girl they're gonna be examining the curves of another in fine biological detail. That's how it goes down in Crongton.'

'Not all bruvs are like that,' I argued.

'Yes they *are*,' countered Naomi. 'You really think Sam's gonna link with you for too long if he can't get to sample your goodness? Wasn't that the reason why he sacked you in the first place? All it took was for Shevray to show a piece of her flesh – you remember that short, skintight skirt she rolled into school with the first day after the summer holiday? If she twerked in that the collateral damage would've been gruesome. Sam microscoped the butt on her and his world was rocked. He went all goo-goo for her after that. He's like all bruvs, Mo – his brains are downstairs and I'm not talking about his feet!'

I was about to fire back but in truth I didn't know what to say. The memory of Sam abandoning our relationship that summer booted me in the gut. I quickened my stride. Naomi and Elaine had to break into a jog to catch up with me. For two hundred metres or so we rolled in silence. Naomi broke the tension. 'Sam *might* be different,' she said. 'He *might* be one of the good ones. Note my swing on *might*—'

'He *is* one of the good ones,' I cut in.

'I'm just being real, Mo,' Naomi replied. 'Trying to protect you. When's the last time you heard of a sister from these ends getting married? Do you ever see chicks from South or North Crong bouncing into that wedding dress shop on the Broadway? Let me answer that one for you. *No.* And you know why that is? Cos bruvs in Crongton can't commit to any girl for a long stretch. After a certain amount of time they get itchy dicks.'

Naomi had a point but I had convinced myself that Sam wasn't like most Crongtonian guys.

'No bruv in these ends can afford to get freaking married,' laughed Elaine. 'Except the Gs. And I can't see them gliding down the aisle in a mad hurry.'

'You're not wrong there,' chuckled Naomi.

'Naoms?' Elaine hesitated. 'Did ... did you give it up for Linval?'

Naomi stopped walking. Her eyes blazed. She angled her head and opened her mouth. Nothing came out.

'What's the score on that one?' Elaine wanted to know.

'What kinda question is that?' Naomi asked. 'That's my personal biz. If you wanna get your freak on, read a *Dirty Shade of Grey* or whatever it's called.'

'I'm asking cos you're not gonna end up flinging some

138

bouquet over your shoulder after a wedding on that one,'
Elaine said. 'Not gonna happen. Linval's moving with hard-
road crims so whatever's going on with you two it's not gonna
end with a reception at the Shenk-I-Sheck.'

Naomi shook her head. 'If I ever have a wedding reception
you might as well make the most of it cos it'll be at a more
top ranking place than the freakin' Shenk-I-Sheck! And I'd
like to spend my honeymoon in Las Vegas or Cancun. Or—'

'Did you, though?' I cut Naomi's flow. 'Or did Linval really
crash out on the couch all night?'

'I'm fifteen for frig's sake!' Naomi raised her voice. 'Do you
have to bash your hips with a bruv all because you wanna get
married or want kids with him one day? Ain't a girl entitled
to have her fun too? You two are going on like you got your
sex education from the pope. Get off my tits!'

'I'm not gonna stop asking until you tell me,' warned
Elaine.

'*No!*' Naomi finally responded. 'There's your answer, OK?
Once Manjaro found out I was only fifteen, he wouldn't leave
us alone together. He kept going on about how he doesn't
want the feds or social services bashing down his gates for
any underage drama. We were sitting around playing cards
till three in the morning, and it wasn't strip poker. Happy
now?'

'He's not stupid,' Elaine said.

'No he's not,' I added. 'But if he hadn't been there ... would
you, you know?'

Naomi didn't think too long about it. 'Yeah, I'm ripe
enough,' she said. 'It's my body. I do what I like with it. And

if I said yes it doesn't make me no ho. I don't leave my DNA on bruvs' pillows all over the ends. One fit guy is enough for me. And Linval's *fit*.'

'Nobody's calling you a ho,' replied Elaine.

'In your heads you are!' Naomi snapped. 'I know what other bitches say behind my back, judging me. You know what? I don't give a silent fart!'

'No one's calling you anyting,' I said. 'Just be ... careful.'

'I was being careful,' replied Naomi. 'Before I touched down at Linval's, I went to Dagthorn's and bought a packet of condoms – strawberry flavoured ones. Old Dagthorn looked at me like he hadn't had any for the longest time. And when I say any I mean *sex*!'

I couldn't help but burst out laughing. Elaine held her stomach and cracked up with me.

'What?' Naomi asked. 'Do you think I'm gonna rely on Linval to buy condoms? Do I have "stupid" painted on my butt? I can't lie, Linval's got two hard, round, rolling ball cheeks but if he got me pregnant I'd saw off his balls with a spud slicer!'

We had to stop stepping, we were laughing too hard. When we'd finished cackling, Naomi continued her flow.

'I'm not gonna be no sixteen-year-old mum pushing some trailer-truck-size buggy with all the little apps to hold your drinks and baby bottles. Have you seen them? Do you see how long it takes for them to jump on a bus? Fruck that! No baby's gonna mash up my life. I haven't got time for that game. How am I gonna rave and go dancing? If I got pregnant I'd have an abortion. Deffo! Wouldn't even have to think twice about it. This girl in my last home had a kid – she had more stretch marks than an elephant's leggings! How's she ever gonna rock a Stella McCartney bikini on a beach in Ibiza?'

For a short second I thought I was gonna have an asthma attack. My ribs were hurting.

'I don't know about an abortion,' I said, regaining my composure. 'Can you imagine a baby booting inside your belly and then getting rid of it? Not sure if I could do that.'

'I couldn't,' said Elaine. 'No way. But I'd never get myself in that kinda mad drama in the first place. I'm not that dumb.'

'Not even with Manjaro?' I teased. 'Rocking cribs, if you paired up with Mr Universe that baby would have the biggest mouth in the world.'

Naomi fell about into giggles again as Elaine chased me in and around the slabs of Wareika Way. She finally caught up with me but she was too tired to give me a beat-down. Naomi was still laughing when she finally reached us.

'For the *last* time,' Elaine panted, 'I *wasn't* scoping Manjaro. Can we put a full stop on that one?'

'Of course you wasn't!' added Naomi.

'We believe you,' I laughed. 'He's too skinny for you – not enough detail in his muscles!'

We rolled on for another few minutes, teasing the living furies out of Elaine. She countered by staring at me. 'What about you, Mo?' she asked. 'If Sam's hands start roaming over your business, what're you gonna do?'

'There's … there's nothing wrong with stirring it up,' I managed. 'You know, showing some love.'

'We're not talking about stroking the bumpers, caressing

wings, brushing the feathers,' Naomi got to the point. 'We're talking about if he's ripping off your knickers and begging the bush bouncer for a *dick* pass. *That's* what we're talking about.'

'I . . . I don't know,' I replied. 'Not . . . not sure if I'm ready.'

'If you're not ready then you might as well touch down at Dagthorn's and buy Sam a goodbye, nice knowing you card,' said Naomi. 'I don't care how polite he might be, how sweet he is to his mum, how many ash heads he helps to cross the road and what top ratings he's getting at school, when it comes to sex he's like any other bruv. They *want it* and they want it yesterday. And if they don't want it yesterday they beg for it last week.'

'He'll . . . he'll wait till I'm ready,' I said.

Naomi nearly fell over in hysterics. *God!* This girl had a laugh on her.

Elaine shook her head. 'If he waits, then you know he's on a level and respects you,' she said. 'If he doesn't, then you know he's counting crotches when he falls asleep. *Know* that.'

In the summer, Sam and I did a lot of appreciating the curves and stroking the bumpers. I always stopped him when I felt it was going too far. I wasn't sure if I could've handled the extra stress if Yvonne had finished her shift early and walked in on us. She would've definitely spilled to Mum.

'The important ting,' Elaine resumed, 'is to not give it up till you're ready – that could be next week or next year. Even two years.'

'Another *two* years?' Naomi raised her voice. 'You might as well lock up your business with one of them chastity belts they used in Robin Hood days and call yourself Lady Virgin of Crongshire. Sex is meant to be enjoyed by women too you know – it's not an unforgiveable sin.'

'Naomi!' Elaine shouted. 'I'm trying to give Mo some proper advice.'

Naomi nodded, finally putting her giggles on lock. 'She's not wrong. Don't follow me or anyone else – follow your own mind.'

Ten minutes later, we arrived at Naomi's house. As we approached her pathway, net curtains twitched at the windows. A fat man emerged from the front door. He was wearing a loose-fitting sweater that couldn't hide his belly. His hands were in his pockets as he watched Naomi with controlled rage.

'That's Mr Cummings,' Naomi whispered. 'I hate him.'

'He's got a weight problem – he can't *wait* till he gets to eat,' Elaine chuckled.

'*Stop* taking the piss,' I hissed. 'He might hear you.'

'See you at school tomorrow,' Naomi said, trying to lock down her laughter, 'if they let me go.'

We group-hugged for a long minute. It felt good. Tears filled Naomi's eyes.

'Naomi!' Mr Cummings called. 'I'm glad to see you're safe. We've been worried sick. Your father's been calling constantly. Where've you been?'

'I'm here aren't I?' Naomi replied. She wiped her eyes. 'I know how to look after myself.'

'You're not *meant* to look after yourself,' said Mr Cummings. 'We're here for you. Would you like to talk about ... this?'

Naomi pretended to retch and vomit with full sound

effects. 'With you?' she finally answered. 'I'd rather have a case review with a slug.'

I could sense Mr Cummings' fury but he let it go. Naomi gave us a last squeeze before she rolled up to her front door. I thought of the hugs Elaine's fam always gave me – they made me feel loved, wanted. Naomi and Mr Cummings? They just glared at each other. No wonder she craved intimacy.

Suddenly, Naomi hot-toed back to us. '*Promise* me you'll be there when I step to court?' she pleaded. 'They might send me away. *Promise?*'

'Of course!' I said and held her hand tight in mine. 'It's not even debatable. It's in the diary.'

'Even if we have to hop school,' added Elaine. 'When it's all done we'll step to the Cheesecake Lounge.'

'Frig the Cheesecake Lounge!' mocked Naomi. 'We'll hit the Shenk-I-Sheck! Sink some shots and cocktails! Dance to some block house grime.'

Naomi mopped her cheeks, forced a smile and reluctantly stepped inside. Mr Cummings gave us a dirty look before closing the door. I was about to give him a full Crongton ear-savaging but thought better of it.

16

The Sound Of Silence

My instincts were telling me not to march into Elaine's flat and face Granny Jackson. Guilt smacked my conscience for skipping brekkie and sneaking away. I just wanted to wait on the B of the block for Sam.

'Mo!' Elaine insisted. 'If you're there with me, Gran will only half merk me. If you're not there you'd better buy yourself a black hat and ask Early B to write my eulogy.'

Reluctantly, I followed Elaine into her yard. It was more nerve-wracking than stepping into Folly Ranking's den. The TV in the lounge was on – Del Boy and Rodney were raging at each other in another repeat of *Only Fools and Horses*. Granny Jackson was ironing Elaine's school uniform. She glared at Elaine as if she had swapped her rum bottle with mud blood before she concentrated on her work again.

'Gran,' Elaine called. 'We found Naomi. She's back in the home.'

Granny Jackson refused to look up. Instead, she folded Elaine's school trousers and placed them carefully on the back of an armchair.

'Gran. I'm sorry that you cooked brekkie and we weren't here to sink it,' Elaine tried again. 'Sorry to the max! But I had to go and get Naomi – she wasn't picking up her phone.'

From a basket on the floor, Gran picked up one of Lemar's school shirts. *'Hmmmpt!'*

'I'll do all my chores this afternoon,' Elaine offered. 'And some more on top of that – just tell me what needs doing? Gran ... *please* talk to me. I'm sorry for stepping out but I *had* to go.'

Granny Jackson stopped ironing. *'Hmmmpt!'* she repeated and chewed the corner of her gum. She finally looked up. There was enough venom in her glare to scare off a sky full of Death Eaters. 'You sure Naomi reach home safe?'

'Yes.' Elaine nodded.

'We walked her to her gates,' I added. 'Mr Cummings was there.'

'And where was she?' Granny Jackson wanted to know. 'Where was she yesterday afternoon and all night?'

'Er ... can't say,' Elaine replied.

'What do you mean you can't say?' Granny Jackson raised her voice.

'Just can't,' said Elaine. 'Isn't it all nice and good that she's home safe though?'

Granny Jackson resumed ironing the sleeve of Lemar's

shirt. 'Me suppose so,' she said. 'Your mother called over an hour ago.'

I could see the dread in Elaine's eyes. Her lips thinned and she swallowed a ball of spit or something.

'Don't worry yourself,' Granny Jackson said, smiling at the tension in Elaine's face. 'Me told her you two were sleeping.'

'Thanks, Gran.'

'Appreciate it,' I added.

'*Don't* think you get off lightly. Oven needs cleaning, kitchen floor wants mopping and blankets have to be taken to the launderette. And don't you girls have homework to do?'

'No problem, Gran. Take it as done.'

'*And* you can do your own ironing!'

'I'll . . . I'll start with the oven,' I offered. 'When I'm done I need to pick up a few things from home.'

'You're not going anywhere,' Granny Jackson said. 'Me lied for you once today, me *not* doing it again. Let me tell you that. The Good Lord will be offended. Yes, sah! And because of you two, me couldn't go to church today. Me good friend Miss Belinda wasn't too happy with me. You should've heard her cuss-cussing on the phone – she hates to sit alone.'

'But, Gran,' Elaine cut in, 'Mo needs her garms – she's not wearing *my* underwear.'

'Trust me,' I said, 'I don't wanna wear your underwear.'

Granny Jackson nibbled her gums again. 'After you've done the oven you can go and get your clothes, but *don't* take too long. You better reach home before me daughter finishes work. And that oven better be cleaner than the one in Saint Peter's kitchen.'

17

Basketball and Welfare Juice

An hour and a half later, I was wondering why I didn't offer to take the bedding to the launderette. Granny Jackson had given me pink rubber gloves and wire wool pads to clean the oven. I grazed my knees. I hurt my already bruised hand. Every muscle in my arms and shoulders ached. Before Elaine fixed up my hair to link with Sam, she massaged my neck and shoulders. It was like having a real sister.

'Where are you two soul bloods gonna stroll before you pick up your garms?' she asked as she brushed my hair in front of her dressing-table mirror.

'Somewhere on the low tip,' I replied. 'Crongton Heath. Not many peeps cruise up there on a Sunday. Only the keep-fit freaks and the Sallys without sistrens.'

'Good move.' Elaine nodded. 'Whatever you do, don't bounce to Crongton Park. Someone from school is bound to scope you there and before you know it your business is broadcast all over Crong and beyond.'

'I hear you,' I agreed.

'And remember what I said,' Elaine reminded me. *'Don't* let him sample your goodness till you're sure he's given Shevray the sack.'

'He was meant to see her yesterday.'

'Good,' Elaine said. 'I'm sure there'll be nuff bruvs waiting for her and her short skirts when they find out she's on her ownsies.'

At 1.45 p.m. the waiting was cranking up my anxiety. I just had to head for the balcony. Elaine followed me.

'Elaine!' Granny Jackson called. *'Don't* even think about going anywhere. I need you to do someting for me.'

'I'm saying bye to Mo.'

I looked down to the forecourt. There he was. Sam. Waiting on the B of the block. Fifteen minutes early.

'He's proper keen,' remarked Elaine. 'Have a blessed afternoon – but not *too* blessed an afternoon. *Don't* give it up.'

'I won't give it up, *Sister* Elaine,' I mocked. 'Don't fret, I'll be back in time for my last supper and prayers.'

Elaine pulled a face and went back inside.

'Yo, Sam. Up here!'

He looked up. 'Mo!'

I skipped along the balcony and almost broke my ankle bull-frogging down the stairs. He greeted me with his easy smile. As usual, half of his hair was in cornrows and the other afro. He was wearing blue jeans and a sky-blue hoodie. *Cute.* He hugged me tight and I could feel the baby hairs of his chin. Even the sun came out to nice up the afternoon.

149

'What's gwarning, Mo. How did Saturday treat you?'

'Didn't do too much. Watched some DVDs at Elaine's. Drama happened later though.'

'Why? What happened?'

I took a deep breath. We started walking. 'Feds clipped Naomi after she went on a shoplifting spree. She has to step to court. Feel bad cos Elaine and I could've done more to cosh her mission.'

I told him about our trek to Manjaro's flat to find Naomi.

'Don't step to their yard again,' Sam warned. 'They go on about how they're protecting the ends but they're hard core. Believe me on that one.'

'Manjaro made us brekkie,' I said.

'Manjaro?' Sam stopped striding. He gave me a hard look. 'Mo, that is one messed-up bruv with a globe-load of problems.'

'How do you know?'

'Nuff peeps whisper,' Sam replied. 'He's got mama issues. Didn't you hear about how Manjaro cracked Welton Blake's face against the kerb? They were proper bredrens. They were swapping banter when Welton joked about Manjaro's mum being a ho. *Wrong move.*'

'Didn't hear about that drama,' I said.

'Welton's got stitches laced across his forehead. They branded him Triple-Brow. Trust me, Manjaro's so far off-key they haven't built the lock yet. And I heard his pop's a mad woman-beater.'

'But he seemed all right to me,' I said.

'Listen to me on this one, Mo – keep outta his circumference. And the bruvs he trods with.'

I linked arms and pulled him towards me. 'You're getting a bit over-protective in your old age,' I said.

'You gotta be on red alert when you're around those bruvs,' he replied. 'You drop one wrong word and they force you to headbutt the concrete.'

I wanted to change the subject. 'Did you miss me? You know, not being upstairs from you?'

'Yeah, it was weird,' he said. 'Your room's on top of mine. Knowing you weren't there was a major switch for me.'

I searched his eyes. I believed him.

'At least you can't bang on your ceiling with your football boot to wake me up on a Sunday morning,' I said.

'Sunday morning? More like Sunday afternoon. You love your sleep more than you love b-ball.'

'And you love that lame *Big Bang Theory* more than you love me, that's for real. When you're watching it I might as well start a convo with your screensaver.'

'Half an hour!' Sam raised his voice. 'An episode is only half an hour. I would park with you for a whole afternoon watching *Boardwalk Empire* with you—'

'Park?' I cut in. 'I remember it differently. Hands wandering, my zip sliding, testosterone bubbling and you trying to give me a love munch on my neck.'

'You wouldn't keep still!'

'How am I supposed to keep still with you draining me of my bodily fluids like a vampire?'

'Anyway, not my fault *Boardwalk Empire* is soooo boring. What's a bruv supposed to do?'

Suddenly Sam looked uncomfortable.

'Let's head out,' I said.

We rolled out of the southern ends of our estate until we hit the Heath Road.

'Did ... did you chat to Shevray?' I asked.

Sam hesitated.

'Don't go mute on me, Sam. Did you?'

'Her mum wouldn't let me see her,' he replied. 'She's got an evil dose of plague and her mum has her on lockdown in bed. She said she's on the Night Nurse.'

'So you didn't get a chance to broadcast our situation to her?'

'No, Mo. And even if her mum had let me in, I couldn't sack her while she was lying in her sick bed. That's just too wrong.'

Sam was right but I just couldn't help punching him in his back.

'What was that for? Mo! Trust me, as soon as I see her I'm gonna lay it down to her. I'm gonna roll the end credits on that one. Promise.'

I boxed him again. 'You'd better.'

We stepped on, passing the wood where evil PE teachers forced us to run cross-country.

'Where're you taking me, Mo? Don't forget I'm supposed to be helping you pick up your garms.'

'That's number two on my agenda but I thought I'd take you up to the rec first,' I replied. 'Thought we'd play some one-on-one b-ball on the new AstroTurf.'

'Mo. You know me and a b-ball are not good bredrens.'

'Did I say the same ting when you wanted a chess partner? No! So stop your bitching and get your stride on.'

'Can't we go up to the leisure centre and play water polo or something? I've got skills at that.'

I guessed he had played water polo with Shevray. I blazed him a look that could've barbecued the spare ribs of a rhino. 'Basketball!' He grinned away his awkwardness. 'I can only get better.'

We arrived at Crongton Heath rec fifteen minutes later. The hills beyond it seemed to kiss the clouds. The sun was playing peek-a-boo. A few peeps in tracksuits were jogging around the track. A couple of others styling white headbands were performing mad stretches – I almost felt tired watching them. They were studied by a guy smoking a rocket in the small stand. He was wearing a yellow dayglo top and heavy boots, and wielding Crongton's longest, hairiest broom. An old lady peered through binoculars behind him. In the infield, a woman with a voice deeper than Megatron was drilling hockey girls on shooting practice. *What does* she *drop in her pumpkin juice?* A guy on his lonesome was zooming down the long jump lane. The sandpit didn't look too fresh. A dog was sniffing around the discus circle before it raised a hind leg and took a piss. Straight outta Crongton.

I could hear shouts and curses from the AstroTurf behind the stand. 'Come on, Sam. Beat you there!'

I stole a lead from him but as always, despite me trying to trip him up, Sam won the race. Eight bruvs and two fit chicks were playing soccer on one of the three five-a-side pitches. Another two guys were balling on a basketball court – three were empty. We paid our five pound deposit for a ball and started playing on a vacant court. Sam was pretty tall but he wasn't any LeBron

James or Kevin Durant – a drunk bruv pissing in a doll's teapot had more accuracy. In any case, if he even remotely looked like scoring, I would jump on his back, dig my nails into his shoulders, tramp on his toes or try to pull off his hoodie. *Nice chest!*

'*That's* another reason why I don't like playing you cos you *always* cheat!' Sam complained. 'Haven't you heard of rules?'

'Grieve to the referee,' I replied as I shoulder-bumped him and scored again. 'Boo-freaking-hoo.'

He retaliated by wrestling me to the ground, rolling up my tracksuit legs and tickling behind my knees – he knew that was my vulnerable spot. It was good to laugh. I booted his chest but it wasn't easy to brush him off and truth be told I wasn't so sure I wanted to. I couldn't lie – it was nice to feel his body pressing against mine.

When we actually got up and played some ball, it was a good workout. I beat his ass thirty-two to sixteen. When we finished we both lay flat on the court, staring up at the sky. We both puffed hard. Sweat poured off me. My hair frizzed. His face was filmed in perspiration too but it just made him sexier. Kiss-a-licious. *Man! Sam Bramwell's lying down with me on Crong rec! He chose me! Not Shevray with her* America's Next Top Model *sway, bigger tits, name-brand garms and showcase trainers.* I tried to forget about the fact that he hadn't actually given her the Wellington boot yet.

'What d'you think you'll be doing in five years' time?' I asked him.

'Probably at uni,' he replied. 'If I don't go my mum will definitely shoot me and send me there in a box anyway. I'm gonna need a good degree to be a history teacher.'

'You seriously still wanna teach?' I challenged him. 'Have you been dropping brain cells? Have you clocked the stress levels on teachers at South Crong High? Half of 'em are on Prozac and the other half are popping dragon hip pills to get them through the day.'

Sam laughed. 'Mo, do you really think I wanna teach at a school like South Crong? No freaking way! Did you hear about Miss Soares?'

'The Asian teacher who talks proper quiet? Biology?'

'Yep – that's her.'

'You have to go up to her desk to check what she's saying.'

'She had a breakdown, Mo. She's only been teaching at South Crong for six months.'

'Seriously? That's not too bad. Most new teachers flop out after two.'

I laughed at my own joke but Sam wasn't feeling it.

'Yeah,' he said. 'Miss Soares had to be helped out of the science lab after some Year 8 kid told her to stand on a ladder and suck her mother.'

I couldn't help but leak a chuckle.

'It's not funny, Mo. That's one of the reasons why I don't wanna be stuck in some low-ranking school in the ends – kids here are too renk and run up their mouths too much – they need some *heavy manners* as my mum would say.'

I rolled on to my side to face him. Man hairs were sprouting above his top lip. 'So where would you like to teach?' I wanted to know.

He considered it. 'Somewhere different. Somewhere far. Not too far cos I wanna be able to step to a decent trimologist to get a proper snip. I don't want any C-class hands sabotaging my fro and my rows.'

'You're so vain,' I said, punching him in the chest.

'I just wanna be somewhere where there's not so much badness going down twenty-four-seven. All everyone's chatting about these days is what happened to Marshall Lee, which Gs gonna be blazed next and who's gonna paint the RIP mural. I'm tired of it, Mo. That's why I don't want you near those hardback crims.'

'I can look after myself, Sam. Jeez and peas! Didn't you learn anyting from watching the *Hunger Games* films?'

'Yeah I did actually – chicks need help now and again.'

'Wrong!' I argued. 'We don't need any bruv saving our butt.'

Sam shook his head. 'By the way, you won the game so you have to get the drinks.'

'I haven't got any funds, remember? I'm a fugitive without a budget.'

Sam dug into his pocket and tossed me over a few coins. 'Get me a welfare juice and a Mars bar. Get yourself something. You owe me.'

There was a drinks and chocolate vending machine just outside the changing rooms at the back of the small stand. As I queued to get our refreshments, I wondered if I'd play a starring role in Sam's life in five years' time. The wifey of a history teacher? That wasn't too tatty. Much better than being the floozy of a South Crongbanger – I needed to have a proper one on one with Naoms to discuss the Linval situation. Sam and I wouldn't drop babies till our thirties. We'd holiday in cool places like Shanghai and New Orleans – one day Sam could even jet me to the US to watch a live NBA basketball game. That could be a sweet treat for my twenty-first.

I returned to Sam with our snacks.

'You got my juice?' he asked.

'Yeah,' I replied, holding up his bottle of water. 'But before you get it, you have to do your Obama impersonation.'

'Mo. Stop playing, girl. Give me my welfare juice! I'm proper thirsty.'

'Nope. Do your Obama ting.'

'Here?'

'Yes, here.'

'But them brothers playing ball over there might see.'

'So – if you do it good, charge them a fee. If they give you top ratings you should do your Kanye West as well.'

'Mo, stop messing.'

'I'm not messing,' I said. 'Come on, Sam. Do it for me.'

'Blackmail!'

'You're damn right it's blackmail. Now stop your griping and get your Obama sway on. Entertain me!'

Sam shook his head before checking if anyone else was watching. He stood up, cleared his throat and flexed his fingers. 'No, I can't do this,' he said. 'Not here.'

'Sam! Come on, Half-Fro. Cheer me up, man. Press my funny buttons! Are you a hamster or a rhino?'

He flicked me an offended look. *Good!*

'*I'm at a loss why so many of you Republicans detest me,*' he began, looking to his right and then to his left just like Obama. He even pointed like the former president. I could almost picture Michelle standing beside him. '*I haven't eaten your children, bombed your churches, never gained illegal entry into your homes and stolen the Thanksgiving turkey. I haven't set dogs on you or lynched you or even pissed on your white picket fence. Nor have I chained any of your menfolk to the back of a pickup truck and driven down a rocky road.*'

By now I was busting with laughter. His American accent was so on point. If he didn't make it as a history teacher there was a career waiting for him as an impressionist.

'*And I certainly haven't assaulted any women,*' Sam resumed, maintaining his presidential stare. '*I apologise if the fact that my mother was white has offended your sensibilities and I'm sorry that I haven't bleached my skin and straightened my hair like Michael Jackson. Perhaps that would've made me more acceptable. But I'm at a loss at why you folk hate me so much ... I have to ask ... is it just a black thing?*'

Finally, his face creased up and he burst into laughter. We rolled about in giggles until my ribs begged me to stop.

'You should join the school drama club,' I suggested. 'Ms Crawford would love to have your funny bones on stage. She's looking for more guys. I'll get Elaine to big you up to her.'

'Nah,' he said. 'Remember in Year 7 when I did the school play? Pure abuse I got for that. Some haters called me a chi-chi boy.'

'Them hoodslugs are just jealous,' I said. 'Don't let them put you off.'

'Now can I have my welfare juice?' he asked.

I tossed him over his bottle of water and his Mars bar. It didn't take me too long to sink my Twirl and can of Coke.

18

Falcon's Ridge

'When's the last time you climbed up to Falcon's Ridge?' he asked.

'I've never been up there,' I admitted.

He scooped me to my feet and without even asking he set off towards a dried mud path that snaked into the woods. I had to bust into a jog to catch him up. 'Do I get a choice in this?' I asked.

'No,' he said. 'You'll love it. It's the living view when you get to the top. You can see all over Crongton and the ends of the wilderness.'

'You can see all over Crongton?' I repeated. 'It's not exactly like breezing in a balloon and kissing the Jesus statue over Rio.'

'Mo, *cease* your bleating and get your stride on.'

'What about the ball?'

'We'll take it with us.'

The climb was proper steep. The path wriggled this way and that. My calf and thigh muscles screamed for mercy but I didn't want to flake out in front of Sam on this mission. I kept going. We passed through pine and oak trees, past the fenced-off Scouts' complex. Birds sang in the branches above our heads and squirrels hot-pawed in and out of sight. On the ground, bugs crawled everywhere and we even caught sight of a fox with a tail thicker than its body – it stood still as a statue and scoped us go by.

By the time we reached Falcon's Ridge, I was puffing hard. No wonder not too many peeps got their hike on up here. The wind jungled-up my hair. We were all alone. Sam led me to the viewing platform – four steps leading to a waist-high concrete circular wall built within an arc of pine trees. Copper plates set into the circle indicated with arrows the towns and villages in the distance: Monks Orchard, Spenge-on-Leaf, Shrublands, Miller's Pond, Elm Park Gates, Biggin Spires, Corkscrew Spa, Nobbler Fields.

'Close your eyes,' said Sam, putting down the ball, 'and make a wish.'

Before I shut my eyes I had to appreciate the stunning views all around. You could see our estate, North Crongton and even Notre Dame to the north-west. Forests, hills and fields made up the rest of the panorama. All of a sudden my world was broader than Broadway.

'My mum used to bring me up here and make me do the same thing,' Sam revealed. 'I think she first took me up here after Pops left. "Make a wish," she'd always say. You made yours yet? When you do, keep it to yourself.'

My wish was easy. To be part of Sam's life in five years'
time. Maybe we'd be engaged by then, living in some
cramped-up flat paying a jacked-up rent. Elm Park Gates
sounded like a cool place to live. I hoped to be nine-to-fiving
by then – not in an office – that'd drive me nuts. Working as
a photographer – that was what I wanted to do in college.
Maybe I'd even work for a sports mag or a happening website,
get freebies to any sporting events that tickled my fancy. Yeah,
I could do that. I'd have basic wheels, not too boasty – as long
as I could get from A to B. I'd support Sam in his studies. I'd
test him every now and again to make sure he was keeping
up his ratings. He could teach me how to cook West Indian
meals like his mum. I'd scholar him in how to roast a decent
joint of beef and get the Yorkshire puddings on point.

'Made it?' Sam asked again.

I nodded.

He gazed into my eyes, grabbed my shoulders and kissed
me hard. Elaine's voice boomed inside my head. *Don't give it
up!* I deleted that thought. All resistance left my loved-up ass. I
opened my mouth wider. The pressure of his lips almost made
me tilt over but I regained my balance and tenderly placed my
palms on his cheeks. Baby beard. If he ever thought about
growing a full one I'd smack it all the way to Nobbler Fields.
I twiddled his earlobes. He smiled. His hands slid down and
rested on my butt. He slipped in the tips of his digits on the
top of my crease. I didn't stop him. I tasted the chocolate and
caramel that sweetened up his tongue. We smacked lips till I
ran out of breath. He stroked my neck. I pulled back. A hard
breeze caught my hair. Weird things were happening inside

my head. The rest of my body was tingling to the max. I looked around. I felt as if I was in my own movie. The thought did crash into my head that we could bash the hips out of each other right here. *Right now.* It might have been uncomfortable and a bit grimy but – fruck it all – we were all alone ... I wondered if he had brought protection. He gave my bumper another squeeze and kissed me again. I reached out for his firm chest. I felt his heartbeat. *Mo! Control yourself. You don't wanna lose your big V on a muddy viewing platform with twigs, leaves and crawlies blowing up your ass.*

'Let's get back to our slab and get your things,' Sam said, retreating. 'You have to land back before Elaine's mum gets home, right?'

My heart pounded repeatedly against my ribcage like a cherry blossom tree smacking down a castle's gates. I wanted him to kiss me again. *Grab my ass!*

I could barely get my lyrics out. 'Er ... yeah, right.'

'And I've heard what Elaine's mum's like when she gets vex – peeps say you can hear her voice from Ripcorn Wood. *Don't* spill I said that.'

'I won't,' I laughed. 'They're not far wrong.'

We made our way down to the sports rec. Before we dropped the ball back I pulled Sam towards me. I explored his eyes for a few seconds.

'What is it?' he asked.

'This time, is it for real?' I asked. 'Not just a temporary ting? You're not gonna plug out our connection at the first excuse?'

He cupped my jaw and kissed me on the forehead. 'For real,' he said.

162

'Soul blood?' I said.

'Soul blood,' he repeated.

I wasn't sure how long we stood there hugging the intestines outta each other. My heart was fully charged.

19

Revelation Time

I wanted him to hold my hand as we rolled towards our home slab – Slipe House – but you hardly see young soul bloods doing that kinda thing in South Crong. And I didn't want him to think of me as too damn clingy.

As we neared our block, the memory of Lloyd and Mum attacking me grew large. Mum's rigid fingers. Her twisted face. The revulsion in her eyes. Lloyd's broad feet. The searing pain in my hand. The beer on his breath. His wonky teeth. I fiddled around with the keys in my pocket. I didn't have to return home just yet. Maybe it would be better if I skipped into central Crong and window-shopped for a couple of hours. Hike back to my yard when it was late. When *they'd* be in bed. I slowed my stride.

'You OK, Mo?' Sam asked.

'Yeah,' I lied, remembering Lloyd's right fist. My hand twitched at the memory of the power of it.

'I'll go up with you,' Sam offered. 'If your mum's there with Lloyd, don't stop to chat – just grab your tings and hyperspace outta there.'

'I hear you,' I said.

Sam pushed his key into the communal front door. 'You sure you don't wanna drop into my yard for a minute before we go up to yours? If I remember rightly, Mum's got some jerk chicken patties in the fridge. We could—'

'No,' I stopped his flow. 'Let's get this over and done with.'

I gave Sam my front door keys. He hugged me and kissed me on the forehead. My insides felt nourished. I closed my eyes and imagined I was back at Falcon's Ridge with the breeze blowing through my hair. 'No worries, Mo. This'll be over in a short minute.'

We climbed the stairs slowly. New graffiti on the walls promised three wet necks for the Marshall. The mat outside my front door was at a crooked angle. I fixed it. A spider eight-legged its way through a hole in the wall. A crisp packet and a couple of chocolate bar wrappers polluted the landing. That had to have been Lloyd. He was the living slob. We swapped a fretful glance. 'If you want, Mo,' Sam said, 'just tell me what you need and I'll get it for you. You can bounce downstairs.'

'No way, Half-Fro! Do you really think I'm gonna allow you to go through my undies' drawer? You'll have to merk me before I let you do that.'

Sam didn't know how to answer that. He inserted my key into the latch. As he slowly opened the door we heard a creak – it had surely never been that loud before. We paused. I tuned in my lobes. I couldn't hear any voices. No sound apart from the distant hum of the fridge. Taxi business cards were piled on the doormat along with a flyer about some new Thai restaurant. I didn't pick them up. I switched on a light. The naked bulb was partially covered in dust. We walked along the hallway. I turned left into the kitchen. It was clean. I could smell the recently mopped floor. The table had a shine to it. Mum had really got her spick and span on. I opened the fridge. Cans of beer were inside. Mum had cooked –cabbage, carrots, roast potatoes and slices of pork in see-through containers. *Frig my chefs!* I couldn't remember the last time Mum dished up a Sunday roast. I grabbed a carton of apple juice.

'Want some?' I asked Sam.

He nodded.

I poured juice into coffee mugs. Sam sank his in two gulps. I downed mine in three. I collected two shopping bags that were hooked on the kitchen door handle.

'Come on, Sam.'

He followed me to my bedroom. It was tidy. I closed the door behind me. My bedding had been changed. I could sniff lavender rising from the sheets and pillows. Clothes had been folded and placed at the foot of my bed. My DVDs were in a neat pile in my bedside cabinet. My dressing table was in proper order. Even my windows had been wiped clean. For a short second I thought of better times with Mum: my bouncy castle ninth birthday treat; trampolining with Sam on my eleventh; the trainers I had wanted for my twelfth. Smacking down skittles on my thirteenth—

'Mo,' Sam interrupted my thoughts. 'Get yourself in motion.'

I moved quickly. I packed the garms I needed into the shopping bags. Sam stood near the door. I collected all my lotions and creams. Just when I was picking up spare pairs of trainers and flats, Sam heard something.

'Someone's coming in,' he said.

For a moment I stopped what I was doing. I swallowed. Then I joined Sam by the door. We both pressed our ears against it. We heard rattling keys. A high-pitched creak. Footsteps. Mum's voice.

'Thanks for helping me out, My Tonkness. I owe you a treat.'

My veins came alive. Fear opened a trapdoor in my head and a storm of adrenalin surged through me.

'Am I on a promise?' Lloyd replied. 'Glad to help out my girl at work, and nice of that posh lady to give you a tip – ten notes ain't too shabby.'

'Not it's not,' Mum said. 'We'll put it into next weekend's pot.'

'Maybe we can shuffle up to that new bar up by the Broadway – I think it's called Ruby's or Cubies. Something like that. They play some eighties and nineties stuff on a Friday night. You fancy doing your kinky chicken and giving your toes a twirl up there?'

What the hell is the kinky chicken?

'Why not?' Mum replied. 'If I can find something to wear. I might head to Crong market during the week and get some-thing. I could do with a new pair of shoes as well. Do you wanna cup of tea?'

'Yeah, tea's nice but . . . don't I get a sexier treat than that?'

'Good things come to those who wait,' chuckled Mum.

'Is that a promise?'

'It could be, My Tonkness.'

They both laughed. Sam made a face. I returned it, double.

'Keep your beak on pause,' I whispered, pressing my finger to his lips.

I placed my hand on the door handle, squeezed the lever and pulled the door open. I sucked in a long breath.

'Do you want me to carry the bags for you?' asked Sam.

'No, it's all right. I want *her* to see them in my hands.'

We tiptoed into the hallway, not that it was any use creeping around – in a flat this small they were bound to see us. We took another two strides. Lloyd was sitting at the kitchen table, his feet up on a chair. He spotted us first. He didn't say anything, but glared at me and tugged Mum's arm. She was filling the kettle. She turned around. Our eyes clashed. Her cheeks were pale. Shadows darkened her brows. She seemed five years older than the last time I'd seen her. A smile just grazed the corners of her mouth. Then she looked down and saw my bags. *Good! That's what she gets for wanting that human sandbag Lloyd more than her own daughter.* She glanced up at Sam. Then she turned her back on me, took out two mugs from the cupboard and switched the kettle on.

'Come on, Sam,' I said. 'Let's stroll.'

Lloyd stood up, his chair screeching behind him. He scoped me like his mortal enemy. Mum looked over her shoulder. 'Leave it, Tonks,' she said, sensing the tension. 'Let her go if she wants to go.'

I didn't know why but I paused. I suspected it all along

but hearing it, casually like that, came as a shock. *Let her go?* I wasn't the freaking family pet! Bitterness stir-fried inside of me. I gave Lloyd a brutal eye-pass, challenging him to say something. I could feel the rest of my body tensing up.

'Mo,' Sam said. 'Let's drop into my yard – there's a jerk chicken pattie with your fangs on it.'

Lloyd's eyes followed my every move. His lips wobbled. I returned his glare like a Serena Williams smash. *Hate him.* Mum reached for a bag of sugar.

'Do you know what you're doing to your mum?' Lloyd exploded. 'Do you know she's not well? She hasn't slept a wink since the day you left. She went to the doctor's yesterday morning. She's on pills again. But you wouldn't know that, would you, Mo, cos you walked out on her.'

I said nothing. I just stared at Mum, wondering if she might try to beat me down again. I was ready for her this time. She scooped a teaspoonful of sugar, spilling a few granules as she stirred it into a steaming mug, her fingers trembling at the tea.

'You don't freaking care, do you, Mo?' Lloyd raised his voice. 'I know you don't give a shit about me but . . . your own mum? She could've given you up. The social were on her back about it. Did you know that?'

'Yeah but she didn't, did she?' I couldn't help myself. 'She chose to keep me and that means she chose to be a mum, but then you gatecrashed us – she cares more about you than me. If she gave a shit about me she would've booted your gut to the rough side of the kerb a long time ago. So why don't you get your bad breed self out of my freaking eyesight.'

'At least my bad breed, fat ass is a lot better for her than your old man ever was!'

'Leave it, Lloyd,' Mum tried to interrupt.

'*No!*' Lloyd yelled. 'She thinks she's all grown so she has to hear it!'

Sam was pulling my wrist. I wanted to stay. The furies danced in my head. I needed to offload my rage.

'Hear what?' I asked.

'Why d'you think that your mum can't stand to mention your old man's name, even now?' Lloyd shouted. 'And it's not because he never had a penny that ever stuck to his foot.'

He stepped towards me. Hate swam in his eyes. His teeth were yellow. I didn't crumble. I wasn't sure what happened. A bravery app downloaded itself into my heart. I took a stride towards him. *Go on, lick me. I'll fly-kick you so hard in the balls you'll be tasting a brand new flavour of lollipop!*

'Mo!' Sam called. 'You don't *need* this. Let's bounce down to mine.'

'You freaking look down on me?' Lloyd ranted. 'On *me*? Your old man can't even compare to me, Mo! Do you wanna know the truth? How it went down with your old man and your mum? What he did to her? How he messed her up?'

'*Lloyd!*' Mum screeched. '*That's* enough.'

'He's a *rapist!*' Lloyd raved. 'A freaking *rapist*! That's *your* old man, Mo! *Surprise, surprise! That's* the blatant truth!'

'*Lloyd! No! Please!*' Mum tried to intervene again.

He ignored her. 'Do you still wanna track him down? *Do ya?* That's what your mum says you're always throwing at her. And you go on as if I'm not good enough.'

'You're lying!' I screamed. *'You're freaking lying!'*

'I'm not!' yelled Lloyd. He turned to Mum. *'Tell* her. *Go on!* Tell her the truth! Tell her how she came about. Tell her about her rapist old man!'

Mum held my gaze. The tea was forgotten. Everything went quiet. Time took a breather. Nobody could move. I felt my blood spitting through my arteries. Then Mum dropped her head and covered her eyes with her left palm.

I'm the result of a rape? Mum . . .

I felt tears forming behind my eyes. My stomach made a weird scrunching sound. Sam pulled me into the hallway. I almost tripped over. 'Go, Mo! You don't need this. Get out!'

I went to open the front door but suddenly my bodyweight seemed too much for my knees to bear. I was giddy and felt myself buckle. Sam helped me to sit down on the floor. He opened the door. A gust blew up from downstairs. He gazed at me for a long second, placing a gentle hand on my cheek. I didn't like him seeing me like this. Fury brewed in his eyes. His eyebrows angled towards the bridge of his nose. He clamped his fists. He returned to the kitchen. *Oh no!*

'You're something else, prick-head!' I heard Sam shout. 'Really, something else! Do you realise what you've just done? You know she's vulnerable. Do you have any frucking idea the damage you've just caused?'

'What *I've* just done?' Lloyd ranted. 'I gave her the truth. I'm not the one who left home and broke her heart.'

Curses and swear words fired out of Sam's mouth like a West Coast rapper cussing out the feds. *Straight outta Crongton!*

I was a dose unsteady but I managed to get to my feet. I returned to the kitchen and used all the strength I had to wrestle Sam out of our flat. 'They're not worth it.'

Lloyd cursed and chased us.

'Don't ever look down on me again, Mo!' he fumed on the stairwell landing. 'Now you know I'm better than your old man by a long mile! You should be grateful that I'm around, trying to make your mum happy. *Go* if you have to – go on, go! But remember you're the one breaking her heart! Not me!'

Sam escaped my hold. He rushed Lloyd. He crunched his right fist, levered it behind his back and took one wrecking ball of a swing. It crunched Lloyd's left cheek. *Booofff!* Lloyd staggered back against the door frame and spread out his arms to break his fall. He shook his head and blinked twice.

'Stop it!' I screamed. 'STOP IT!'

I wouldn't know how to describe the sound Lloyd made as he charged Sam. It was something primal – something animal. Sam was smashed by over one hundred and twenty kilos of big-boned flab. He fell backwards into the balcony and down the stairwell. I heard a sickening *budoof* as he landed on his head. He somersaulted the rest of the way down and ended up crumpled outside his own front door, his arm resting on the WELCOME mat. For a short second shock paralysed me but I quickly regained my wits and leaped down the steps. Sam wasn't moving. His eyes were closed. His legs were all wrong, pointing in different directions. Blood oozed from his left ear. His top lip was twitching. *My poor Half-Fro!* I cradled his head. I gently tried to revive him. No response. *Oh my God, oh my God, someone help him. Please someone . . .*

help me. I pressed my ear to his nostrils. *Thank God!* He was breathing.

I didn't even realise I was crying till a tear splashed on his cheek. I glanced up. Mum stood outside our front door, her left hand held over her mouth, her eyes Imax-size. Lloyd crept down the stairs as if they were made out of paper mache. 'I . . . I didn't mean to . . . I never meant to . . . '

'Call an ambulance!' I wailed. 'Call a freaking ambulance!'

Mum rushed back inside. Lloyd had reached ground level. Dread had knocked all rage from his expression. He lumped towards me. Undiluted hatred swelled in my gut.

'Mo, you gotta believe me,' Lloyd said. 'I didn't mean for this to happen . . . I just wanted to push him away from me. That's all. I swear . . . Don't move him too much. I'm . . . I'm . . . Wait for the ambulance, Mo. Stay with him. Your mum's calling for one right now. He'll be all right . . . he's just knocked out. That's all. He's a strong boy that Sam of yours.'

I carefully placed Sam's head on the ground. His lips stopped moving. I wiped the blood from the side of his face with my sleeve. I kissed him on the forehead. I turned to Lloyd. The sensible part of my brain exploded like a *Lord of the Rings* climax. I clenched my fists till my knuckles cracked. The flesh beneath my fingernails turned red. I launched myself at him. I mauled, brawled and clawed him with everything I had, screaming as I did so. He tried to hold on to my arms and legs. I stretched my jaws as far as they would open and guillotined my teeth into his forearm. His hairs got trapped in my gums. He yelped in agony. Blood spotted the concrete. *Double good!* I couldn't quite get out of the way before receiving his right hook. *Cooooffff!* My head snapped ninety degrees. I felt an agonising whiplash. My senses dived overboard.

In my blurred vision I saw Lloyd opening the communal door and foot-slamming it into the night. I slumped against the wall. Then I remembered Sam. *My soul blood.* My legs wouldn't carry me so I crawled over to his motionless body. Blood and grit stained my palms. I checked his breathing again. *Thank the Buddhas!* Some of his blood had seeped on to his cornrows. I wasn't sure why but I didn't want him going to hospital with his hair messed up. I held his head with one hand and with the other I tried to swab away the blood the best I could. *Stay with me! Please stay with me!*

20

Crongton General

Flashing blue lights roused me from my daze. Arms lifted Sam away from me. My chest felt suddenly cold. People seemed to be moving in grainy slow motion. Colour returned to my sight. Medics in yellow dayglo jackets. Green surgical gloves. Shiny black shoes. Concerned faces. Soft conversation. I couldn't make out what they were saying. They were fitting some kind of brace around Sam's neck and head. Someone else was pressing a dressing against the back of his head. A woman was holding up three fingers in front of my face. She had green eyes and black hair. Pretty. She smiled. 'What is your name, love?'

'Maureen,' I answered. 'Maureen Baker. Everyone calls me Mo.'

'You're doing really good, Mo. How many fingers am I holding up, love?'

'Three,' I replied. 'Can you get out of the way? I want to see what they're doing with my boyfriend.'

'He's your boyfriend?'

'Er . . . sort of.'

'And this is where he lives?' she asked, pointing at the door.

'Yes,' I said. 'Number three. I live upstairs at number thirteen. Is he gonna be all right?'

She turned to look at Sam. A tube was placed into his mouth. Behind him someone was holding up a bag of clear liquid. A doctor held his temples with his fingers while checking his eyes. 'They're doing everything they can,' she said. 'He's in the best hands.'

'But will he be OK?' I asked again.

'Let's get you sorted out, shall we?' she said. 'That's a nasty bump you've got.'

'But what about Sam?'

'They'll be taking him to hospital soon. They're just checking if it's safe to move him.'

'What are they checking? Is it his back? His head?'

The medic forced a smile but kept her lips on lock.

It was at this point I realised Mum was sitting beside me, ashen-faced. She went to put her arm across my shoulder and I tried to shrug her away with a 'Get off!' but I didn't have the energy to resist.

The medic gave us a confused look. 'Listen to me, love,' she said. 'You're suffering from shock and mild concussion. You should be all right but as a precaution we're gonna take you to hospital for a CT scan.'

'What's that?' I wanted to know.

'A scan of your brain that can tell us if anything is damaged – just a precaution.'

My attention was diverted as other medics lifted Sam on to a stretcher. 'What's wrong with him? Has he opened his eyes yet? He *pushed* him!'

I tried to push Mum away again but I could barely lift my arm. 'Why aren't the feds here? Where's Lloyd? *He* did this; he's an animal; they need to lock him up.'

'Your boyfriend is going to be well looked after,' said the doctor.

I felt Mum's hands on my wrist and I jerked suddenly. 'Get your hands off me!'

The front communal doors opened. A blinking blue light caused me to squint. Sam was wheeled away. I tried to stand up but my legs weren't cooperating.

'We'll help you into the ambulance,' said the doctor. 'Just try to relax.'

'I want to go with Sam,' I said. 'Who's going with him?'

'Lorna's making her way to the hospital,' Mum said. 'I just called her.'

'*Don't* talk to me, don't even look at me, just stay the freak away. *Your* man did all this!'

They lifted me into a wheelchair and took me to an ambulance – Sam's had already left. Once inside I was helped on to the bed. Mum climbed in to escort me – I didn't love it, but I had to give her ratings for persistence. Unable to fight any more, I turned my back to her and tried to kiss my teeth the way Elaine does, but it went all wrong and I bit my gum. *God!* My head hurt chronic.

All I remembered from that journey was the kind medic stroking my forehead and telling me I was gonna be OK while Mum looked on. She braided her fingers and pressed her lips tight together and by the time we arrived at Crongton General she looked like a ghost with the world's worst migraine.

I was seen to immediately. They checked my eyes and my reflexes before I had a CT scan. They took X-rays of my brain from different angles. I wondered if the scans would show me thinking about Sam, how he was, whether he'd opened his eyes, and hoping he knew how much I loved him. I was so scared.

When he comes around, will he be the Sam I know? Will he remember our one-on-one b-ball game at Crong rec? The everlasting kiss at Falcon's Ridge? The soul blood connection?

Mum was the silent observer. A part of me wanted to ask her to go and check on Sam but I couldn't bring myself to talk to her. Whenever I looked at her, I saw Lloyd. I swore to God, if he ever brought his ass around to our gates again, I'd be waiting. I'd carve him a new belly button and slice him a third nostril.

I asked for a wheelchair so I could check on Sam. Instead, they sent me to a ward to recover from my concussion. I launched a cuss attack but they ignored me. Once I reached the ward, I felt proper drowsy. Sitting beside my bed, Mum was shaking her head and babbling on about how sorry she was and what a damn fool she'd been.

'You know how to pick your men,' I said to her. 'A rapist and now an attempted murderer.' I blanked her sorrys after that.

I drifted off to sleep but was woken a few hours later by a nurse checking on my condition. Again, I begged to be taken to Sam. The nurse shook her head. I tried to get out of bed. The nurse held me down. 'Maureen, you're not in any fit condition. You have to rest.'

I lost my cool, again. Desperation to see Sam made my volume levels rise. Other patients gawped at me. One even got out of bed looking quite afraid. I didn't care. Mum tried to calm me down. I wanted to bang the cheekbones outta her.

'What are you even doing here?' I ranted. 'Stop pretending you care. You have the front to call yourself my mum? You can't even freaking spell it. Why don't you frig off to your *Tonkness?* I don't want you here. Your sell-by date has long gone! I *swear*, if he ever comes around again I'll *kill* him. I'll carve his guts out and feed it to the rats down Beggars Dike.'

She crossed her legs, stared straight ahead and locked her fingers. A lonesome tear appeared on her left cheek. I knew she was peckish for a cancer stick. *Good!*

I wasn't sure how long I slept. Sunlight streamed through the windows. Whatever they used to mop the floor was waging war with my nostrils. I glanced to my left. Mum wasn't there. I realised I was only wearing a hospital gown and knickers. *Who undressed me?* My hands were clean. *Who scrubbed me?* Hunger licked me. *Sam! My belly can wait.* I managed to sit up. I climbed out of bed. Just as my toes touched the floor, Mum entered the ward carrying a cup of coffee and a croissant that looked as dry as a king-size crisp.

'Where are you going?' she asked.

'To see Sam.'

'Not like that you're not.'

'D'you think I care how I'm dressed? And d'you think you can stop me?'

'No ... but his mum might.'

I thought about it and returned to bed.

'What's the score?' I asked. 'Has he woken up yet?'

Mum dropped her head. She fell on to the chair beside me as if guilt had given her an uppercut.

'How is he?' I raised my voice.

'He's ... comfortable ... He's ... sleeping.'

'What the frig does that mean?'

She held her handbag tight against her stomach. She lowered her head. Another lonesome tear. She wiped it away.

'You're *useless*! How long do I have to stay in here?'

She raised her head but didn't dare face me. She directed her answer to the wall. 'The doctor said she didn't find any damage on the CT scan. She wants to check you over again. If everything's OK she said you can go home.'

'Some freaking home,' I muttered.

'Elaine sent you a text wondering where you are,' Mum said. 'I told her you're in hospital. She's coming down at lunchtime.'

'Lunchtime?'

'It's Monday, Mo. They let you sleep through the morning. Elaine went to school this morning. She'll be here soon.'

'Good,' I snapped, hoping she understood that I would rather have Elaine than her by my side right now. 'Where's Lloyd?'

'I . . . I don't know. I tried to call him.'

'You're *lying!*'

Mum didn't respond. She started her silent tears and finger clamping again. I turned my back on her once more and cursed my bad luck.

I had to wait another three hours before the doctor checked me over. 'You're good to go,' she said. 'You might suffer from mild headaches in the next few days but if it gets worse than that, come back to hospital immediately. You need rest.' She turned to Mum. 'Make sure she has plenty of rest.'

Mum nodded. The doctor smiled and went on her way.

I had dressed and was tying up my laces when I heard Elaine and Naomi bounce into the ward. They gave me big hugs and we fell on to the bed. Mum watched silently from her chair.

'What happened?' Naomi wanted to know.

I wasn't sure how to answer. I glanced at Mum and she twined her fingers again. I couldn't lie.

'Lloyd happened,' I replied. 'He banged the DNA outta me. I mangled up his arm good and proper though. Bit him.'

I glanced at Mum to check her reaction. Not a flicker.

'No offence, Ms Baker,' Elaine said, 'but the feds need to seize that waster's ass and Guantanamo him in a stone cell for fifty years. No, Mo! This wouldn't have happened if—'

'All right, Elaine,' I butted in. 'Mum knows the score. Are you gonna come up and see Sam with me?'

'Of course,' said Naomi. 'That's the second reason why we touched down. How is he? Everyone at school is proper worried. A big get-well card is going around our year – everyone's signing it, even all the teachers.'

Mum and I swapped glances. I wanted her to explain but she kept her tongue on lock. Instead, she stared at the wall without twitching a muscle, as if Michelangelo himself was sketching her portrait.

'How is he?' Elaine repeated.

'He's ...' The words got jammed in my throat. 'He's in intensive care.'

The intensive care unit was in a different building – a ten minute trod away. Naoms, Elaine and I linked arms. Mum followed. As we stepped into the lift to take us to the third floor, Naoms couldn't take any more. She broke down and cried in my arms.

She dribbled on about losing Crumbs ... How he was like a proper bruv to her in the home. He got shanked and the feds found his burst body left in the Crongton stream. He went toe to toe with Death for a few long days and she sat by his bedside – right here, in the same intensive care unit – for the duration.

In the end, Death won.

I wasn't really hearing her. I didn't *want* to hear Crumbs' full drama – especially not while I was fretting over Sam. *What if ... what if ... what if ...*

We almost missed our floor but Elaine placed a foot against the lift door so we could step out. We followed the directions to the intensive care unit – the ICU. I spotted Lorna, Sam's mum, sitting in the waiting area. She was on her lonesome and holding a cup of coffee but not really paying it any mind. It was as if she just wanted to hold on to something. She stared at the floor. Along a short corridor, doors were marked A, B and C. Doctors and nurses clopped here and there.

'Lorna,' Mum called.

Lorna stood up, saw Mum and they hugged. No words were spoken. It pissed me off big time, that hug – none of this would have happened if Mum hadn't linked with Lloyd in the first place. Lorna then embraced me. 'How are you feeling?' she asked. 'I heard you got punched up pretty bad.'

'I'm good,' I replied. 'Just a little bit giddy. How's Sam?'

Lorna's mouth opened to draw in a big breath. Her shoulders rose. They dropped. She momentarily closed her eyes. Her head fell a few centimetres. My pulse hardened in anticipation.

'He ... he was bleeding from the brain,' she explained. She inhaled once more. I sensed she was holding back a lake of tears. 'He has internal swelling ... on the brain. So they induced a coma to give his brain a chance to recover. He'll be in that ... that state ... for as long as necessary.'

A coma? How long was as long as necessary? Mum hadn't spilled any of that info. I wanted to know what chance he had but I daren't ask Lorna right then ... I suddenly felt strange. My head blazed ... Elaine caught me as my legs buckled and she helped me into the chair Lorna had just emptied.

'Get her a drink,' said Lorna.

Elaine had a bottle of water in her rucksack. I drank greedily from it and even tipped some over my head. I stood up again, gingerly. *Sam in a coma! That's for people in soaps. Not for peeps you know.*

'Maybe we should take you back to A & E,' said Mum. 'You're still a bit groggy, Mo.'

'I'm *all right!*' I protested.

'You sure?' asked Lorna.

'Can I see him?' I asked. 'I have to see him.'

'He's in room B,' Lorna replied. 'Only two can see him at any one time. Make sure you put that antibac stuff on your hands before you enter.'

'Elaine, you go,' said Naomi. 'You've known him longer than me. And he's your ... I'll see him afterwards—'

'Er ... hold up,' Lorna interrupted. 'Someone's already in there.'

'Who?' I asked.

Lorna exchanged looks with Mum. They didn't answer me.

'*Who?*' I repeated.

'Shevray,' revealed Mum. 'Lorna messaged me. I should've told you back in A & E.'

I almost doubled over. My ribs seemed to be grinding against each other. Sensing my agony, Mum reached out a hand but I moved away from her. I opened my mouth to holler something.

'Maureen!' Mum said firmly. '*Remember.* You're here for Sam. Drop it before you enter.'

I didn't argue. Lorna nodded.

I walked unsteadily to room B. I paused when I reached the door. I pressed the antibac dispenser and rubbed my hands with cold liquid. It smelled of alcohol. I hate alcohol. I closed my eyes, sucked in a long breath and knocked.

'Give him nuff love from the whole school!' called out Elaine.

'And from everybody else,' added Naomi.

A nurse opened the door. Her hair was in neat cherry-coloured braids. She was wearing rectangular-shaped glasses and held a clipboard. She smiled at me the way good nurses do. 'Are you a relative or close friend?' she asked.

'I'm Mo, his ... very close friend. I was with him when it happened. I live upstairs from him.'

'He's over there,' she said, pointing to a bed. 'Don't be too overwhelmed by all the screens, blips and tubes. He's quite comfortable. And now he doesn't need a ventilator to help him breathe.'

Four screens were on a shelf beside Sam's bed. Two of them had visible graphics with green and red light indicators. Beneath them were what looked like a row of hard drives. The nurse returned to her stool where she copied something down from a monitor. Different sized tubes were fitted into Sam's mouth, nostrils, throat and wrist. His eyes were closed. His face was swollen and his complexion patchy. A white dressing covered the back of his head. For a moment the stark reality of things struck me – this was live or die. Actual life or death. I wondered what I'd do if I lost him and then I started to think of all the things he'd never do again ... No more treks to Falcon's Ridge together. No living in a flat, rating him on his uni studies. No *future*. I couldn't stop the tears.

Shevray was sitting beside Sam. She was holding his other hand and hadn't even noticed me enter. She watched intensely over him. Grief filled her eyes. I couldn't help but feel a long, sharp shank of jealousy. My legs suddenly felt weak. My stomach whisked and churned.

Her! Just yesterday, that hand she's holding now was

appreciating my butt. It had tickled the back of my legs. His arms had held me close. The face she's gazing at was gazing at me. Now he's lying there. With her holding his hand! I had to keep my emotions on lock but couldn't help grinding my teeth and pressing my hands together.

At last Shevray noticed me. Tiredness pinched her eyes. Her nose was a shade lighter than the rest of her face. Her nostrils were blistered. I remembered Sam telling me she had been suffering from some kinda plague. She didn't say anything. She tried to force a smile but it only reached her lips. She kissed him on the forehead before standing up. She slowly walked towards me and opened her arms. I accepted her hug. I couldn't lie – it felt good. She rubbed my back before we separated. We gazed at each other for a long second, acknowledging the pain we both felt. 'Have your time with him,' she whispered. 'I know … I know how you guys …' Then she dropped her head and left. I would never spill a bad word about Shevray Clarke ever again.

I glanced at the nurse. She was still monitoring the screens, jotting notes on her pad. I kept staring at the graphs and charts and blinking lights but I couldn't understand their meaning, no matter how hard I tried. I filled the chair Shevray had vacated. I gazed at Sam. Long, pretty girl-like eyelashes. I'd tease him about that when he woke up. So peaceful. So still. This couldn't be the full stop to his life. *No!* He had so much to live for.

I touched his hand, held it in mine, stroked his fingers. *No response.* Anger tidal-waved inside me. Tears flooded my cheeks. Then I felt a reassuring hug. It was Elaine.

'He'll come good, Mo,' she said. 'Remember, the doctors induced him into a coma. They can bring him out of it. You just gotta be like a lioness for him right now.'

We sat with him for half an hour. Like Shevray, I kissed him before I left. Elaine helped me to the door. We linked arms to the waiting area where Lorna embraced me once more. *Jeez and peas! If I'm feeling like this, how is she coping?*

I sat down. Mum had sympathy in her eyes for me but I wasn't ready – I turned away from her. There was no sign of Shevray. Meanwhile, Lorna escorted a weeping Naomi to room B. I put my arms around Elaine's neck and rested my head against her shoulder. I leaked tears into her school sweater. Mum could only look on.

I recalled Sam's seventh birthday party. Lorna had emerged from the kitchen with a chocolate cake that had Maltesers set into the icing – Sam loved Maltesers. Mum had baked it – there was one ball of chocolate missing cos I had swiped it. She walked proudly behind Lorna wearing a paper party hat. The candles were lit. Sam only needed one puff to blow them out. He was wearing a big number seven badge that covered half his chest. We all sang 'Happy Birthday'. Shortly afterwards, Sam discovered he had received two games of Connect Four. Without even thinking, he offered me one. 'Take it,' he said. 'Go on!'

I'd hesitated. There were six other boys at the party. I was the only girl. I didn't scoop anything from the pass the parcel rounds. 'Take it!' Sam insisted. 'That way, when I come up to your flat I won't have to bring my one, will I?'

I was the last kid to leave that night. Sam and I were

warring over Jenga – I remember I wobbled the table as he was carefully trying to pull a block out. Lorna gave me an extra slice of cake to take home. I went to bed that night wondering what to get Sam for his eighth birthday. *God!* I'd had it bad even then.

'Are you coming back to my yard?' Elaine asked.

'No,' I replied. 'I'm going home.'

'Are you sure, Mo? What if Lloyd comes back?'

'If he does,' I raised my voice so Mum could hear, 'I'll go all samurai on his kidneys.'

Elaine struggled to find words. 'My mum ... yeah, she said ... if you want you can coch with us for as long as you want. It's not an issue. Gran don't mind either. And you know my liccle bruv's got untold love for you.'

'I'm going home,' I repeated.

'Is ... is there anyting you want me to do?' she asked.

'Yeah,' I said. 'Can you bring me my photo album?'

'Of course, Mo. I'll bring it around later after school.'

21

The Beg-Mother

That night I tried to nap in my own bed. I placed the bread knife under my pillow. I could feel the handle under my head as I struggled to catch sleep. The image of Sam lying motionless outside his front door wouldn't leave me. I turned and rolled. I fidgeted and scratched. The night was longer than double chemistry. Finally, the cold grey light of morning framed my curtains. I got up and sought comfort by flicking through my photo album: Sam and I crashing the dodgems at Crongton Heath fair; me shouldering the shove-a-penny at Brighton pier; me holding a screwdriver, about to help assemble Sam's new bed. Sweet memories.

A knock on my bedroom door. I didn't answer. I flipped over another page. Mum opened the door and poked her head in. 'How're you feeling?'

I refused to reply. I gave her one of my stone-cold sideway glares.

'Breakfast's on the table,' she said.

I was hungry to the core. The last time I'd had something to nibble was at Crong rec – I just couldn't munch the brekkie the hospital offered. I closed my eyes and tried to wish myself back to Falcon's Ridge. I opened them again. Reality gave me a left hook. *I'm gonna have to face her. I'm gonna have to spend time with her. Maybe I should just lick her down and get the furies out of my system. Maybe we should just merk each other and put a full stop to our Channel Four docudrama lives. Let the feds and the social people try to work out what drove us to it.*

I climbed out of bed. I had a slight brain-ache but the doctor warned me about that. I made my way to the kitchen. Mum was parked at the table, lipping a mug of tea. A cigarette burned between her fingers. Laid to rest in a saucer were three dead fag ends. She was wearing her baby-blue dressing gown. Two croissants and two curled-up rashers of bacon were waiting on a plate for me. A napkin was beside it. That was new. We didn't do napkins.

I dropped myself into a chair and tuned my facial expression to 'strop'.

'Eat up,' Mum said. 'You must be starved.'

I went to the fridge, took out the margarine and buttered my croissants. I got up again and took the brown sauce from the cupboard. It was a mad effort to squeeze out the dribbles. Mum watched my every move.

'D'you *have* to smoke while I'm eating? You know I hate it.'

She killed her cigarette as I took a first bite. The bacon was good – nice and crispy. The croissants were dry.

'We have to talk,' Mum said.

'About what?' I replied. 'About *your man* trying to kill my man? Nice liccle convo for the morning. What shall we chat about this afternoon? Paedos hogging the park swings?'

She took another sip and picked up her box of cigarettes but decided against sparking another one.

'I hope he gets done for attempted murder,' I said. 'And gets at least ten freaking years for it.'

She didn't say another word till I finished my brekkie. I washed it down with water. Then she lit another cancer stick. 'I'm really sorry for what happened to Sam,' she said. 'I didn't expect Lloyd to ... I'm really sorry, Mo. I know how much you ... care for him.'

She reached out and touched me on the shoulder. I looked at her hand as if it was infected with Ebola. I spoke very slowly. 'Get ... your ... freaking paw ... off me.'

She pulled her hand away. 'I ... I wanted to talk about what happened to me. You know ... with your dad. It's about time you knew about that stuff. It whacked me sideways and round in circles at the same time. It was very traumatic for—'

'I don't wanna hear it, Mum.'

'It might help you understand—'

'No, Mum!' I raised my voice. 'You just want the sympathy to swing to you and I'm *not* gonna do that. *Sam's in a coma!* Has that news downloaded into your brain yet? The next time we see him on the B of the block he might be rolling in a wheelchair. He's fighting for his life! Do you get that? Have you any idea how Lorna slept last night, thinking Sam might never wake up – that's what kept me awake and she must feel a world worse than me – and *your* man, *your* freaking Tonkness, is the waster who's responsible. I tried to clang the bell for you – when he beat me down that first time, what did you do, Mum?'

She turned away.

'Don't turn your freaking back on me! What did you do?'

She sucked hard on her cigarette. Her exhale was long and slow. The smoke dragon-hipped around the naked light bulb. Her lips wobbled.

'Yes,' she finally answered. 'When he put his hands on you I shoulda ended it with him. He treated me a lot better than some ... well you know about the disasters I've dated over the years. I just thought I could change Lloyd's way with you. After he said sorry I thought—'

'NO!' I cut her flow. 'You didn't think! You shacked up with a woman-beating waster and you let him smack your blood outta her own bed. If I ever have kids you think I'll let any man even place a finger on them? *No freaking way.*'

Mum stubbed out her new cigarette. She rubbed her forehead and mumbled something I didn't quite hear.

'Where is he?' I asked.

Mum shook her head.

'Stop trying it, Mum.'

'I don't know – he's not answering his phone and I don't think he's at home. I've sent him loads of texts.'

'You're lying.'

'I'm not lying to you. I even tried to call one of his, er ... friends, Sean.'

'What did he say?'

'He's not picking up either.'

'If he steps his foot in here again, I'll—'

'He won't,' Mum interrupted me. 'I've told him in a text it's all over. It wasn't down to him to tell you about your old—'

I screamed, cutting her off mid-sentence.

'You know what?' I said, my voice softer. 'Hear this good and proper ... I swear to God, as the clock ticks right now, you're not my mum. I'll never call you that again. You're just the bitch who pushed me out.'

My cuss attack smacked the bullseye. Mum's eyes did something strange. She dropped her cigarette into the saucer. She pressed her palms together. Her chest heaved up and down. She looked about ripe to collapse. *Good!*

A solid knuckle rapped on the front door. The sound of it momentarily stilled me. Mum was too crushed to open it. I went to my room to get the knife. I held it so hard the big vein in my wrist stretched my skin. I returned to the hallway. Mum spotted the blade in my hand but didn't say anything. The letter box rattled. I stared at the door and gripped the knife even tighter, trembling.

'Who is it?' I asked.

'It's the police,' came the answer.

I went back to my room and replaced the shank under my pillow. I had to take a long second for my adrenalin rush to simmer down. I closed my eyes. Deep breaths. In, out, in, out. The letter box clattered again.

Finally I opened the front door. Two feds were waiting outside. One male. One female.

'If you're looking for Lloyd, he's not here,' I said.

'Is it Maureen?' the female fed asked. 'We would very much like to ask you a few questions if you're up for it. Is your mum home?'

'I wouldn't call her that.'

I opened the door and led them to the kitchen. Mum was busy arranging chairs – we only had three so the male fed had to stand. Mum wiped the table. She emptied the cigarette butts into the bin before parking herself down again.

'We came to your bedside in hospital but you were sleeping,' said the female fed. 'How are you feeling now?'

I directed my reply to Mum. 'Alive ... at least I'm not in a coma.'

'Any ... side effects?' asked the female officer.

'Slight brain-ache,' I replied.

'Are you able to answer a few questions? Make a statement?'

Again, I addressed my response to Mum. 'Most def. Go for it.'

Mum interrupted in a weak voice. 'Would you like a cup of tea?'

'No, thank you,' said the female fed. She took out her notebook. She had a silver pen clipped to her breast pocket. Her colleague shook his head. 'My name is Sandra, by the way and my colleague's name is Rahul.'

Rahul nodded.

Mum picked up her cigarette packet. 'Do you mind if I smoke?'

'No, go ahead,' said Sandra.

Mum took the longest time blazing her fag – her hands were shaking.

'You have already alleged to my colleagues that Lloyd assaulted you on a previous occasion,' said Sandra. 'We did hope that you would return and complete your statement. We take any assaults on minors very seriously and they are investigated thoroughly, I can assure you of that. Now, in your own time, Maureen, what happened on Sunday afternoon?'

Before I got to what happened yesterday, I told the feds about Lloyd back-handing me out of bed. I even admitted to pissing on his precious Real Madrid number seven shirt. I told them about him grabbing me over the fiver and spilled everything about me wanting to leave home and staying at Elaine's. Finally, I got to the drama of Lloyd telling me my old man was a rapist.

'What happened then?' asked Sandra.

'Sam was calling me to go,' I replied. 'He wanted me to go down to his flat.'

'Yes?' Sandra pressed.

'Lloyd followed us out,' I answered. 'Sam didn't love the way he was hounding us, and what he was telling me about my dad. So Sam went to defend me.'

'How did Sam defend you, Maureen?'

I hesitated. I glanced at Mum. She was sucking hard on her lung merker. Vertical lines creased above her top lip. Sandra stared at me. Her pen was ready to strike.

'You have to understand Lloyd's ten times bigger than Sam,' I said. 'Sam's only fifteen. He's a slim ting, not too broad. Lloyd was saying some toxic shit; he really got our blood brewing. Sam just wanted to shut it down.'

'We know how big Lloyd is,' said Rahul. 'We just need to know how Sam reacted.'

'He ... he ...'

I stopped again. I glared at Mum. I could've lied. I thought of Sam lying there with all those tubes attached to his body. So still. So beautiful. He would tell the truth.

'He banged him,' I admitted. 'As I said, he was defending me—'

'When you say *bang*,' Sandra said, 'what do you mean?'

'He ...' I hesitated again. 'He punched him.'

'Then what happened after that?'

'Lloyd charged him!' I raised my voice. 'Like a freaking rhino. Sam crashed down the stairs, landed on his head. I tried to ... I tried to get him to open his eyes but he wasn't moving. *He wasn't moving!* His light was out. I thought he was dead. It was horrible. I asked him to open his eyes but he didn't hear me. He didn't hear me!'

Sandra reached out her hand and placed it on my own. Mum offered me a tissue but I swatted it away. My memory of Sam lying outside his front door was fully formed in HD colour. I could almost feel his breath on my hands. Blood seeping from the back of his head. So still. So quiet. Pretty eyelashes.

Tears fell from my eyes.

'I think that's enough,' Mum intervened. 'She's still suffering from shock.'

'Yes,' agreed Sandra. 'I don't think we have to—'

'But what about Lloyd?' I wanted to know. 'Have you

clipped him yet? Are you gonna charge him with attempted murder? Sam's in a coma. He might not wake up from it.'

'We're doing all we can to find him,' said Rahul. 'And we will.'

'You should ask his friend, Sean,' I suggested. 'You know he's a G, right? He runs tings in North Crong. Sean must know where Lloyd's hiding out and Mum knows the lowdown on both of 'em.'

'We've already checked their addresses,' said Rahul. 'No one was at home.'

'Ask Mum anyway,' I urged. 'Lloyd's gotta pay! He can't get away with what he did to Sam. No freaking way!'

'We're doing all we can to locate him,' said Rahul. 'He'll be in custody soon enough.'

'He *better* be.'

I stood up and poured myself another mug of water. Everyone watched me. I returned to my chair.

'Maureen,' Sandra resumed, 'I need to chat to your mum and get her statement.'

'Go on then – don't let me stop you.'

Mum and Sandra swapped a glance.

'I need to chat to her privately,' Sandra explained. 'If you can go to your room and—'

'*No!*' I protested. 'She sat down listening to my statement so why can't I park myself listening to hers?'

'Perhaps we can discuss the child protection issues first,' said Rahul. 'You have the option of going to a safe house while Lloyd is at large. If you like you can make an appointment with the police family liaison officer and they can advise—'

'Safe house?' I repeated, cutting his flow. 'I'm not going to any safe house. *Fruck that!* Lloyd and his lumpy self aren't gonna make me shift from my own flat. It's not even negotiable.'

The feds looked at Mum. *She better be on point on this or I'll give her the full cuss blast.*

She shrugged.

'So you don't want us to get in touch with social services about emergency accommodation?' asked Sandra.

'*Shit, no!*' I replied.

Three cigarettes later, I slow-toed to my room as Mum began her statement. They shut the kitchen door. I couldn't make out her whispers but I heard her bawling. Before they left, the feds promised that they would step up the hunt for Lloyd and check on us every day. I thanked them for their concern but I didn't have much hope that they'd find Semolina Butt.

Mum still wanted to chat about what happened with her and my dad but I wasn't having it. I blanked her and returned to my room. It was a relief when she left for work. I Chubbed and bolted the front door.

22

No Rest, No Peace

The next four days I established a routine. Get up at seven. Sink a brain-ache pill or three. Shower, breakfast and take the 345 bus to Crong General. Sometimes Mum came with me, sometimes she didn't. I bumped into Shevray twice – we hugged, held hands and cried together. We didn't need to talk.

Get-well cards filled Sam's room – it was nice seeing peeps' messages among all the tubes, screens and blips. I would sit with him for half an hour, holding his hand and stroking his fingers. I would kiss him on both cheeks on arrival and peck him on the forehead before I left. I would talk to him about the mad, bad and crazy times we had, but the only response I received was a beep from the monitor or a computer. His face wouldn't even twitch. His eyelids didn't flicker once. Elaine would keep me company in the evenings. She tried to get me to step to the movies but I wasn't feeling it. 'We'll bounce through legally,' she said. I didn't change my mind. She brought me carrot cake that her grandma had baked and a home-made card from her brother.

Thinking of you and Sam!
  Luv, Lemar
  PS I've grown two centimetres since you last seen me but everyone's still branding me Liccle Bit xx

Too cute.

On the sixth morning since Sam was induced into a coma the feds called – they still hadn't clipped Lloyd.

'What d'you mean you still haven't hunted him down?' I snapped. 'His fam and peeps are in North Crong. It's not exactly the same size as London or New York. Can't you put up one of them drone things and find his butt? Jeez! It can't be too hard – when it rains he gets wet in two different postcodes! Someone *knows* where he's locked down. *Make* them spill!'

I went to hospital that morning with the furies dancing inside my head. Sam hadn't changed his sleeping position since the first day I saw him in the hospital. I held his hand, caressed his fingers. I watched his toes. I listened to his breathing pattern. I spoke to him. I tried to read the screens. Nothing. *Why won't you wake up? Please wake up.*

I knew it was all wrong but I was mad with him. I hot-footed out. I recognised one of the doctors who had been treating Sam and flew towards him, blocking his way. 'Why are you leaving him like that? He's a frigging cabbage.'

'We can't rush it,' he replied. 'His brain will heal itself in time. We just have to be patient and wait for the swelling to go down.'

'But he's been lying there for nearly a week. What's he gonna be like when you bring him out of it? Will he recognise anybody?'

'Mo!' someone called. 'Mo!'

I snapped my head left. It was Lorna. She was sitting down in the ICU waiting area with Mr Holman, our student council someting or other. He was Naomi's English teacher too. Lorna stood up and walked slowly towards me. The doctor smiled and went on his way. Lorna grabbed my hands and closed them together as if she wanted me to pray. She searched my eyes, trying to read my thoughts. Again, I couldn't barricade the tears. Nor could I fight the righteous anger that was building inside me.

'*Don't* become shattered,' she said in a tone just above a whisper. 'Remember what I said about that? *Don't* let it happen to *you*. It's almost impossible to reassemble a mirror when there're so many sharp tiny pieces.'

'But he's not gonna wake up! He's—'

'Mo!' Lorna raised her voice. '*Stop it!*'

She wrapped her arms around me. For the first time I saw moisture in her eyes. The lines in her forehead seemed deeper. *So tired.* Guilt right-hooked me in the gut.

'Have you had breakfast, Mo?'

I nodded. 'Only a slice of toast.'

'Will you follow me outside to get something to eat?'

'Of course.'

Mr Holman stepped up to me, hands behind his back. He was wearing a tartan bow tie. He had kind eyes. He gave me a reassuring tap on the shoulder. 'How're you doing, Maureen?'

'Doing the best I can,' I replied.

'You've been through so much lately,' he said. 'If you want to talk, my door's always open ... or I could come to you if that works better. If you feel uncomfortable talking to me I can arrange for you to see the school counsellor.'

Normally, I would have given Holman zero attention. But he was here. I hadn't seen any other teachers. He did give a shit.

'Maybe ... maybe later,' I said.

He smiled as Lorna and I stepped to the escalator.

She bought me a bacon bagel and an orange juice at a nearby cafe. I drowned my snack in brown sauce. She had a coffee and a slice of chocolate gateau. 'This is so rich but what the hell,' she said. 'Stress is killing me anyway.'

I finished my treat and studied her. 'You know the feds still haven't found Lloyd, right?'

Lorna nodded. She gazed aimlessly through the window.

'Aren't you vex, Lorna?' I said. 'Don't you have a hot urge for revenge or someting? Lloyd is out there. He's probably living it up big time, drinking his liquor and sinking his pizzas.'

Lorna thought about it. 'At times, yes I do,' she admitted. 'I lie in my bed. I can't sleep. I get up. A stupid part of me says Sam's sleeping in his room. I go to his room and he's not there – just an empty bed. I even open the curtains in the morning as if I'm waking him up for school. I close them in the evening – how crazy is that? I don't know how many times I have made his bed in the last few days.'

'I'll *never* forgive Lloyd,' I said. 'I think of revenge all the time. It's burning into me.'

'Don't crack yourself up,' Lorna stressed once more. 'It passes. Even if I killed Lloyd – and the thought has passed my mind – afterwards, I would still get up in the middle of the night, wander to Sam's room and he *still* won't be there. I'd still go back to bed thinking he'll never wake up . . . Mo, you gotta let it go.'

'Let what go?'

'This feud with your mum.'

'If she hadn't linked up with that waster, Sam wouldn't . . . '

'It wasn't her that pushed him down the stairs.'

'She might as well have.'

'Mo, listen to me.' Lorna put down her cake and held my hands. She scanned me again. 'I know you're hurting. We're all hurting. We're all angry. But this thing with your mum is not helping me.'

I pulled my hands away. I turned away from her and looked down at my trainers.

'Mo,' Lorna said, 'maybe some counselling would help. In fact I'm thinking about getting some support for myself – I just don't know where to turn any more. We're all worried about you, Mo. I hear they've got a new student counsellor at your school – a Mrs Samantha Watson. She can help you. You've been through so much—'

'I *don't* need counselling,' I spat. 'I just need my mum to be a proper mum. That's all. Then I'll be on the level.'

'She's been through a lot too,' Lorna said. 'And the way you've frozen her out I doubt there's anything she could do to reach you right now. What ... what happened to her still traumatises her. I know it's hard for you to understand, but believe me – that is one of the biggest traumas a woman can ever experience. She's never found closure and she hasn't healed from—'

'I don't wanna hear it, Lorna. I don't wanna think about it. Don't even say my dad's name.'

'Mo, *please* listen to me,' she appealed. 'Give her a chance to explain. Listen to her. Give yourself a chance to find peace—'

I shot up out of my seat.

'Are you serious? Sam's in a coma, Lloyd's out there somewhere, probably shacked up and hidden by his North G crew, my mum wants to tell me all about how I'm the frigging daughter of a rapist – and you wanna talk about finding peace!'

'Mo, please sit down. I don't wanna argue with you.'

'No!' I felt the tears forming. I didn't want Lorna to see me bawling again. 'You're the last person I wanna offend but God can *frig* His peace! *He* doesn't have any peace for Crong sistrens like me.'

I sank the rest of my orange juice and hot-stepped it out of the cafe. As soon as I reached the end of the street I felt bad, very bad. I thought about returning and apologising to Lorna but my pride stopped me.

In an effort to simmer down I trekked up to Crong rec and sat in the small grandstand. The breeze there cooled my temper. I took off my trainers and flexed my toes. I watched girls from the posh Joan Benson school playing hockey in their neat sky-blue socks, skirts and T-shirts. I wondered about their lives, how safe they must feel. Their teacher seemed happier blowing her whistle than allowing them to play. I forgot about my worries for a while until I started to imagine Sam lying still in the middle of the field as the girls played around him.

When I returned home, some bruv wearing dungarees and army boots was changing the locks on our front door. He smiled at me and said hello. I ignored him. I just wanted to crash. Mum was cooking something but I couldn't be bothered to investigate. I rolled to my room and flopped out on my bed.

23

The Shenk-I-Sheck Club

Sometime later, I realised somebody was rocking me by my shoulder. I rolled on to my back and opened my eyes. It was Naomi. She was all garmed up in a black leather pencil skirt and a pink top. Purple lipstick sexed up her grin.

'Mo,' she called. 'Mo! Come on, sistren, wake the freak up!'

I sat up and checked my phone – 10.15 p.m.

'What the blouses are you doing here at this time?'

'Taking you out,' Naomi replied.

'I'm not stepping anywhere, Naoms.'

She opened my wardrobe and started to flick through my garms. 'You need to sketch a smile on your face, Mo. You're turning into the Grim Weeper.'

'Girl, it's quarter past ten! And aren't you on lockdown for your shoplifting mission?'

'Mo, in all the time that you've known me, have I ever bowed when they tried to give me heavy manners?'

I couldn't argue with that one. 'Will you stop nosing through my wardrobe? There ain't shit to see.'

'Mo, if you're gonna bubble with me then I don't want you looking all wrong – sometimes you don't know how to colour-match. No, delete that – you *never* know how to colour-match.'

She pulled out a pair of light blue slacks, a dark blue top and a black leather short-sleeved jacket. She threw it down on the bed.

'Get wrapped. Have you got any white stacks?'

'No.'

'Then put on a pair of black shoes then. *No trainers!* I'll park in the kitchen. Oh, and do someting with your hair.'

'Like what?'

'Brushing it could be the start of that box set. And clip on some blue earrings or someting.'

'I haven't got any.'

'I need to take you shopping.'

'No thanks, Naoms. I know your kinda shopping.'

Naomi disappeared. I took a quick shower. I dressed and went to war with my hair. *Shit! No conditioner.* I braided it into a ponytail and tied it with a blue band. I gazed into the cracked mirror on my dressing table. Not too tatty.

I found Naomi sitting with Mum in the kitchen. They were both blazing cigarettes but not saying a word to each other.

'You see!' Naomi said. 'When you brush out your hair you look all *Hollyoaks*ish! All you need now is a dose of blue make up on your eyes and a splish of red on your cheeks. You're a liccle bit pale – I don't want you looking like the psycho in the *Scream* mask.'

'She doesn't wear make-up,' cut in Mum.

Mum wasn't wrong.

'It clogs up my skin,' I explained. 'Gives me spots.'

'The raving will do her good,' said Naomi. 'Mo needs to get out of here and forget her dramas for a liccle while.'

'What time are you gonna be home?' Mum asked. She inspected her fingernails as if she had just painted them. 'And aren't you gonna eat before you go? I've cooked some lamb chops, parsnips, carrots and baby potatoes – your favourite. I made some gravy too.'

Gravy! She hasn't brewed any gravy since she poured it over the head of an ex-boyfriend. She's deciding to play mum now?

'I'm not hungry,' I lied.

Naomi answered the first question for me. 'No later than one,' she said. 'I'm locked on that. We're just gonna bubble to a few tunes; take our minds off tings.'

'Be ... be safe,' Mum managed. It was obvious she didn't want me to go. I didn't care. If she tried to stop me I'd fling her down the stairs.

'Let's go missing,' I said.

'How're you getting home?' Mum wanted to know.

'My bredren's driving,' replied Naomi. 'Don't fret about nothing. He'll drop her off.'

Mum took out a latch key from her purse. 'Here,' she said, handing it to me. 'You'll need this to get in. Be safe. Look after yourself. Don't be too late getting home.'

I took the key and hooked it on my key ring.

I didn't say goodbye.

We stepped outside. Sitting in the driver's seat of a dark blue Peugeot 207 was Naomi's boyfriend, Linval, bopping his head to a slamming beat. He was boasting a fresh number one trim. A diamond stud niced up his left ear and a black Louis Vuitton shirt wrapped his torso. Reptile skin shoes hugged his toes. I felt seriously underdressed. Naomi climbed into the passenger seat and I got in the back. 'Mo,' Linval said. 'Sorry to hear about all the drama you've been going through – nuff commiserations.'

'Commiscrations? Sam's not nibbling worms yet,' I snapped.

'I know, I know,' Linval quickly added. 'I mean, I hope he sparks out of his coma quick time.'

'Who else knows about this?' I wanted to know.

'The Lloyd–Sam drama has CNN'd all over South Crong ends,' replied Linval. He turned the ignition in the car. The engine rocked into life. Rihanna's 'Work' boomed out from the stereo. The audio system could've played the pyramid stage at Glastonbury.

'Can you deflate the bass a bit?' I asked.

Linval did what he was told.

'So everyone knows?' I said.

'Everybody,' said Naomi. 'Sam's well popular in the slab zones.'

'And South Crong soldiers know that a North Crongbanger put Sam in a coma,' added Linval.

I wanted to change the subject. 'So where are you taking me?'

'The Shenk-I-Sheck,' replied Naomi. 'It's old school soul and disco night.'

'Don't you have to be eighteen?' I wondered.

'I'll look after that,' said Linval.

We cruised up to Crongton Gardens, a green square opposite the town hall. The fountain in it hadn't sprung for two years. One drunk was pissing in it, another was singing some mad Christmas song. Then we hot-wheeled down Parchmore Drive where the council had their vehicle depot. Blue and white vans and coaches filled the forecourt. At the end of the street was an old church building. Behind it was a graveyard full of ancient, angular tombstones; alkies, dragon-hippers, the cuss-happy and the confused hung out there, righting the world's wrongs. In the basement of the old slab was the Shenk-I-Sheck club. Cars with sexed-up wheels were double and treble parked but Linval managed to find a space. As soon as I stepped out of the ride I could hear a Godzilla-stomping bassline – it was rumbling beneath my feet. We passed a couple lip-smacking in a Benz, a suited brother in a smartcar scoping porn on his tablet and three chicks sparking rockets in an Audi Sports. *Straight outta Crongton.*

Linval led us down an iron spiral staircase. I glanced below. Above the entrance a red, blue and white neon light spelled out THE LEGENDARY SHENK-I-SHECK NIGHTCLUB. I couldn't lie, a rush of excitement charged through my veins. I felt proper grown up.

'Back in the day they branded this club "The Crypt",' said Linval.

'Why?' asked Naomi.

'They used it as a morgue about a hundred years ago.'

Naomi pulled a face. *'Eeewwww!'*

Two bears wearing white shirts, black velvet jackets and black bow ties guarded the doorway – the both of them had arms big enough to hurl the Millennium Falcon into hyperspace. They patted down Linval for any shanks and weapons. They recognised Naomi and let her through.

'And who's she?' one of them asked, pointing at me with a broad finger.

'She's with me,' said Linval.

'How old are you?' the other grizzly asked me. 'Do you have any ID?'

Before I could answer, Linval took out a solid bundle of twenty pound notes from his back pocket, peeled off one and slapped it into the palm of the man-bear.

'She's old enough,' said Linval.

'Of course she is.'

I'd almost forgotten Linval was a South Crong G who nine-to-fived for Folly Ranking.

We stepped along a hallway lit by white Christmas tree lights. The ceiling was low and painted black. The carpet was red. Framed black and white portraits of great ancient-school musicians filled the walls. They had their names and bios underneath the pics. I recognised one or two from my mum's old stash of LPs: Jelly Roll Morton jangling on his piano; Louis Jordan and his Tympani Five, all wearing baggy pants that could've sheltered a Scout troop on Crong Heath; Cab Calloway bragging his white suit and the world's biggest fedora; and a young Mavis Staples singing into an old-school mic that was big enough to hit a home run. I paused to read more info about these old time chanters but Naomi told me to keep my butt in motion.

The club opened out before us. To the left of us was a long bar. Waitresses were wearing pink blouses, chocolate-coloured lipstick, spangly red hair ribbons and black bow ties. Glitter sexed up their cheeks. They were shaking cocktails and serving chicks with long heels and even longer hair extensions. Brothers wearing silk shirts, trimmed goatees and heavy watches scoped the girls. A few ravers had permed and afro-wigged up for the occasion. The dance floor was in the middle of the room, glitter balls and rainbow lights shining this way and that above it. Bubblers were already Crong-hustling, electronic-sliding, shoulder-juggling and South-Crong-Jerking – a dance that kinda involved nodding like a chicken and walking like an Egyptian ... well strange. To my right were partitioned cubicles with candle-lit tables and velvet-covered seating. Sia's 'Cheap Thrills' was thundering out from the sound system. I found myself nodding to the beat and flexing my toes.

'You chicks want something to sink?' Linval asked.

'I'll have an orange juice,' I replied. 'And if they sell any nibbles I want all of that too – I'm peckish to the core.'

'You don't wanna try a cocktail?' asked Naomi.

'I don't sink alcohol,' I said. 'Don't wanna end up like my wot'less mum.'

'Just one shot won't hurt,' said Naomi. 'It'll relax you a dose.'

'Nope.'

Linval led us to a cubicle. As I sat down I felt like a proper VIP. I could understand the attraction Naoms had for G boys.

'Soon come,' Linval said before he went off to order.

'What d'you think?' Naomi asked.

I looked around. For the first time in days, I smiled. 'I can't believe that bouncer let me in. Oh my days! I'm in the Shenk-I-Sheck. It's … it's bubbling. I always thought it was some kinda C-class hole where Gs sold dragon hip pills and road chicks twerked the poles.'

'Nah,' Naomi giggled. 'Someone bought out the last owner. She niced up everyting, slapped a decent piece of carpet down, brushed up the walls and ceiling and got a proper sound system in.'

'A woman owns this place?' I asked.

'Yep,' replied Naomi. 'Lady Mellow.'

'Lady Mellow?' I repeated. 'Who the freak is she?'

'Her dad is Brazilian; her mum is South Korean,' answered Naomi. 'No one knows too much about her apart from the fact she speaks about six languages – she's like a proper C3-PO. I saw her once – seriously pretty. She loves her high boots, power shoulder-padded jackets, hot pants and sailor hats. If I swung the other way she'd be top of my agenda, for real.'

As Tinie Tempah's 'Girls Like' rampaged from the sound system, I tried to imagine what this Lady Mellow looked like.

Linval returned with the drinks and a silver bucket of fries. Naomi sipped this mix called a Vasco da Gama – some rum and coconut frothy thing. Linval had a straight beer. While they sunk their liquor I sampled most of the fries. Linval had to return to the bar to order some more.

Sister Sledge's 'Lost in Music', one of Mum's faves, came on and Naomi took my hand. 'Time to dip the lollipop,' she said.

I followed her on to the dance floor. The bassline punched a Muhammad Ali combination right through me. We started to bust some serious moves. Naoms taught me how to do the South Crong Jerk and the Ashburton Stomp. She was giggling a mad giggle at my attempts but it was all good. I couldn't remember all the moves but I joined in this weird foot-shuffling, praying mantis dance that everyone loved to the max. I couldn't lie – I had some big fun.

Half an hour later, we rolled off the dance floor and found somebody else mingling in our cubicle. It was the wordologist, Early B. He was showboating a sky-blue suit, white shirt and blue bow tie. A blue and white polka-dot hankie niced up his breast pocket. A royal blue Kangol beret topped off his long, skinny frame. White shoes bottomed him out. He was grinning as if he was dragon-hipped to the max. 'Naoms! Mo! You reach! The word is good! The word is beautiful!' he hailed.

Naomi and I went to the ladies' to swab off our sweat. By the time we returned, Linval and Early B were back at the bar. They bought more drinks and fries. Naomi sank another cocktail, Linval drained a cola and Early B had this vodka, Red Bull minty thing. I concentrated on the chips.

'Mo, I'm gonna dip and bubble a liccle more right,' said Naomi. 'Linval, look after her.'

I sipped my orange juice as Early B sided up to me. 'I'm hearing that the wot'less blue bloods still haven't clipped Lloyd?' he said. 'Am I right? You know I'm right.'

'You're too freaking right,' I replied. 'The feds are not fit to give a shit.'

Early B leaned in closer. I could sniff his aftershave. 'Do you know he's Sean O'Shea's bruv?'

'Yeah,' I replied. 'I know they're bredrens – I know Lloyd's a North Crongbanger.'

'No,' said Early B. 'You're not comprehending. They're blood bruvs – same mum and even the same pops. I'm not spinning this, sis. Lloyd is Lloyd O'Shea.'

I looked at Early B hard. I digested this news and chased it down with the rest of my orange juice. Mum linked with the brother of the top ranking North Crongbanger? She must've known. She was more reckless than I thought.

Early B sank half of his mix before whispering into my ear. 'Maybe you should do to him what he did to you.'

'What d'you mean?' I asked.

'Didn't he lame your man's brain?' he said.

'*Don't* put it like that!' I said.

'He put your man in a coma right? That's *too* scandalous! Outrageous! You can't let that blasphemy go. Everyone's been telling me that Sam was a noble bruv, got top notch ratings at school and was a blessing to his mum. He didn't deserve that gross calamity!'

Crack! Sam's legs pointing in different directions. So quiet, so still. Blood oozing.

'What's your point?' I wanted to know.

Early B spoke slowly. 'Lloyd O'Shea hurt you to the core by laming your man, right. We all can feel that cos we're still grieving over Marshall Lee. Nuff eye-water was dripping at the funeral. His mum's still bawling two Mississippis.'

'Get to the climax, bruv.'

'We all know the feds are not gonna find Lloyd O'Shea,' Early B said. 'North Crong soldiers are gonna make sure of that. No one's even gonna leak a dribble. And we all know that Lloyd and his bruv are close like licked cigarette papers, right? So to get to Lloyd, we have to *get* to Sean. *Capish?*'

I understood what Early B was getting at. I did want to get to Lloyd. Hurt him. Leave some lasting damage. I wanted him to feel the pain I'd had to carry these past few days. Let him have sleepless nights. Let him spin and fret in his bed. Let him dread when his phone dings.

I watched Naomi on the dancefloor. *Jeez!* The girl could move. She was bubbling, dipping and grooving to the max.

'You might be able to help us get Sean,' Linval said.

Another one of my mum's faves, Earth, Wind and Fire's 'Let's Groove Tonight', spanked out from the speakers. Naomi spun like Michael Jackson. She foot-shuffled like James Brown. Ravers formed a circle around her. They clapped and hollered. The disco ball spun like a glammed up Harlem Globetrotter b-ball.

I seized Linval with a stone-cold stare. 'How?'

'Are you sure you don't want anything stronger?' Linval asked, looking at my orange juice.

'No,' I said. 'What the freak is wrong with your attention span? I don't sink alcohol ... How am I gonna help you get Sean O'Shea?'

Linval and Early B swapped a glance.

'You could help us set him up,' said Linval. 'Neatly.'

Early B nodded.

'Set him up for what?' I wanted to know.

Dumb question.

A rocking disco beat pulsed out of the sound system in its entirety before Early B spoke again. He leaned in close once more. I could sniff the drink on his breath. 'Sean O'Shea's a bad breed,' he said. 'He needs taking out like one of them outta control dogs; disposed of like a surgeon's gloves; sliced and quartered like a biology experiment. He ain't no gent. He smacks down chicks, beats down cadets for no good reason. The blue bloods can't or won't put a full stop to his shit. *We* can write the requiem on his messed-up life. Nuff South Crong peeps will be chanting when that glorious day happens.'

'Requiem?' I wanted someone to explain.

Linval nodded. 'The end credits. The last post. The final word.'

I searched for Naomi once more. She had found a dance partner. He was wearing an enormous afro wig. She was twirling, spinning and laughing. Linval didn't seem to mind.

'You think you can get to him?' I asked. 'You're not just running up your mouth?'

'Yeah, we know where he hangs on the last Friday of every month.'

'Where's that?' I asked.

Naomi rolled back off the dance floor. Sweat dripped from her fringe. She squeezed in between Early B and myself and sunk the rest of her cocktail. 'That was good!' she said. 'Mo. Step with me.'

She grabbed my hand and led me to the ladies'. She refreshed herself and fixed her make-up. 'So, did they drop it on you?' she asked.

'What d'you mean?' I asked.

'About helping set up Sean O'Shea?'

'You knew?'

'I only found out the other day that your mum's boyfriend was Sean O'Shea's liccle bruv. Linval wouldn't give me the full song at first but I got it outta him. So they asked you to do anyting?'

'Yeah.' I nodded. 'Early B told me the score.'

'You can say no if you want to, Mo,' Naomi said. 'It's up to you. You're the only voter on this election. All of them have nuff respect for you so if you blank them there's gonna be no comebacks.'

'Lloyd has to pay,' I said. 'And if the only way I can get him to pay is to set up his bruv then let the roses drop into the grave.'

'You sure?' Naomi pressed.

'Double sure,' I said.

An hour and a half later, Linval dropped me home. Naomi stepped with me to my gates. She had to lean on me for support cos she was a little charged. Before I took out my new front door key, Naoms grabbed my arm. 'I've got someting to tell you too,' she said.

'Tell me what?' I asked.

She sparked a lung merker. She toked on it as if it was the last drag she'd ever have, staining the butt with her purple lipstick. Her voice dropped to a whisper. 'I'm gonna go miss-ing with Linval.'

I widened my eyes and swallowed the shock. 'You're ... you're what?'

'I'm gonna hot-toe it away with him. What do they call it? Elop? Elope?'

'Where to? You've only known him for a few weeks!'

'*Keep* your voice down, Mo!'

'And he's into all shades of crookery. The man's a serious G!'

'He has to do one last mission with Folly Ranking and Manjaro and then he can cut loose.'

'What last mission?' I asked.

Naomi pulled on her cancer stick again. She blew the smoke over my left shoulder.

'Sean O'Shea – and that's proper classified.'

'Naoms, isn't this all a bit last minute dot com? You're on lockdown as it is. Don't you have to go to court soon?'

She snatched me with a glare. 'Mo, I don't give a freak any more. I *hate* my drunk-up dad, I *hate* living in a home, I *hate* school, I *hate* Crongton ... and I lost Crumbs. If I don't jet out soon I'll probably end up in a nut yard.'

'What about us?' I said. 'Me and Elaine?'

Naomi paused. A dose of sadness passed her eyes. She looked at the ground.

'Linval's got some funds saved,' she said. 'And if he carries out the mission he'll have a sweet-looking bank balance. He's got some fam who live up north in Elmers End. We're gonna stay with them. I'll tell them I'm seventeen. The only nega-tive is that those ends are dry – bumpkin country – nothing much going on up there but at least I can keep a low profile. As soon as I kiss sixteen I'm gonna skip to fashion college or someting. Linval's gonna flee from the G game and learn to be a mechanic – he's into cars—'

'Naoms,' I cut in. 'They're gonna satnav you down and if that don't work they'll probably resurrect a Red Indian to scope your trail.'

'Even if they find me, they won't send my ass back to Crongton,' she reasoned. 'They'll post me to somewhere else. And if I don't like it I'll go missing again. I'll keep doing it till I lick sixteen.'

'You didn't answer my question,' I said. 'What about us?'

'Don't fret. You girls will still be the most important blips on my radar. We'll link up again and do some shopping or clubbing or someting. Oh, by the way, *don't* leak anyting to Elaine yet. You know the play – she'll get all sensible on me and try to chat me out of it.'

'My jaws are locked on that one.' I nodded. 'But I'll have to spill about this Sean O'Shea mission.'

'Good luck with that,' she said. 'She's not gonna love it. And remember, it's classified. For my sistrens' lobes only.'

'Elaine won't snitch.'

Linval smacked the car horn.

'I'm dusting out,' Naomi said. 'Remember, don't even hint anyting to Elaine about me going on a magical mystery tour with Linval.'

'When are you gonna tell her?' I wanted to know.

'Oh, about five minutes before I hit the Crong ring road,' she laughed. 'I'm gonna need a head start.'

Naomi hugged me tight before she climbed back into Linval's ride. He waved at me before revving his engine and pulling away.

The new key was stiff but eventually I opened my front door. I could sniff cigarette smoke coming from the kitchen. The radio was playing on a low volume. It was a phone-in show. Somebody was asking where young people were gonna live if they couldn't afford rip-off rents. I thought of Naoms and Linval trying to make a start.

Mum was sitting cross-legged in her pink dressing gown. Tobacco polluted the air. She looked at me, killed her cancer stick in a saucer and said, 'You're home and safe. I'm turning in.'

She got up and made for her room. We didn't say goodnight.

24

Never Forget the Cheese on the Pasta

Nine days since Sam had gone into a coma. It seemed like months. Elaine touched down at my flat after school. She was carrying a shopping bag. I had been fretting how to tell her that I was willing to help Folly Ranking's crew set up Sean O'Shea and now she was here – the scene of the crime – it was now or never.

'Thought I'd pass by and cook you someting,' she said, making her way to my kitchen. 'Is your mum home?'

'Er, no,' I replied. 'She's doing her shift at the launderette.'

'She can have her portion when she gets home.'

'If she wants.' I shrugged.

I emptied the groceries on the table. Elaine had bought mince, pasta, a block of cheese, a red pepper, an onion and a jar of tomato-garlic mix.

'So when are you coming back to school, Mo? Everyone's asking for you.'

'I was gonna come back today,' I said. 'But Sam's still . . . '

'Yeah, I get it. How can you focus on anyting when Sam's where he is? Did you see him today?'

I hung my head and nodded. I didn't want to talk about it. The same sleeping position. Stroking his fingers. Watching his toes for any sign of movement. Listening to his breathing pattern. A nurse staring at the screens and filling in numbers on an A3 chart. Her colleague adjusting the blue and white tubes in his mouth. The white plaster securing another tube against his nostril. Feeling helpless. Useless.

'I'm not sure how much more I can take of this,' I said.

Elaine wiped my tears away and hugged me for a long minute. I didn't even realise I was crying.

'He'll be out of it when he's ready,' she said. 'Don't give up on him.'

Elaine browned the mince in a pot while I boiled the pasta. 'You know, the feds still haven't clipped Lloyd yet,' I mentioned.

'They never will,' said Elaine, now slicing the red pepper and onion. 'Trust me, if it was somebody rich and famous lying there in a coma they would've hunted Lloyd down within hours.'

'It's *not* right, Elaine,' I said. '*Not* right.'

'Karma will lick him down one day when he's not expecting it.'

'*Trig* karma! Somebody should take him out. Plain and simple.'

Elaine offered me a long look. 'Mo, you sure you're OK?'

I took in a deep breath. I stirred the pasta. I added a little salt. Elaine didn't take her eyes off me. 'I'm gonna help set up Sean O'Shea. Did you know? He's Lloyd's older bruv.'

She didn't say anything. She just lasered me with a long Crongton stare. The power of it almost knocked me over.

'That's the only way I can get to Lloyd,' I reasoned. 'Do to him what he did to me.'

Elaine put her knife down on the table. She washed her hands in the sink and wiped her eyes. 'I'm waiting, Mo,' she said.

'What d'you mean you're waiting?' I asked. 'Say it. Let the rat outta the cage.'

'I'm waiting for your common sense to make a re-entry back into your brain!' Elaine snapped. 'What are you think-ing, Mo?'

I chucked the wooden spoon into the sink.

'You know what I'm thinking? Every day I go to see Sam and he doesn't move a freaking muscle from the day before! Not even a liccle twitch. Nothing! He might as well be dead!'

'Mo, he's in a coma. You're gonna have to be patient, sis. It's gonna be a long ting. It might be weeks or months—'

'Exactly!' I raised my voice. 'And Lloyd's out there some-where sinking doughnuts, living his life, not giving a freak. Right now he's probably watching his *Sopranos* box set.'

'Mo, trust me. The cookie's not meant to crumble this way.'

'You're not feeling what *I'm* feeling.'

'That's not fair, Mo.'

'Yes it is!' I screamed.

I think she was freaked out by my rage. She spread her arms out and moved towards me. 'Mo, all this stress is squashing your brain. Let the feds do their work – they'll clip him.'

I turned away from Elaine, rejecting her hug. 'No they *won't*!' I raised my voice again. 'You know and I know that North Crong soldiers are gonna hide Lloyd's flabby self. No, Elaine! I'm done with waiting for the feds.'

'Then at the end of it, the feds might clip you,' warned Elaine. 'Mo, hear me out. You're not thinking right ... maybe ... maybe you should take a break from visiting Sam at the hospital? Put a full stop to that for a few days. It's traumatising you.'

I faced up to her. 'You're my girl, Elaine, and I appreciate that you don't want me to get slammed down for any crime. But if it was your liccle bruv lying on a hospital bed, twenty-four-seven, week after week, and you don't know when the freak he's gonna wake up again cos his brain's on a permanent pause, would you take it?'

She glared at me hard for more than ten seconds. I didn't blink. She finally diverted her gaze. She poured the red pepper and onion in with the mince and began to stir furiously. I could hear the spoon scraping the bottom of the pot. 'No, I wouldn't take it,' she admitted. 'I'd have to do someting.'

I grated the cheese in silence and drained the pasta. Minutes later I sprinkled the cheese over Elaine's meal. 'Can't sink pasta without cheese,' I remarked.

As we began to eat, Elaine stared into her plate for what seemed an eternity. I wondered if she'd just sink her meal and hot-step it out – I'd been a bit coarse on her. She lifted her head and studied me. 'If you're gonna be active on this mission, I'll be rolling with you, every damn step of the way.'

'You don't have to,' I replied. 'Besides, I don't think Folly Ranks and Manjaro want anyone else to be in this task force.'

'It's not negotiable.'

'It's my war,' I protested.

'And now it's mine too,' Elaine insisted. 'What do they want you to do?'

'I'm gonna find out tomorrow evening,' I said. 'Everybody's linking at Manjaro's flat. Folly Ranking, Linval and Early B will be there . . . and Naomi.'

'Naomi?'

'Yep, she's on it too.'

'I thought she was on lockdown,' said Elaine.

'I don't think she looked it up in the dictionary,' I replied.

I was tempted to spill about Naomi going missing with Linval but I couldn't betray her trust. 'Elaine, you get the jeopardy level on this one, don't you? It's well in the danger zone. I don't give a drip of what my mum would say but your mum?'

She swallowed a mouthful of spaghetti bolognese, gripped my eyes and nodded. 'I get it,' she said. 'My mum will probably carve out my eyeballs and grill them slowly over a barbeque but, hey-ho, you're my sistren. If one of us falls then we all fall.'

'Elaine,' I called out, 'we're not the three musketeers!'

'As I said, Mo, I'm on your agenda from now on. I'm not gonna flex on that.'

My bones were roasting, like hot Jamaican jerk. I got up and gave Elaine a King Baloo hug.

25

Sococheeta

It was 11.57 a.m. the following Saturday. Thirteen days since Sam went to sleep. Naomi and I were waiting on the B of Elaine's block. Elaine finally appeared carrying shopping bags in each hand – her mum, Yvonne, was pulling a trolley beside her. They approached us. Yvonne headed straight for me, let go of the shopping trolley, embraced me and rubbed my back vigorously.

'How's Sam?' she asked.

'The same,' I replied.

'Are you going to see him today?'

I nodded.

'If you like you can still stay with us,' she said. 'You know . . . if things aren't too good at home with your—'

'That's OK, Yvonne,' I cut her off. 'I'm good for now. Thanks for offering.'

'You sure?'

'Yes, Yvonne, double sure.'

'Mum,' Elaine called. 'Can we drop off this shopping? We have to step somewhere.'

Yvonne kissed me on the cheek. I couldn't remember the last time my mum had pecked me. 'Send him my best,' she said.

Five minutes later we were on our way to Manjaro's.

'What's their programme?' Elaine wanted to know.

'Linval hasn't told me the full get-down,' replied Naomi. 'But he did leak that Sean O'Shea lurks at this club in North Crong.'

'What club?' I asked.

'Sococheeta,' Naomi answered. 'It's on the west side of the North Crong estate, near the railway line – not too far from the ring road. It's not on the same level as the Shenk-I-Sheck but they've got a small dance floor and a DJ booth.'

'Don't they have untold bears on the gates there?' asked Elaine. 'Doesn't everyone get a pat-down? North Crong soldiers will be mingling all over the place.'

We looked at each other. No one came up with a reply.

'You can still change your mind, Mo,' said Elaine.

'No,' I replied. 'The cheerleaders have left the court and the ball's in motion.'

My heart battered my ribcage as we approached the gates of the South Crong crew. I tried to control my breathing when Elaine rat-a-tatted Manjaro's letter box. Linval opened the door. He hugged and kissed Naoms. He grinned at me. 'You reach,' he said, looking relieved. 'We appreciate that to the max.'

Linval led us into the hallway. We turned right into the lounge. Manjaro was parked in an armchair. He was wearing a white string vest and grey tracksuit bottoms. His naked toes were as thick as spring rolls. Folly Ranking was parked on a stool. He was bragging a white beaver beret, a black denim jacket, a *Reservoir Dogs* T-shirt and black jeans baggy enough to wrap the trunks of a couple of oaks. He was pulling on a rocket when he nodded his greeting. Early B was standing. His eyes were slightly bloodshot. His headphones were big enough to trap two tarantulas. He was fiddling with his phone. *Tipping Point* was broadcasting silently on a large flat-screen TV. I could sniff a recent coating of paint. The beige walls were slick.

'The sofa's for you,' said Folly Ranks.

I had a sudden urge to foot-slam it out of there – *What the hell am I doing?* – but I told myself to Crong-tough up, for Sam's sake. Naomi parked herself and I joined her. Elaine followed.

Linval switched off the TV. He shut the blinds. Early B pocketed his phone and took off his headphones.

'Do you ladies want anything to nibble or to drink?' Manjaro asked.

I shook my head. Elaine did the same. 'I'll have a Coke,' Naomi said.

Linval went to the kitchen. Folly Ranks climbed off his stool, killed his rocket and slowly stepped towards me. 'We really appreciate you coming,' he said. 'I didn't think you . . .'

'That's all right,' I replied. I studied his face. Close set eyes like an owl. Eyebrows that nearly shook hands. Nostrils that promised a fiery temper. He had a small scar just below his bottom lip.

'I'm not gonna talk fart and rate the weather with you,' Folly Ranks said. 'And if you want you can say no and skip out of here. That'll be cool on my part. No pressure. No comebacks. When I see you on road I'll nod my greeting, show my respect and move on.'

'What do you want me to do?' I pressed.

Linval returned with a glass of Coke for Naomi. She took a sip and lit a cancer stick.

Folly Ranks exchanged glances with his crew. He stroked his cheeks with his thumb and forefinger. 'We need you to smuggle in a blade at Sococheeta,' he said.

The room went quiet. Naomi exhaled smoke. Linval asked Naomi for a cigarette. Suddenly, Elaine stood up. 'How's she gonna do that? Isn't there nuff bears on the gates of Sococheeta? And I'm guessing they're not too cuddly.'

'If you're smart there *is* a way,' remarked Manjaro.

Folly Ranks' eyes never left me. 'How's that sitting with you, sis?' he asked me. 'If you're not up for that we'll download another programme.'

All eyes on me. I could feel the heat in my head. I wiped a dose of sweat that was dripping on to my eyelid. 'Can I have a glass of water?' I asked.

Linval fetched my drink. I downed it in one gulp. I shifted uncomfortably in the sofa. I even thought about asking Naoms for a lung merker. I tried to breathe slowly. Elaine sat down.

'OK. I'm on it,' I said. 'Till the last whistle.'

It took me a few seconds to realise that I was clenching my right fist.

'Are you bona fide?' Folly Ranks wanted confirmation.

'You're gonna burst Sean O'Shea right?' I asked.

'Trust me, I would love that, but it won't be me,' replied Folly Ranks. He looked at Linval then returned his hard gaze to me. 'They know me. They'd never let my ass in. And even if they did they'd swarm me in a mad rush. They know Manjaro and Early B too. But ... they don't know Linval. It has to be on the surprise tip – they say it's the punch the boxer isn't expecting that knocks his ass out.'

Linval pulled mightily on his cancer stick, lighting up the ash. By the look of his eyes he wanted something stronger.

'You never answered my question,' Elaine said. 'How's she gonna get a blade through their customs?'

'Cycle shorts,' said Folly Ranks. 'Duct tape and well thick jeans. We'll look after all of that.'

'And where are you gonna be?' Elaine wanted to know.

'Waiting outside in a car,' replied Manjaro. 'With the engine humming.'

Folly Ranks turned to Early B. 'Has Lady P bought the wheels yet? You've given her the notes, right?'

'Yeah,' Early B answered. 'She's got the funds. She's going to an auction in Ashburton tomorrow.'

'Make sure she registers it in her name,' said Folly Ranks. 'And I don't want any big-dick wheels. We need a ride on a low-profile tip. And something dark so peeps can't be sure of the colour.'

'Who's Lady P?' I wanted to know.

'Our source,' replied Folly Ranks.

'And she's already got the phones,' added Early B.

'Phones?' I queried.

'Yeah, we all need brand new mobiles for that night,' said Folly Ranks. 'When the mission's done we smash them up and fling them in the Crong stream.'

'Why do you need the phones?' asked Elaine.

'So we can synchronise,' explained Folly Ranks. 'When the shank is passed over to Linval, he texts all of us at the same time. The countdown begins at that point.'

'Countdown?' I wondered.

'Thirty seconds,' said Manjaro. 'Linval counts to thirty and at the same time Folly Ranks, Early B and I count to thirty-five. Then we rush the gates of Sococheeta to get your asses out of there.'

'If they know you, how are you gonna get in?' I asked.

'Cos when Linval rips Sean O'Shea there's gonna be a mad Crongfusion,' Folly Ranks explained. 'Chicks are gonna be wailing. Pussies are gonna be scrambling. The mice will hit the holes. Grizzlies will fly from the door to see what's going down.'

'How many bears on the gate?' I wanted to know.

'For the last four Friday night open mic sessions, there have been two,' said Manjaro. 'They're not tiny. They do a proper search on the men but with the ladies they just pat them down on the sides. And if they're still at the gate when we reach, we'll deal with them neatly.'

I pictured in my head what dealing with them neatly meant.

'We'll get you out,' added Manjaro. 'You've got my exclamation mark on that.'

'I'll be with Mo,' said Elaine.

'That's not in the programme,' said Folly Ranks. 'One strange chick not from the ends you can get away with ... but two? That's a virus we don't need. I don't want anyone else in the game.'

'We won't step in together,' Elaine said. 'Maybe Mo can go in before or after me? I'm *not* letting her step into Sococheeta on her lonesome. *No way!*'

'Linval will be there,' said Folly Ranks.

'Linval will have other tings on his mind,' Elaine countered. 'He's got to burst Sean O'Shea. I'm all about defending Mo if anyting boots off. *She's* my main priority.'

A warm sensation filled me. *God! I'm lucky to have Elaine.*

'Thanks,' remarked Linval.

'Don't take it personal,' said Elaine.

Folly Ranks thought about it. He took out a cigarette, split it in half, carefully placed the tobacco in a large cigarette paper, added cannabis and expertly wrapped a rocket. He didn't speak again until he took his first pull. Smoke filled the room. The Mary Jane invaded my nostrils. It was sweet. 'That can work,' Folly Ranks said after a while. 'But make it at least a fifteen minute gap before Mo steps in. When it all kicks off I don't want you two chicks involved – just hyper-toe it out of there.'

'Are you good with this?' Manjaro asked Elaine.

Elaine nodded.

'So when is this all gonna go down?' I asked.

'Next week,' Folly Ranks announced. 'Friday – the last Friday of the month. It's when Sococheeta hold their open mic slams. For the last few months Sean O'Shea's been correct and present at that gig – some of his soldiers and cadets spit a few bars.'

'Where d'you get that info from?'

Folly Ranks swapped a glance with Manjaro. 'Tell her,' he said.

'Lady P,' Manjaro revealed. 'She used to live in North Crong ends – James Baldwin House. She was a regular at the Sococheeta in them days. She was linking with one of O'Shea's soldiers – it didn't end too sweet.'

'What does the P stand for?' I wanted to know.

'Patricia,' said Manjaro. 'She's eighteen.'

'And where is she now?' Elaine asked.

'Safe in South Crong,' said Folly Ranks. 'We look after people who step over to our codes.'

'She still has fam in North Crong,' explained Manjaro. 'A younger sis, an aunt and two cousins.'

'Do they know that she's skipped to South Crong ends?' I asked.

'No,' answered Folly Ranks. 'We have to keep her under-cover. Even from her fam. You'll meet her on the night – she'll be driving.'

'How many of us are gonna be there?' asked Early B. 'Might need another set of wheels.'

Folly Ranks thought about it. 'You're not wrong. Give P the funds. Again, I don't want no big-willy car.'

'I could respray my wheels, black out the number plates and drive that,' offered Linval.

'Gonna have to put an embargo on that one,' said Folly

Ranks. 'What if you break down? You're registered to that car. The feds will have a trail.'

'What do you want me to do when I touch down at the club?' I asked.

'Listen carefully,' said Manjaro. He pointed a finger at me. 'Whatever you do, don't link with or say *anything* to Linval once he gets inside, you receiving me?'

'I hear that.' I nodded.

'You go to the ladies' and wait. After a few minutes, he's gonna follow you there,' Manjaro advised. 'He'll knock so you'll know it's him. That's when you give him the blade – *inside the cubicle* though – and make sure it's locked; make double sure. Receive that.'

'Try to make sure no one sees you and Linval together,' added Folly Ranks. 'And when you give him the shank, wait thirty seconds after Linval leaves before you come out.'

'And what do I do while Mo's in the toilet?' Elaine wanted to know.

'You roll to the ladies' too,' instructed Manjaro. 'Wash your hands or something and wait for Mo to come out of the cubicle. When Linval shows, *don't* say a sweet prayer. Don't even watch him go in to see Mo. Act like you don't know him.'

'I don't want you chicks being caught up in any warring or crossfire when it all kicks off,' added Folly Ranks. 'You following me? Just deliver the blade, keep your heads low, and get the freak out of there.'

'I'm following.' I nodded. 'Where are we meeting on Friday?'

Folly Ranks took his time in answering. 'Not here.

Crongton rec. Nine on the bang,' he said. 'There's a small car park behind the grandstand. You'll be given your phones then.'

'And your caps,' Manjaro added.

'Caps?' Naomi wanted an explanation.

'Cameras are always higher than face level,' Folly Ranks reasoned. 'They put them up outta reach so road peeps can't jack them. CCTV's a bitch but if we're all wearing baseball caps and pull them down over our eyebrows it makes it impossible for the feds to scope anybody. When the mission's done we burn them all.'

'Smart,' I remarked.

'We have to be,' said Folly Ranks. 'Any other questions?'

'What happens after the mission?' I asked.

'We hit the wheels and cruise to Notre Dame,' said Manjaro. 'We respect the speed limit at *all* times. Then after an hour or so, we head back down to South Crong, taking the ring road back to Crong rec.'

Elaine gave me a reassuring squeeze on my shoulder.

'Say bears find my shank when I try to get in?' I asked.

'Then you don't put up any resistance, let them confiscate the blade and step away peacefully,' said Folly Ranks. 'Tell them you were only carrying cos someone in the ends had threatened you. That's a standard reason for anyone in Crong to be packed and shanked. They know the get-down; they confiscate arms on the regs.'

Manjaro cut in, 'No North Crong soldiers will be tooled up in Sococheeta. They think they're in the safety zone there. They won't be expecting any G drama.'

'And before they know what's happened,' said Early B, 'we'll be on the ring road wiping the blade.'

We all looked at each other. It all sounded too neat and easy.

'So everyone knows the programme?' Folly Ranks asked. 'If any soldier isn't feeling this then I beg you to holler a protest now ... or forever stitch your lip.'

I could sense Elaine's eyes boring into me. Naomi sucked hard on her lung merker. Linval wiped his brow.

I took in a deep breath. 'I'm good,' I said.

'One more thing,' said Manjaro, scoping my face. 'You look sixteenish – we need you to look a liccle older so you get through Sococheeta customs with no worries. Before the mission I'll ask Lady P to mask you up a bit. Is that OK?'

'As long as she doesn't make me look like a clown,' I said.

Folly Ranks grinned. He took out an envelope from his pocket. He handed it to me. 'For your devotion to our cause,' he said. 'You'll get another slice when we debrief.'

'I'm not doing this for the notes,' I said. 'I just want to see Lloyd suffer.'

'Then give it to Sam's family,' Folly Ranks suggested. 'Lloyd will be screaming perfect storms – he loves his bruv. Trust me on that.'

I glanced at Elaine. She nodded. So did Naomi. I accepted the envelope. I banked it in my back pocket. Folly Ranks smiled again. 'You're one of us now,' he said. 'A South Crong GI. There's no gender bar in our crew. If we complete this mission I'll make sure your name goes up on the tall slabs – bright capital letters.'

I didn't argue with him.

'Can I use the toilet?' I asked.

'Yeah, of course,' Manjaro said.

He led me to the hallway and pointed to the toilet. I bolted the door, sat down on the seat and counted the notes. A wad of twenties and fifties. Two grand.

I can't give it to Lorna. She'll want to know where I got the cash from. When Sam sparks out of his coma I'll give it to him. I'll tell him I won it on a scratch card or someting. Maybe he can buy that new Apple laptop he's always wanted. Then again, knowing Sam, he'll probably lock it down in a high-interest bank account.

I looked at the notes, and thought about the mission. Sam fighting for his life in hospital; me about to step into danger ... Who knew what would happen – who knew whether Sam was going to pull through; whether I'd make it out of the club alive? I stood up, pressed the flush, stepped over to the sink and stared at my reflection in the mirror. I would have to work out a way to give the notes to Sam before this last reel played out.

26

Rendezvous

Nineteen long days since I watched Sam fall. It was 7.50 p.m. on Friday evening. I pulled on an old pair of trainers and tied my laces three times before I was satisfied – I didn't wanna trip up if I had to hot-step away from a situation. I was wearing blue jeans and a baggy black pullover that reached down to just above my knees – Folly Ranks had advised us all to wear dark clothes. My hair was tied in a black band – I didn't bother braiding it. The money was beside me on the bed. I counted out one grand, then another, wrapped each wad in an elastic band and pushed them into my back pockets. I headed out of my room. Mum was washing up in the kitchen. She had cooked dinner – tuna and rice. There was even a side of sliced tomato and cucumber. That was new. I had dined in my room even though Mum had set a place for me at the kitchen table.

'Going out?' she asked.

'A bit later,' I replied. 'I'm just going downstairs to see Lorna.'

'Where are you going later on?'

'You don't need to know,' I answered.

Suspicious glance. Silence. *Good!* The less she knew the better.

I walked carefully down the concrete stairs. It was the seventh step where Sam had cracked his skull. I couldn't bear to look, stepped straight from eighth to sixth, and continued to his front door. I tickled the letter box. Lorna answered wearing a brown headscarf, a black cardigan and black leggings. Her eyes were moist. Tiredness licked her forehead. Stress stroked her cheeks. I could hear her washing machine spinning.

'Come in, Mo,' she said. 'How're you doing?'

'I don't know, Lorna,' I replied. 'Every day is the same, isn't it?'

'Maybe you should go back to school,' she said. 'It'll help take your mind off things.'

She led me to her lounge. I dropped myself in the sofa. There was an uneaten plate of chicken, rice and broccoli on the coffee table.

'I find it hard to concentrate on anyting,' I admitted. 'Until Sam is up and about my brain will be on a permanent go-slow.'

'Would you like a cup of something? I've just boiled the kettle.'

'No thanks. I'm just passing to pick up one of my books from Sam's room.'

'OK, Mo. I've just cleaned in there so don't disturb anything.'

Lorna returned to the kitchen. She took the untouched meal with her and scraped it into the bin. I entered Sam's bedroom and closed the door quietly behind me. The carpet was spotless. It smelled of apple air freshener and recently laundered bedding. His bookshelf was as neat as I had ever seen it. There were posters on the walls – Kandace Springs with her hot mad afro, Dreezy in her batty-riders. His computer desk, usually a mess of pens, books, headphones, iPod and CDs, was clear of all but a laptop and mouse on its mousepad. A framed photograph of Sam's grandmother stood on his dressing table. It suddenly smacked me – Lorna had lost her mum earlier this year and now Sam was lame-brained in a hospital bed. How much more could she take?

His footwear was lined up tidily beneath the window. I opened his wardrobe. Shoeboxes filled the bottom section. I pulled one of the boxes out and lifted the lid. It was full of football and basketball cards – in his junior years, Sam had collected hundreds. Lionel Messi, Ronaldo, Neymar, LeBron James, Kobe Bryant, Michael Jordan – they were all there. I pulled out the two bundles of notes, tucked them beneath the mass of cards and replaced the lid.

'Are you all right, Mo?' Lorna called from the kitchen. 'Have you found what you're looking for?'

'Yes, Lorna,' I quickly replied while putting back the shoebox into the wardrobe. 'I've got it.'

Hurriedly, I picked out *The Black Jacobins* by C. L. R. James from the bookshelf.

I found Lorna parked on her sofa, absently stirring her tea, staring into it. I sat down beside her. We were silent for a while. I stood up, wanting to leave. I didn't want my emotions to conquer me.

'You're not going yet, are you?' she asked. She was sniffing the tea, not sipping it.

'I've got to meet a friend soon,' I said.

'I won't keep you long.'

I parked myself once more.

'If it's about how I behaved in the cafe, I'm sorry,' I apologised. 'I was well out of order.'

'No, no, it's not that,' she said. She placed her hand on my shoulder. 'You were upset, grieving. I understand. There are times I want to climb on to the roof of the highest building and just scream. There are moments I can't get Lloyd's face out of my mind and I just want to smash his head in. Sam might never recover from what that man did.'

'Sam will come out of it,' I managed. 'He's in a good place. Being looked after well.'

'The doctors and nurses are so kind but every night I can't help thinking ... maybe Sam won't come back to us. They don't induce you into a coma for nothing. It's been weeks.'

'Two weeks and five days,' I said.

'Maybe this is the way it's meant to be,' Lorna continued. She dabbed her eyes with a tissue. 'God's will. We have to prepare ourselves for the worst.'

'Don't say that, Lorna. *Please.*'

'I see the way you look at him, Mo. Even when you were kids you gazed at him that same way. I know you love him.'

For a while I didn't respond. I stared into space. Eventually I closed my eyes and nodded.

'Then I know that if he doesn't make a full recovery and I have to look after him, you'll help me. I'll have your support.'

'Of course. It's not even debateable.'

'I might have to give up work,' she said.

'Let's hope it won't come to that.'

It was all proper distressing hearing Lorna switch negative. I put up resistance to my tears. My guts resumed their war with the scrambled eggs and bacon I'd sunk that morning. She stroked my hair. Tears fell down her cheeks.

'I'm sorry, Mo,' she said after a while. 'Don't listen to this foolish woman. Sometimes I have my bad days.'

'Lloyd did this to Sam and he did this to you,' I said. 'Justice has to smack his ... behind. He's messed up our lives.'

Lorna didn't disagree. She put down her mug and hugged me. Her hands trembled against my back. 'I didn't mean to scare you,' she said in a whisper. 'He'll be all right. God willing.'

'Yes he will.'

'Are you going to see him tomorrow?' she asked.

'Of course,' I replied. 'I wanna be there if he wakes up – you never know.'

Lorna smiled and reached out to place a hand on my cheek. 'Thanks for your hope,' she said. 'I lost mine so I needed yours. I'll pray for all of us tonight. I hope He's still listening.'

I left Lorna gazing into her cup of tea.

Mum was smoking a cancer stick in the kitchen when I returned home. The plates were gleaming on the draining board.

243

Poor Lorna. At least Mum and I could eat a decent meal and sink our hot drinks.

'How's she holding up?' Mum asked.

'As best she can,' I replied. 'It's not easy for those of us who love him.'

I turned to walk away.

'I love him too,' Mum called out. 'Didn't I used to babysit for him? I taught him how to swim that time on holiday. I cared for him, spoon-fed him and changed his nappies. Didn't I used to bake his birthday cakes?'

'You loved Lloyd more,' I said.

'We all make mistakes,' she said.

'Not major ones like you.'

'I've . . . I've tried my best to find a decent guy to be a father figure to—'

'Don't even bother, Mum,' I ripped her flow. 'You might try, but you always flop. And you never learn.'

Mum's head dropped. *Good!* She stared at the floor as if it would hide her shame.

'Where're you going tonight, Mo?' she asked after a while.

'If you don't ask me any questions I can't tell you any lies.'

'Mo, I'm *still* your mum, and you're not a grown woman yet! I have a right to know where you're going.'

I gave her a stone-cold glare. 'You lost any right the day you let that child-beater step into our flat.'

Mum looked away and tipped her ash on to a saucer. I glared at her, ready for a cuss war. I wanted a response but there was none.

I made for my room. Slammed the door behind me. I

crashed on my bed and opened my photo album. I looked through the past, remembered good times and big fun in more innocent years, and then I imagined Sam taking me in his arms and kissing me hard. I dreamed of him undressing me, caressing my shoulders, tracing my spine with his fingertips, giving me little kisses all the way down to my belly button, interlocking his fingers into mine. I released the sight.

My rage hardened.

Twenty minutes later someone knuckled the front door. I went to answer it. It was Elaine. She was dressed in black jeans and a dark blue hoodie. Grey Nikes wrapped her toes. Her hair was in loose braids. 'Are you ready?' she said quietly.

I heard Mum rise from her chair and step into the hallway. I searched Elaine's eyes. I nodded.

'Elaine!' Mum called. 'Can you tell me where you're going?'

Elaine didn't answer.

'Let's step off,' I said.

I closed the door. I didn't look behind.

We didn't say much to each other until we hit the Crong Heath road. She seemed to sense that I didn't wanna chat about my mum.

'Naoms making her own way to the rec?' I asked.

'Linval's picking her up,' replied Elaine.

We arrived at Crong rec at 8.50 p.m. Two lamp posts lit the red-gravel car park. A bin was overflowing with drink cans and crisp packets. A strip of overgrowth behind the grandstand stank of piss. Owls *tu-whit tu-whooed* in the surrounding trees. The pathway leading into the woods was Transylvanian dark. Gnats orbited our heads. There was no breeze to refresh my cheeks. No night chill to cool my revenge.

'A good place for a merking,' remarked Elaine.

'Don't say that,' I replied.

'Who knows?' Elaine said. 'They might not turn up. You can still step away from this, Mo.'

I shook my head.

Moments later, two pairs of headlights lit up the tree trunks. A squirrel danced along a branch. The owls paused their hollering. Wheels crunched the gravel. Two cars pulled up. The first was a black Mini. Black paint had been sprayed over the number plates. A pretty girl with blonde hair streaked with green highlights was sitting behind the wheel. Lime-coloured mermaid earrings sexed up her lobes. It must have been Lady P. Manjaro was sitting beside her in the passenger seat. Behind the Mini was Linval's dark blue Peugeot 207. Naomi was next to him, smoking. The windows were wound down. His stereo banged out grime beats.

'*Turn* that shit down!' ordered Manjaro, climbing out of his ride.

Linval did what he was told.

Manjaro approached us. He reached out. 'Respect,' he said, shaking my hand. 'Respect to the fullest that you're supporting us on this mission. We're shoulder to shoulder; blade to blade.'

He greeted Elaine the same way. His eyes locked on to her face. He threatened to smile. Interesting.

'Good that you're wearing dark or black,' Manjaro said. 'We'll blend in neatly when we reach North Crong.'

Lady P switched off her car engine but left the headlights on. She opened the door, stepped out of the Mini and rolled towards us. Manjaro did the introductions. 'This is Mo and Elaine,' he said. 'Mo, Elaine, this is Lady P.'

I searched Lady Ps eyes. I recognised the hunger for vengeance behind them. I'd seen it in my bathroom mirror for nearly three weeks. 'Good to finally link,' she said. ''I've got your bike garms and a make-up bag.'

'P, you wanna park in the corner to give Mo a liccle privacy?' said Manjaro. 'She has to change.'

'No probs,' replied Lady P.

She returned to the Mini and drove it twenty metres towards the bushes.

'Where's Folly Ranks?' I asked.

'On his way,' replied Manjaro.

As Elaine and I stepped towards the Mini, Lady P took out a brown package and a small see-through bag from the boot. She placed them on the back seat.

'I'll fix up her face,' offered Elaine.

'Coolio with me,' replied Lady P. She looked at me. 'OK with you?'

I nodded.

'First thing you do is tape up the blade,' Lady P advised, pointing at the parcel. 'You don't wanna slice yourself. When you strap the knife, fix it to the *inside* of the leg – the club's for ever using male security guards and they always gotta pat down chicks on the outside edges. The cycle shorts and tape are on the back seat already. Before you open the parcel, make sure you put on your surgical gloves – they're on the back seat too.'

'Will do,' I said.

Lady P stepped out of the car. I climbed into the back seat of the Mini and Elaine walked round the other side and joined me. We closed the doors. We stared at each other. I sniffed lavender air freshener. *Jeez and peas! We're really doing this.*

'It's still not too late,' Elaine said.

I didn't reply.

Instead, I pulled off my jeans. Elaine squeezed on a pair of surgical gloves. I did the same. She ripped open the jiffy bag. A curved knife was hidden inside. On closer inspection I could make out the abrasions and marks on the blade after somebody had sharpened it. The blade was about twenty centimetres long. A few centimetres wide. Sheffield steel. Two brass screws in the black handle. It glinted beneath the Mini's interior light. Elaine peeled off a long stretch of brown masking tape and cut it with her nail file – then carefully wrapped it round the shank. 'Is that enough?' she asked.

'Wrap it a bit more,' I said. 'I wanna have kids one day.'

Elaine did as she was told.

I peered out of the window. The rest of the crew were breezing small talk under a lamp post. Naomi strolled towards us. She opened the passenger side door and filled the seat. 'Everyting all right?' she asked.

'Yeah.' I nodded. 'We're bouncing down to the basket.'

Elaine asked me to part my legs. She secured the blade to the inside of my right thigh. The tip pointed down. The tape felt cold. Elaine wrapped it tightly till I felt numb. Naomi watched.

'How's that?' Elaine asked.

'I can't feel anyting,' I replied. 'My leg's going all white.'

'You are white,' Elaine joked.

'Now I know how a mummy feels.'

'Good,' Elaine said. 'If you slice open your bits you won't feel anyting.'

'That's not funny!' I countered. 'If something happens to my business you're gonna be a surrogate for my kids.'

'I'd rather give birth to crocodiles,' Elaine countered.

I pulled on the cycle shorts. They were padded in the crotch and groin area and reached just above my knees. 'It looks like I've got a dick,' I chuckled.

'And a very long one!' Naomi laughed.

Elaine giggled.

'Is it comfortable?' Naomi asked.

'No,' I said. 'It feels like I'm wearing an iron nappy.'

'See if you can walk,' Elaine suggested.

I opened the car door, climbed out and stood up. It felt weird but OK. I tried a few paces. Gradually, sensation returned to my upper leg.

'How is it?' Naomi wanted to know.

'Not too bad,' I said. 'Just don't ask me to jump the vault.'

'Come back in and put your jeans back on,' said Elaine. 'Then I'll do your face.'

I returned to the car. As I was pulling the gloves off, light flared up behind the grandstand and another car appeared through the dark. It was Early B. He was driving a dark blue Renault Clio with blacked-out plates. Folly Ranks was in the passenger seat. I pulled on my jeans and secured my belt. I pushed an extra pair of surgical gloves into my back pocket. A bird squawked high above.

Elaine began to apply mascara to my lashes. 'Keep your head still!' she said. She finished my eyes with liner, then brushed some blusher across my cheekbones and painted ruby-red lipstick on my lips. I felt like someone else. I felt totally uncomfortable.

'I would groove up your brows too if I had time,' mentioned Elaine.

'Not in this lifetime,' I said.

'You do look a liccle older,' remarked Naomi. 'Like about *forty-five*!'

'Burn you!'

'Keep your lips still!' barked Elaine. 'Just finishing the corners.'

I checked myself in the rear-view mirror and didn't like what I saw.

Early B switched his engine off and Folly Ranks stepped out of the car. He was dressed all in black, with Delta Force boots – they were Trooping-the-Colour shiny. He scoped the scene. A fly buzzed around his nose. We all went to greet him. My pulse banged in my veins.

'Everyone correct and present,' Folly Ranks said. He swatted the fly, then scanned my mask and nodded approvingly. 'Good. We're on track to smack the skittles. B, give them the caps.'

Early B stepped out of the ride. He was wearing black trainers, black jeans and a black hoodie. He handed out black baseball caps to everyone. I pulled mine over my eyebrows. I didn't like the taste of the lipstick. Folly Ranks bounced up to me. 'Comfortable?' he asked.

'Not comfortable,' I replied. 'But I can tolerate this. Just don't ask me to do the splits.'

Folly Ranks laughed. 'I love that,' he said. 'We're ticking to zero hour and you're busting jokes. A good sign – it shows confidence.'

It wasn't confidence. I was shitting breezeblocks.

'Right,' Manjaro said. His cap barely fit his large head. 'Everyone primed? Linval, leave your wheels here. Elaine and Mo, you can go with Early B and Folly Ranks. The rest of us will cruise in the Mini.'

'Before we roll off,' said Folly Ranks. 'Once we dust away from here, we're all in the game. Are you following me?'

The South Crong crew hollered a loud yes and raised their fists. Elaine, Naoms and I nodded.

'Let's do this,' said Folly Ranks. He climbed back into his ride. 'For the Marshall and for Sam!'

Elaine and I stepped into the back seat. I sniffed fish. 'I can't ride with that smell,' I said. 'It'll make me sick.'

'What smell?' asked Early B.

'Fish!' Elaine raised her voice. 'Her gut doesn't get on with anyting that swims. This chick will erupt if she watches *The Little Mermaid*. Trust me on that.'

Early B and Folly Ranks looked at each other with confused expressions. I sprung out of the car. 'No way I'm riding with that pollution,' I protested.

'I had cod and chips for my dinner,' Early B explained.

'You two go with Lady P,' Folly Ranks decided. 'Naoms and Linval can ride with us.'

Elaine and I hot-toed to the Mini. Lady P wound her window down. 'What is it?' she asked.

'We have to swap over,' I said.

Five minutes later we headed south along the Crong Heath road. I stared at the satnav on the dashboard. Elaine's view was partially blocked by the crusty frame of Manjaro filling the passenger seat. He took two mobile phones from the glove compartment and handed them over the headrest to us. 'All our digits are in there,' he said. 'F is for Folly, L for Linval, B for Early B and so on. Don't text or call anyone else, even after the mission, you receiving?'

'I get it,' I said.

We joined the Crong circular, cruising in the second lane of three. The lorries and trucks seemed so much bigger, more menacing. Car horns sounded louder. Untold cones slowed the traffic coming the other way. No one said a word. The clock on the dashboard read 9.15 p.m. I wound down the window. The rush of air cooled my face. Elaine was checking out her phone. I looked straight ahead, taking in the road signs. I caught Lady P glancing at me in her rear-view mirror. Manjaro took off his cap and wiped his bald head.

NORTH CRONGTON 4

'Have you got any music?' I asked.

Lady P didn't answer. Instead she pressed a button. Some kinda African choral chanting sounded from the speakers. I had no idea who it was but it was soothing.

NORTH CRONGTON 2

My heartbeat raced into fourth gear. Early B's Clio was four cars behind. Elaine had put her phone in her pocket. She picked her nails. Manjaro pulled his cap on. I adjusted mine.

NORTH CRONGTON 1

We turned off at the Crongton Green roundabout. Slabs and high rises loomed in the moonlight. Manjaro wound down his window. A man with a *Pirates of the Caribbean* beard slowly made his way over a zebra crossing. A kid on a Segway zoomed past him. I read another road sign: WELCOME TO NORTH CRONGTON. CHILDREN PLAYING. DRIVE CAREFULLY.

Lady P drove along narrow roads, twisting lanes and over a mountain of road ramps – she knew the ends well. North Crong soldier tags were everywhere – a black-sprayed small 'n' within a big 'C'.

She eventually pulled up on a street full of five-storey slabs and small terraced houses. An unseen dog barked. A young bruv kicked a ball against a wall. *Keboof, keboof.* Train tracks ran parallel to the street beyond the terraces. Lady P switched off the engine but left the music on at a low volume. She fixed her black cap and pointed to the end of the road. 'Sococheeta's down there,' she said. 'Just past the shops. About another hundred metres.'

I didn't want to get out. My heartbeat cranked into fifth gear. It was now 9.40 p.m. Early B parked up behind us. Folly Ranks stepped out of the car. He had pulled down his cap so far you couldn't see his eyes. He stood for a while, peering down the street. Then he rolled up to Manjaro.

'Is he greased?' Manjaro asked.

Folly Ranks nodded. 'Yep, primed to go. Let's press green on this mission.'

'You told him not to drop the blade?'

'Repeated it on a loop all the way here,' Folly Ranks confirmed. 'He knows the programme.'

'So this is it,' Manjaro said in a raised voice. He looked over his shoulder at Elaine. 'Are you good to go, sis? It's time.'

Before Elaine could answer I cut in, 'I can do this on my lonesome.'

'No.' Elaine stared me down. 'You are *not* mingling in that place on your Jack Jones.'

Folly Ranks opened the door for Elaine. Elaine hopped out. I followed her and hugged her tight.

'You're not gonna stay parked here, are you?' I asked Lady P. 'I can hot-toe the length of a b-ball court but over two hundred metres I'll be wheezing like a dying Darth Vadar. '

'No,' replied Lady P. 'When you're all inside, we'll drive closer.'

Folly Ranks spoke slowly to Elaine. 'Now remember, sis, you're not in there to sketch portraits. You're in the game to make sure Mo gets out. That's your play in this drama.'

Elaine nodded. Manjaro clambered out of the ride. He wrapped Elaine in a massive hug. His gaze lingered on her face. 'Good luck, sis. Any probs before Mo and Linval reach, give us a ding or text as soon as. Wait a second! Have you got any liquor money?'

Elaine shook her head. Folly Ranks peeled off a twenty pound note from his wallet.

'Hold up,' said Naomi, jumping out of her ride and jogging towards us. 'Let me give her some love too.'

Elaine and Naoms embraced for a long minute. I could smell the nicotine gassing from Naomi's breath.

'We're in motion,' said Folly Ranks. 'Start the ball rolling.'

Elaine stepped slowly down the street. She glanced over her shoulder twice. I could hear a train rattling in the distance.

'Get back into the rides,' ordered Manjaro.

We did as we were told. I couldn't help feeling guilty. I wanted to leap out of the car and yell for her to come back.

'Can you turn up the music a bit?' I asked Lady P.

Elaine disappeared up the street to the soundtrack of an African choir. I thought of her mother, Yvonne, her liccle bruv, Lemar and Granny Jackson. What had I done?

Without warning, I opened the door and climbed out. 'I have to step with her,' I said. 'I can't let her mingle in that place on her singles.'

Manjaro was quick to jump out after me. He glanced at Folly Ranks in the passenger seat of the Clio. After ten seconds thought, Folly Ranks nodded.

'OK, Mo,' Manjaro said. 'But don't heat yourself up. Step in slow. Be in control. Don't look anybody in the eye. Don't rush anything. Don't make any sudden movements. And when you hand the shank over, remind Linval *not* to drop it.'

My heartbeat found gear six. I took in a deep breath. Sweat leaked from my armpits. It dripped from my belly button. Ten Muhammad Alis bish-boshed my ribs.

'Remember, Mo,' Manjaro said softly, 'if you're not feeling

this, roll back. Ain't no shame in that. If it comes to that, we'll reboot the game and back up the heathen another day.'

'I've got this,' I said. 'I'll be cool.'

I took my first few strides but I was too hasty – I felt the knife handle poke into my groin. *Step carefully, Mo. Sheffield Steel. Honed to the max.* Elaine waited for me. She tapped her right foot. A brown and white cat slinked under a parked car. The boy was still booting his football. *Keboof. Keboof. Keboof.*

'Glad we're stepping into the club together,' Elaine said when I reached her. 'I was crapping myself.'

'Me too.' I nodded.

We linked arms and moved on. A couple of kids were performing wheelies on mountain bikes. A row of houses stood to our right, their front gardens barely big enough to park a skateboard in. Two of the houses were boarded up. Red graffiti hyped up the North Crong crew.

SOS roois crong! Welcome to the NS! Deadlier than a black mamba! The S merker!

We passed a chicken takeaway hut and a convenience store. Hoodslugs garmed in baggy black jeans and black T-shirts lipped bottles of hard-core drinks outside an off-licence. Young bruvs were swapping macho poses and hype on the pavement. A few of them were bragging black head rags. Some were puffing rockets. Grime beats blared out from a couple of rides. A tall chick fronting a pink spangly headband

and black hot pants whizzed by on roller skates and all the guys she passed studied her behind. A short brother with a number one head trim was handing out flyers about a rave. Elaine pulled me closer. 'That's gotta be it,' she said. 'You go before me,' Elaine advised.

'OK,' I said.

Faking confidence, we bounced up to Sococheeta. It was smaller than I expected. It had a yellow awning over its entrance. A red and green neon light sexed up the front windows. SOCOCHEETA'S! A tonking bassline quaked the pavement. Two chicks were in front of us. False eyelashes filled their faces. Black bangles niced up their wrists. Ripped black jeans snugged their bumpers. They were chatting about a spoken word artist named Shiloh G. Two bears stood either side of the front door. They were giants, big enough to pick me and Elaine up and roll us like dice down the street. They were both wearing black bomber jackets, black polo-neck sweaters and black trousers. The blade suddenly felt mega heavy. It was as if I had the Eiffel Tower taped to my leg. I pulled down my black pullover. Elaine gave my arm a reassuring squeeze. The grizzlies patted down the two chicks ahead of us.

'Shiloh G's gonna mash it tonight!' one of them said.

'Yeah, she's so on point,' said the other. 'Even SOS will give her props.'

'The Lonesome Stranger's blessing the mic tonight too,' the first chick added.

'He spits dark tales,' the other remarked.

The bears didn't say a word.

I worked out who SOS was – Sean O'Shea.

The two girls were ushered through.

'Next!'

I stepped forward two paces. I swallowed. I shifted my weight from foot to foot. My hands clammed up. I wiped them on the front of my pullover.

'Keep still,' whispered Elaine.

'Raise your arms, miss,' I was instructed.

I did as I was told.

The bear looked at me hard before patting me down from my shoulder blades to my waist and the outside of my thighs. His big thumbs and wide palms pressed into me.

I held my breath.

'Go through,' he said.

'Wh-what?' I stuttered.

'Go through,' he repeated.

I managed three paces. I stood still and closed my eyes. Eventually I got my breathing back on the level.

Elaine joined me seconds later. She shook her head and wiped her cheeks. 'That was messed up,' she said. 'Never felt so nervous in all my days.'

'Breaking into the cinema used to give my heart a tumping,' I said. 'But this is *Mission Impossible* scary – rogue ends.'

'But we got in,' said Elaine. 'What next?'

I scoped the club.

A long bar to my left. Varnished wooden counter. Female staff wearing dark blue Sococheeta T-shirts and black trousers. Peeps sat on leather-padded stools sinking cocktails, wines and beers. Others nibbled French fries, roasted peanuts and crisps. Cream-coloured leather chairs and tables were on my right. Framed pics of celebs covered the walls. Taylor Swift, Rita Ora, Rihanna, Drake. There was a small stage towards the back – a microphone stand stood on its lonesome in the centre. Beyond that was a see-through DJ booth. Funky beats rocked the club. The bassline tickled my toes.

'Where's the toilets?' I whispered.

'Past the stage I think,' replied Elaine. 'Let's take a tour.'

We linked arms and rolled through the club.

One table caught my eye – there was a kind of electric energy surrounding it. Two slick chicks were seated there, curled around a bruv garmed in a baggy white suit and a black string vest. He was the centre of attention. Three diamond studs glammed up his left eyebrow. He wore a samurai hairstyle with some sort of wooden clip gripping his long ponytail. He was spinning the ice cubes in his cocktail with a straw. They were all laughing at an image on his phone. He had green eyes and a trimmed goatee. Was *that* Sean O'Shea?

Elaine pinched me. *'Don't* stare,' she warned.

We rolled past the DJ booth. The toilets were on either side of a narrow passage that led to a kitchen. The smell of fries licked my nostrils.

The men's was on the right. We went inside the ladies'. I stared into a mirror above a sink. 'Jeez and peas, Elaine. I'm sweating saunas! I knew I shouldn't have put on this pullover.'

'Splash your face,' Elaine advised. She lowered her voice. 'Remember what Manjaro said about heating yourself up – *stop* staring out peeps!'

I sprayed my face with water. My mascara smudged. Elaine fixed it. I dried my hands.

'Let's get a drink,' suggested Elaine.

We bounced out of the ladies', hit the bar and perched ourselves on stools. Elaine took out the twenty pound note. 'What do you want?' she asked.

'To run out the back and jump on the first train outta here,' I replied.

Elaine wasn't laughing. 'To drink?' she asked again.

'An orange juice,' I replied. 'With nuff ice.'

'I'm having the same,' she said.

Elaine ordered the drinks. I glanced over at the entrance. North Crongtonians were still swagging in, most of them boasting name brand black T-shirts and black string vests. Who'd come up with this suicide mission? Over on the stage, a crusty bruv working an orange waistcoat and a green bow tie tested the microphone. Next to him a girl wrote something on a piece of paper.

A chick with baby dreadlocks and brown lipstick served our drinks. A pink heart tattoo sexed up her neck. I sucked hard on my straw. Relief as Siberian-cold orange guzzled down my throat. *Good.*

'Just relax,' said Elaine.

'You ever tried chilling with the Great Pyramid of Giza sticking out of your crotch?' I whispered.

'Stop it,' Elaine said. 'You can't see anyting.'

I drank the orange juice too fast. I suffered a brain freeze.

'Get me another,' I asked Elaine.

She did as she was told. While she was trying to get the bar chick's attention, I watched the entrance. There was plenty of fist and shoulder bumping going on. *Smoking blisters! We're in the heart of North Crongbanger junction.*

'Maybe we should roll back and reprogram this situation,' I whispered to Elaine. 'Or we can text Folly Ranks and tell him we're surrounded by North Crong slug-rats.'

'Give it a couple of minutes,' said Elaine. 'Let's see if Linval wants to see it through.'

I had just finished my second glass when I spotted Linval. He was standing with the bears at the door, his arms out wide. They checked his behind and the inside of his legs. They asked him to take off his trainers. Satisfied, they let him through. Linval pulled on his name-brands and bounced into the club. He pushed his hands into his pockets. He glanced at me as he rolled by. He took up a position at the end of the bar, opposite the stage. This was really happening.

'Shall I go to the ladies' now?' I suggested.

'No,' Elaine replied. 'Let him sink a drink first. Looks like he needs it.'

I glanced at Linval again. He definitely needed an alcohol dose or three.

Linval ordered a cocktail. He drained it in three glugs before he demanded another. As we watched him, the bruv in the orange waistcoat announced the line-up for the lyrical slam. Shiloh G received the loudest cheer. *'Bo! Bo! Bo!'* the crowd hollered. The Lonesome Stranger got two boos. When Linval had sank half of his next glass, he glanced at me and nodded.

'Now,' Elaine whispered into my ear.

I climbed off the stool. Elaine took out a tissue and wiped my forehead. 'OK,' she said. 'Let's do this.'

I closed my eyes and tried to download a shot of bravery. Elaine took my arm and together we headed for the rendez-vous. We passed by Linval. He didn't look at me. Instead, he gazed at the floor. We went by the DJ booth, into the pas-sageway and turned left into the ladies'. No one was in there. Thank the Crongton Gods for that.

'Go into the cubicle,' suggested Elaine. 'I'll be out here washing my hands. If someone else steps in I'll knock twice. When they leave, I'll tickle it three times.'

I did what I was told. I closed the door behind me. I bolted it. I could sniff piss. Someone hadn't flushed the toilet. I pulled the lever and brought down the seat cover. The flush made an ugly gargling sound. A cockroach would've had trouble wiping its ass with the toilet paper available. North Crong graffiti covered the walls, written in different shades of lipstick.

SOS the Don Dada! If you have a slug problem, call the South Crongbusters.

As soon as I sat down, someone knuckled the door.

I pulled it open a centimetre. Linval's left eye stared at me. Sweat leaked from his forehead. High tension marked his lips.

'Let me in,' he whispered.

I let him in. He secured the door. I looked at him hard.

'Are you gonna do this?' I asked. 'There's untold rag-heads out there. Did Folly Ranks expect so many of them?'

'They're not tooled,' said Linval. 'The security detail are on point with their patting down – the grizzly almost frisked my balls.'

'They didn't stop my ass from getting in with a blade,' I cut in.

'You're a chick,' said Linval. 'They don't pat you down to the max cos they don't wanna be accused of anything.'

'Lucky me,' I replied.

'The rag-heads will mouse out when it all kicks off,' Linval predicted. 'They're not expecting any warring tonight. They think they're untouchable here.'

'So you're going through with this?'

'Most def with a big D,' he replied. 'What d'you take me for? I ain't no lamb! We're behind enemy lines. I didn't cruise up to these ends to scope the bitches and listen to dead-end poets.'

'Cool down your fever, Linval,' I said. 'You want them to hear you in the club?'

I unclipped my belt. I took off my trainers. I pulled off my jeans. I pinched on a new pair of surgical gloves.

'Look the other way,' I said.

Linval turned around.

I peeled off my cycle shorts. I picked off the tape around my thigh and started to unwrap myself.

I heard two taps on the door. Linval brought his forefinger to his lips. I kept very still. I could hear running water. A minute later, three taps knuckled the door. 'They're gone,' I told Linval.

I unravelled the knife. My leg had turned red. Sweat

cling-filmed my upper body. Linval yanked on a pair of black leather gloves. He turned around. I no longer cared about him seeing me in just my knickers. I handed over the shank. Linval stared at it. He twirled it in his grasp.

'You good for this?' I asked.

He nodded. He was breathing deeply. He took out his mobile phone and started thumbing a text message. He had trouble hitting the digits. I dressed myself.

'Don't leave the cycle shorts in here,' he advised.

'I know the programme,' I replied.

'Right,' he said. 'Zero hour. The count of thirty.'

His thumb was poised for ten seconds before he sent the message. A bulb of sweat crashed on to his phone's face. He placed the blade in the inside pocket of his jacket. He opened the toilet door.

'Whatever you do, *don't* drop it,' I reminded him.

'I hear you.' He nodded. 'I know the programme too.'

I read his eyes. Dread with a big D. He took in one more deep breath and was gone. The building shook as another train rattled by.

In, out, in, out I breathed. I counted to ten and then I came out. Elaine dried her hands with a paper towel. She dropped it in an overflowing bin. Tiny sweat beads framed her top lip. We gazed into the mirror above the sink. In my head I had reached sixteen.

'I don't know about you,' I said, 'but I can't wait till thirty.'

Elaine nodded.

'Linval's quaking,' I revealed.

'So would I if I had to complete his mission,' Elaine said. 'The place is heaving with North Crong GIs.'

We stepped out of the ladies'. My heartbeat vibrated my tonsils. I turned right. Izzy Bizu's 'Mad Behaviour' boomed out from the speakers. An Asian chick rocking a multi-coloured headwrap was up on the stage. The crowd looked at her as she adjusted the microphone stand. The brother standing beside her was styling a sombrero and a Lone Ranger mask. A green and white poncho blessed his shoulders. A few peeps at the back stood on stools.

I scanned the crowd for Linval and saw him slowly threading through the throng. I knew I wasn't supposed to but suddenly I had to catch up with him, and tell him he didn't have to do it. Elaine tried to pull me back but I shrugged her off.

'Mo!'

She hadn't seen Linval's eyes in the toilet cubicle. I had. And I'd seen fear right inside them. I had to reach him.

I managed to get within three metres of him. Linval glanced over his shoulder. I shook my head and mouthed a silent 'No.' Terror seized his gaze but he kept on his course.

He bumped through the crowd until he was a right hook away from the guy I'd noticed before. The guy with the haircut. His long ponytail hung down to the top of his white trousers. This was Sean O'Shea. Lloyd's big bruv.

I drew up to Linval and placed a hand on his shoulder. He brushed me off, slipped his right hand into the inside pocket of his jacket and took out the shank. It flashed under the lights. Curved steel. Honed to the max. Someone screamed.

'Man's got a shank!' another hollered.

Sean O'Shea backed away a step. Panic glossed his eyes. He held out his palms. He frantically shook his head but

Linval gripped the handle of the blade between his thumb and forefinger and raised it up. Twenty centimetres long. Two brass screws in the black handle.

A space appeared around the assassinator and the North Crong crime lord. The music stopped. Linval hesitated. His eyes Scooby-Dooed. He faltered and . . . he dropped the knife. It fell heavily and bounced three times before lying flat on the ground in front of him. Sean O'Shea grinned in relief. Linval froze. Sean O'Shea moved to pick up the blade.

I wasn't sure what came over me and made me do what I did next. I just didn't want to see Linval get sliced and diced right in front of me. I didn't want Naoms to suffer another loss. I thought of her babbling and bawling in the hospital lift about Crumbs. Her entire future was right now.

I dived forward and down towards the blade. My cap fell off but I kept going and reached the shank before Sean O'Shea. He crashed on top of me. I wriggled, twisted and rolled on to my back. I could smell vodka on his breath. I gripped the handle tight between my two hands. I held on to it like it was my only child. O'Shea's green eyes bulged.

Suddenly, my hands were wet. So was my face. I tasted something warm. Blood. My vision went dark.

Chicks screamed. Feet thundered around me. A high heel clipped my head. Elaine shoved Sean O'Shea off me, grabbed my arm and hauled me upright. I dropped the shank. A North Crong slug-rat gave Elaine a right cross that momentarily dazed her. I heard smashed glasses. I saw someone swing a baseball bat. It was Manjaro. He was rushing towards us. A bottle crashed against the side of his head. Folly Ranks brain-caned a bear with a car jack he had tied to a short length of rope.

Another guy jumped on Elaine and Manjaro took aim and bashed him senseless. The bruv dropped to the ground as if he had dumbbells looped to his lobes.

'Get out!' Manjaro yelled at us. 'Get out!'

'Folly Ranks is here!' someone roared. 'Folly Ranks is here!'

Elaine could hardly walk. Manjaro kept her upright with one hand and flexed his baseball bat with the other. Ducking under flying glasses, we made it to the exit. We had to jump over a grizzly who had blood dribbling down the side of his face.

Folly Ranks had lost his weapon. I saw him go down under a mob of black T-shirts and black vests, his body concaved by fists, boots and bottles. I anxiously scoped for Linval and spied him brandishing a broken bottle above his head, trying to make his way out.

'Hold on to her!' Manjaro ordered.

Elaine's weight dragged me down but I managed to get us outside. On the pavement I heard the scream of a car horn and looked for the source. The black Mini: Lady P. Bless her green highlights! I'd never been so joyous to see someone in all my days. Early B was parked behind her. He jumped out of his ride, grabbed a cricket bat from under his seat and hot-footed it inside the club. 'Fly! Fly!' he screamed at us as he rushed by.

Lady P bounced out and opened the back door. I shoved Elaine in, got in myself and slammed the door shut. Lady P jumped into the driver's seat and switched the ignition. The green and blue lights on the dashboard glowed bright. She hit first gear. We pulled away. She nearly hit a parked jeep and a young bruv on a scooter.

'Where's Naomi?' I screamed. 'Where's Naomi?'

'She's in the other car,' replied Lady P. 'She wouldn't come with me. She wanted to wait for Linval.'

'You have to turn back,' I demanded. 'You gotta turn back and get her.'

Lady P shook her head.

'You have to turn back!' I repeated louder.

'My play is to get you two off the scene,' Lady P insisted. 'Naomi was told to hot-rev it outta there if she doesn't see anyone in the next five minutes.'

'But she can't drive!' I shouted.

'She can.' Elaine nodded. 'Linval's been teaching her.'

'I'm *not* turning back,' Lady P maintained.

She glanced at me via the rear-view mirror. I was stained in blood. I could feel it moistening my skin. In the same mirror I could see my hair was clumpy with dark red apps. My hands shook. Suddenly, I felt very cold. Lady P kept silent. She drove carefully through the streets. She pressed play on the audio system. African chanting hummed from the stereo. It didn't cool my dread. I wound the window down.

'Are you OK, sis?' I asked Elaine.

'Just about,' she replied. 'I've got a new pulse at the back of my head though.'

We reached the Crongton Green roundabout and took the Notre Dame road. *Straight outta Crongton!*

27

The Ruskin Windmill

'What the eff went down in there?' Lady P wanted to know.

Elaine and I looked at each other.

'I . . . I . . . ' I couldn't get the words out of my mouth.

'Linval flopped,' Elaine revealed. 'He dropped the blade. Mo jumped in, picked it up, but Sean O'Shea dived on top of her. Mo rolled on to her back and that's when Sean O'Shea got ruptured.'

I could see Lady P's mouth open and close.

'Is he?' she asked. 'Is he . . . ?'

'Don't know,' replied Elaine. 'All I can say is that when I pushed him off Mo, he wasn't moving.'

A sharp chill sliced through me. 'Oh my days,' I ranted, 'oh my freaking days – they'll still be serving me oats when I'm on my second pair of dentures. Oh my days.'

Elaine wrapped her arm around me. She kissed me on the

cheek and picked the hair out of my face. 'It's all right, Mo. Would you rather it be your behind lying there? You think he would've hesitated on designing you a new windpipe? It was self-defence, sis. He jumped on top of you. Remember that.'

I shook my head. 'It's in my hair!' I yelled. 'It's in my hair!'

I couldn't help thinking of Sean O'Shea's white jacket turning an instant wet red.

If he's dead, I've taken away everyting pleasure he ever had in one mad moment. No more hollering at his fave soccer team. No more bopping his head to slamming beats. No making out with his best girl or swaggering in expensive garms. No more sipping his vodka cocktail. No more cruising around in sexed-up wheels. All because Mo Baker, from number thirteen Slipe House, ripped it away from him. Jeez and peas! The devil's prepping a place for me at his dinner table.

Lady P glanced at me again. Her expression never switched. Within minutes we headed north, cutting through the wilderness of Fireclaw Heath. The trees and scrub appeared darker than usual.

'Stop the car!' I yelled. 'Stop the freaking car!'

Lady P pulled up sharply. I leaped out of the ride and puked the remains of my orange juice into the bushes. My belly twisted with pain. Elaine followed me. 'Are you OK, Mo?'

I wiped my mouth with my sleeve. 'No,' I replied.

Elaine helped me back into the Mini. She took out a tissue and wiped my face. Lady P turned around. 'Shall I drive on?' she asked. 'It's not good to stay here.'

'Yes,' Elaine replied. 'Rev it up.'

We reached the hillside town of Notre Dame but Lady P didn't stop there. She kept driving uphill along bush-lined lanes. The only light came from the Mini's headlights and the studs of cat's eyes along the road.

'Where're you taking us?' Elaine wanted to know.

'Ruskin windmill,' replied Lady P. 'That's the rendezvous point. I've been scoping it out for over a week.'

Five minutes later, Lady P turned left into a zigzagging dirt lane just wide enough for one car to pass along it. Broad nettles were growing rampant on either side. The windmill and its outbuildings stood at the end of the lane. No lights were on.

The hills beyond were a shadow and a guess but I could just about make them out. To the south were the distant lights of Notre Dame. It looked kinda pretty from our high vantage point. Further away stood the slabs of North Crongton, the scene of the crime. How had it come to this? I'd only ever wanted Mum to sack her wasterman boyfriend. I hadn't meant for any of . . . any of *this*.

Lady P pulled up outside the windmill and switched off the engine.

'There's nobody here, right?' Elaine wanted confirmation.

'No,' replied Lady P. 'The windmill hasn't been in use for the longest time. A history teacher took us up here on a school trip once.'

She grabbed a torch and a box of matches from the glove compartment. 'Mo, your clothes,' she said. 'I've been told to blaze any DNA evidence.'

'You what?' I replied. 'You're not burning *shit*! You know how much my jeans cost me? I didn't get 'em from Crong market!'

271

'If you've got blood all over you that means you're covered with Sean O'Shea's DNA, understand?' Lady P explained. 'Whatever your jeans cost, they're not worth it, believe me. I've got some new garms in the boot you can wear.'

I swapped looks with Elaine. She nodded.

'You're *not* blazing my trainers,' I protested.

I started to undress. To be honest I was glad to be out of the blood-soaked pullover and jeans. The breeze was stronger up here and my skin felt numb. Lady P brought me a pair of light blue jeans and a cream sweater. Elaine nodded approvingly. 'Anyting for me?' she asked.

Lady P returned to the boot and brought back another name-brand bag. Elaine accepted it with a smile.

'When you reach home make sure you scrub your trainers with a wire brush,' Lady P advised. 'Especially the soles. Soak them in bleach or something.' She gathered up my old clothes, picked up a couple of newspapers from the boot and stepped towards a stone wall. She shone her torch in front of her. The windows of the shed-size slab were all blitzed. There was nothing inside save dust, twigs and litter. A dried mud path led from the crumbling entrance of the structure to the black door of the windmill. It loomed high above us like a giant beheaded scarecrow.

Then Lady P arsoned my bloodied garms. They blazed in seconds, the small fire greedy.

'And your hat!' Lady P called out to Elaine.

Elaine tossed it on to the flames. I was just about to join them when I spotted a pair of headlights weaving its way through the blackness.

'Back in the ride,' advised Lady P.

We scrambled back into the Mini. Lady P started the engine. She didn't switch on the headlights.

The car emerged out of the bush. Lady P switched on her headlights and revealed Early B behind the wheel of his Clio. Manjaro was in the passenger seat. He was holding a t-shirt against the side of his head. Linval and Naomi were in the back. They braked sharply. Early B slowly climbed out. Cuts and bruises mapped his face. He rolled towards us. His head was down. His hands were in his pockets. Lady P wound her window halfway.

'Where's Folly Ranks?' Lady P asked.

Early B shook his head. He paused for a while, staring at the ground beneath him. 'We couldn't get to him,' he finally replied. 'Too many of them. They chased us out, flinging bottles at us. We had to get back to our ride. If we didn't, we all woulda ended up worm-meat for real. Everyone flew when they heard the sirens.'

Lady P hung her head.

'So you don't know if he's . . . ' Elaine wanted to know.

'Whether he's alive or not?' Early B completed the sentence. He shook his head. 'No, we don't know. But he's probably . . . ' Early B didn't finish this one.

'What about Sean O'Shea?' I asked.

'Two chicks were trying to stop the bleeding,' Early B revealed. 'When we winged outta the place, he wasn't moving. His eyes were closed. Worms in Crong cemetery are waiting to feast on his slug-rat ass.'

A cold swirl disturbed my stomach. *I'm a murderer*, I

thought. *Orange is gonna be my new black. My new sistrens are gonna have cell block attitudes and untold scars on their wrists.*

'Manjaro's been gashed bad,' added Early B. 'He needs sewing up as soon as. We're gonna take him to Ashburton hospital. As soon as I drop him I'm gonna rev down to Crongton General and see if I can find any intel about Folly Ranks.'

'What shall I do?' asked Lady P.

'Drop the ladies back in South Crong,' Early B replied. 'All of you are South Crong warrior queens. For real! Manjaro wants you to know that.'

I didn't feel like a warrior queen. I felt like a killer. The cyclone within my belly wouldn't quit. I wanted to vomit again but I held it down.

Elaine hopped out of the ride and checked on Manjaro. She helped press the T-shirt against his wound. 'You're gonna need untold stitches,' she said. 'Next time, don't cruise up to foreign ends headbutting flying bottles.'

Manjaro laughed. They shared a moment.

'Did you burn all the evidence?' Early B asked Lady P.

Lady P pointed to the smouldering fire.

'What about the blade?'

I shook my head.

'We can't sweat about that just now,' Early B said. 'We're just glad that you ladies are still trodding good. I'm gonna dust now. Linval and Naomi are gonna ride with you.'

Early B returned to the Clio. He hugged Elaine before climbing into the driver's seat. Naomi and Linval stepped out. Naomi and Elaine joined me in the back of the Mini. Before

Linval sat himself in the front he chucked his black leather gloves and cap on to the fire. He watched them burn as Lady P revved the engine. Early B steered away. We followed his tail lights.

'Manjaro saved my ass,' said Elaine, staring vacantly ahead. 'Some crusty bruv tried to choke me. Them North Crongbangers don't play! I could've been dead, sparked out in that mother-freaking club. If I ever see them slug-rats again see I don't take off my shoe heel and lace their foreheads with it!'

I held Elaine's hand. Linval remained silent.

'What do we do now?' I asked.

'We hit the pillows,' replied Lady P. 'No one leaks anything. We keep a low profile. We respray the rides in bright colours.'

It wasn't until we hit the Crong circular that Linval mumbled something.

'Sorry,' he said. 'I flopped out big time. Mo, you're bolder than any man I know. You saved my sorry behind. I'll never forget that. Respect to the fullest. Your name should be written large.'

I nodded. I still didn't know what had made me reach for that damn knife, but I had respect for his thankfulness. Somehow it made it less . . . wrong.

The journey back to South Crong rec was completed in silence. Lady P had switched off the music. Faces spoke of disbelief. I was sure everyone else had the same questions as me reeling in their brains. *Is Folly Ranks alive? Is Sean O'Shea dead? Are CSI Crongton scooping up our DNA? Has*

Lloyd heard what went down? How did I get caught up on this revenge tip?

Sam's still lying in a hospital where the bleeping never quits.

I recalled what Lorna said once, about how your soul mirror can be shattered if you allow trauma and rage to control you. Mine was in a million pieces.

Lady P pulled up in the gravel car park behind the grandstand, where this evening's drama had all started. Nobody moved to get out of the car. I couldn't help but think of that dreadful moment when Sean O'Shea had pitched forward on to the shank in my hands.

'Linval and me are going off-grid,' blurted out Naomi.

'Wh-what?' Elaine stuttered. 'What d'you mean you're going off-grid?'

Linval stared aimlessly through the windscreen. Lady P wound down her window. She sparked a cigarette.

'We're sick of this game so we're bouncing off the board,' confirmed Naomi. 'We're leaving tonight. I'm already packed.'

'But you'll only make things worse,' argued Elaine. 'You've got the court case coming up and—'

'*No*, Elaine!' shouted Naomi.

'It'll be even more—'

'For just a second can you shut the freak up and hear me out!' yelled Naomi.

Lady P blew her smoke out of the window. It was obvious she didn't wanna offer her thoughts on the argument. Linval gazed ahead. Elaine was about to say something but changed her mind. The silence was intense.

'I wanna start afresh,' Naomi said after a while, dropping

her tone to just above a whisper. 'Yeah, they'll probably catch me after a while. I know that. But if they do, at least they'll send me somewhere else, somewhere better. I'm tired of all the drama in Crongton. I lost someone close to the warfare a while back . . . '

Naomi paused. Emotion filled her eyes. Her gaze fell on me. 'Crumbs,' she resumed. 'I'll never forget him. A sweet bruv. He always looked out for me. He always had time for me. Nearest ting to a big bro I've ever had. He just wanted to belong to someting cos no one gave a shit about him in the home. Now he's *dead.* And right now they're probably wheeling Ranks' body to the death crib too. We've paid our dues. There'll be no comebacks. We're *done* with it.'

'So your mind's made up?' Elaine said. 'You're Shawshanking out on us?'

'To be honest I would've dusted out a long time ago if it wasn't for you and Mo,' said Naomi. She started to cry – unlike her to the max. I could tell she didn't love us seeing her like this. 'And don't fret about me, I'm still fifteen. They're not gonna send my ass to Guantanamo Bay for jacking a few garms and hot-toeing away from a stupid kid's home.'

'So what Mo and I did tonight doesn't matter?' Elaine's voice was shrill with anger and disbelief. 'So *we* have to deal with all the fallout and shit on our own cos *you're* dusting out with your flop-a-dop lover boy? That's so freaking convenient for—'

'Leave her!' I yelled. 'Let her go! I was on this mission cos I wanted to be . . . I was on a revenge tip. No one forced me to do anyting and I'm not gonna lie about that.'

I glanced at Lady P. She nodded.

'Life in Crongton *is* shit,' I continued. 'Let's get real about that. Even if we do spend all our time hitting books there's no freaking career at the end of it – unless you wanna spend your nine to fives spitting chocolate goo in a biscuit factory. It's a www dot nobody town in the middle of nowhere dot com. No one gives a frig about young peeps here. If Naomi wants to flutter off and try somewhere else, I say the best of luck and solid blessings to her.'

Elaine crossed her arms. Her top lip was twitching. 'But . . . but this *is* our home,' she mumbled. '*Our* ends. What about your pops, Naoms? Don't you wanna keep in touch with him?'

'*Not* my ends,' Naomi snapped. '*Not* any more. And if my pops can rehab himself to a respectable level then I'll give him a ding.'

Naomi opened the car door. We all climbed out. I approached Linval. 'Look after her,' I said. 'And don't get your ass involved in any G warfare.'

'Not intending to,' he replied. 'I could've been merked tonight. I don't wanna dose of that dread again.'

'And don't let her go shopping for garms on her own,' I joked.

Elaine managed a smile.

'I'm locking down any shopping assignments,' said Linval. 'She knows I'm on that.'

'Good,' I said.

I couldn't help wondering if Elaine would be visiting Naomi and myself in a prison somewhere soon.

'Where're you heading?' Elaine wanted to know.

'Elmers End,' replied Linval. 'It's about forty miles north of Notre Dame. I have a cousin who lives up there – he's got a spare room.'

'Do *not* get her pregnant, Linval!' I warned.

'If you do, I'll take the bumpkin bus to Elmers End and mangle your bits with a NutriBullet,' said Elaine.

Linval shook his head. 'That's not on our agenda.'

Naomi, Elaine and I clung together in a group hug. Tears flowed. Linval and Lady P looked on.

'OK, let me go missing,' Naomi said. 'I'll be on your radar as soon as I get a new phone. We'll link before the next Tom Cruise movie.'

'Has Elmers End got a cinema?' Elaine wanted to know.

'Yes it does,' replied Linval.

'Has it got an emergency exit?'

Linval nodded. 'Marked in green.'

'Can you get to the door from the inside?' Elaine wanted to know.

'That's standard,' Linval replied. 'It wouldn't be much use as an emergency exit if you couldn't get to it.'

'Then we're on it,' I said.

Naomi pulled herself away. Linval opened the front passenger door for her. Naomi hopped in. She wound down the window and poked her head out. 'Mo, give Sam nuff love,' she called out. 'He's a bit of a book-slapper but you've got a good specimen there. Claw on to him tight. And stop fretting – he'll get better. And Elaine! Don't think I haven't noticed you scoping Manjaro's bod. Here what. He's on you too!'

'You better stop trending that gossip, Naoms!' Elaine snapped.

'You *know* it's true,' laughed Naomi.

Linval started the engine. Hard grime beats blared out. He hot-revved away and we waved goodbye. I couldn't quite believe she was leaving. None of us moved until the red tail lights faded in the darkness. The owls started their chorus. *God! I'm gonna miss her.* I fell into Elaine's embrace.

28

Shampoo and Conditioner

Ten minutes later, Lady P parked outside my slab – Slipe House.

'Do you want me to go in with you?' Elaine offered.

'No,' I said. 'I'll be good.'

'You sure?'

'Yeah, sis. Better Sean O'Shea burst rather than me, right?'

'You're not wrong.' Elaine nodded. 'Live another day. Mum's been ringing off my phone – she'll probably lock me down tomorrow but I'll fly up and see Sam with you when I get probation.'

'Cool,' I said. 'Thanks for stepping up with me to Sococheeta. You didn't have to. I'll never forget that. You're a sistren for real.'

We hugged for a long minute. I couldn't stop the tears. I missed Naoms already. I wanted Elaine to spend the night with me but she was in enough trouble as it was.

Lady P stepped out of the ride. She waited for me and Naomi to put a full stop to our goodbye. I might've merked a man – the bruv of my mum's boyfriend. How messed up was that? My frigged-up life was a Channel Five documentary waiting to happen: *Teen Female Psycho Killers!* God.

'Just wanna say thanks too,' Lady P managed. 'I could've never done what you did.'

'I don't know how I did it,' I replied. 'I've got *reckless* running in my DNA I guess.'

'I don't know how you did it either, but you did. Try not to koof yourself about it. If it's any consolation, Sean O'Shea's a proper wolf-heart ... Nuff North Crong girls hate him and his crew. It's karma that a chick pricked *that* dick.'

'I can't lie,' I said, 'it's not a consolation ... But thanks for everyting. And thanks for dropping me off.'

'Thank *you*, Mo,' she said. 'Keep a low profile. My blessings to Sam.'

Elaine climbed in to the Mini. I stood on the pavement and watched Lady P perform a U-turn and drive away.

I stepped up to my front door with a jagged feeling in my gut – as if piranhas were feeding on my intestines.

I inserted my key into the front door and walked along the hallway. The light in the kitchen was on. I could hear Little Richard's 'Rip It Up' on the radio. I checked the time. 11.40 p.m.

Mum sat at the kitchen table. She was filling in a crossword in a celeb mag, smoking. The ashtray was full. A beer can stood next to it.

I ignored her and went straight to the sink. I ran the tap

and poured myself a glass of cold water. I sank it in one go. I caught my breath and refilled my glass. Mum looked up and squinted as she scoped my hair. She killed her lung merker and stood up.

'Mo, what's happened, baby?'

I didn't answer. Instead, I drank from my glass. I noticed that Sean O'Shea's blood still soiled my hands – it had gotten under my fingernails. I squirted two doses of washing up liquid and tried to scrub it off with a tired Brillo pad.

Mum picked up a few strands of my hair for closer inspection. 'Mo! What's happened? Please tell me what's happened? What have you done? Whose clothes are you wearing? Is it Elaine? Have you been in a fight with her? What has she done?'

I parked myself at the kitchen table. I finished my water. Some song about a ghost town played on the radio. Mum's frenzied gaze wouldn't leave me alone. 'I'm your mum, Mo! Can't you tell me? What's happened, baby?'

I couldn't say it. I was a murderer. Blood was on my shoulder. I was going to prison. Nothing could protect me from the fate I deserved . . .

'Mo. *Please* talk to me!'

I didn't say anything.

'Mo?' Her voice lowered.

I couldn't look at her. After a while, I opened my mouth and spoke, in a tiny voice I didn't recognise.

'Can you wash my hair please?' I asked.

She was taken aback. I stood up and went to fetch my towel and pillow from my bedroom. I headed to the bathroom where I took off my new cream sweater. I placed the towel around my shoulders. I kneeled on the pillow and hung my head over the bath. Mum entered. She stared at me for a while. She folded her arms. 'Mo?'

I tried to boot out reality from my mind.

'Can you condition it as well?' I asked.

Mum turned on the taps. I closed my eyes.

'Mo, there's so much I'm sorry about,' she said as she rinsed my hair. 'I should've said sorry to you a long time ago. Lorna told me it's never too late, so here it goes. I dunno where to start? I suppose at the beginning if you can bear with me. Despite all my wrongs, you know I love you, don't you, Mo?'

I didn't say a word. Even though my nostrils were soaked with water I could still sniff the tobacco on her breath.

'Your dad, he ... it's true. He raped me,' Mum began. 'That's where all my troubles started. Lorna told me to tell the police ... but I didn't. I have to admit, once you were born, I didn't wanna keep ya. *No way!* Lorna had to babysit you a lot when you were a nipper. You see, every time I looked at you, you reminded me of him – you know, of what he did to me. You've got his nose. It's a terrible thing for a mum to say but that's the truth, Mo. At the time I didn't realise what was going on in my head. Eventually my doctor told me a lotta women get depressed after they have kids. It's hard to describe. I just hope you never go through that kind of bleakness, Mo. It went on for months it did. I didn't wanna get outta bed.'

Mum's fingers massaged my scalp. It felt good. I needed her to wash the stain outta my hair. I wanted to be clean. If only she could have shampooed away everything that'd happened in the last few weeks.

'I think that's the reason why I drink now, you see,' Mum went on. 'I know you don't like it. I don't either, but I wanna forget about what he did to me. I think of it all the time. I can't get rid of it. The drink blunts it a bit but in the morning it doesn't bloody matter – I still wake up and remember it; remember him.'

'You carried that inside you for so many years?' I said just above a whisper. 'Must've been hell. I'm sorry, Mum. Lorna said you were shattered about someting.'

'I haven't told you the half of it, Mo. I'm so sorry.'

She rested her fingers as she gathered herself. She sucked in a long breath. 'But I have to tell you this or my conscience will kill me.'

'Tell me what, Mum?'

'You were one and a half years old, Mo,' Mum went on. 'I wasn't well. Wasn't well at all. Lorna tried to get me help. She gave me loads of leaflets. Lorna's good like that. She told me to go and see this and that counsellor, but I wouldn't listen. Stubborn as a fat mule I was. Then one day I took you to the supermarket. I made sure you had your little soft ball that you liked. Pink and white – do you remember it? I didn't know what I was doing. I left you by the fish section. You were in your buggy. I left a feeding bottle with you, full of milk. I just walked away. Screaming the place down you was but I kept on going. I thought you'd be better off with someone else. So sorry, Mo.'

'Rinse it out good, Mum,' I said.

'In my stupid way, I've been trying to make it up to ya ever since,' Mum explained. 'I wanted to give ya a proper family, you know, find a decent guy who could be your daddy. Someone to love ya. You deserve that. Believe it or not, Mo, there are decent guys out there if you look hard enough. My dad was decent. Sam was ... is ...'

'*Mum!*' I blocked her flow. 'No guy out there is gonna make our lives all sweet and goodness. You can't rely on that, Mum. You gotta rely on yourself. Just me and you is OK.'

'But I tried so hard to find—'

'Mum! Put a full stop on it.'

Mum was thorough with my hair. She dried it, ran a hot tap over my brush and smoothed it out. I spied her via the bathroom mirror. She was humming something. Tears fell over her lips.

'I think I killed somebody, Mum.'

Mum paused. She wiped her eyes. She gazed at me.

'You're winding me up,' she said.

'No I'm not,' I replied calmly. 'I think I murdered Sean O'Shea. I know he's Lloyd's brother.'

She stared into the mirror. She swallowed. 'Mo, baby, don't joke about things like that.'

'Where d'you think the blood came from? Why d'you think I changed my garms?'

Mum backed away a step and brought a hand to her mouth. She retreated again till she hit the wall. 'Mo ...' she managed. Her eyes expanded into panic mode. 'Mo,' she tried again. 'Things haven't been great between us ... but you wouldn't lie to me about this? It's not your idea of—'

'No ... I'm not lying, Mum.'

She gave me a long eye-pass. I held her gaze.

'How?' she asked. 'Where?'

'Sococheeta. It wasn't meant to be me. We both went for a blade on the floor. I beat him to it.'

'But ... How? How did you get in?'

'Mum, it was him or me. I didn't mean it.'

Mum placed her hands on my shoulders. They were shaking. 'They'll come for ya, Mo. Lloyd was very close to his brother. His gang won't let it go. We'll have to move, Mo. Tonight! Did anyone recognise ya?'

'I don't know,' I replied.

'I'll pack our things,' Mum decided. 'Sean's gang are into allsorts. Cold-hearted they are. *Nasty* people. They don't care who they hurt. We gotta get out, Mo. I've got a friend in Anerley – Natalie. Always sends me Christmas cards, calls me on my birthday. She's for ever asking me when I'm coming down. I met her at that place I went to for battered women after I had you. I'll call her. Maybe she can come down tonight and get us. We can't stay here, Mo. Maybe we can—'

'I'm *not* going anywhere till I see Sam,' I cut her off.

'But we can't stay here, Mo! Sean's gang are brutal. *Nasty* people! Lloyd once told me ... I won't tell you that story but they won't care that you're only fifteen—'

'Then you go!' I raised my voice. 'Come for me later if you have to. I've gotta say goodbye to Sam first.'

Mum thought about it.

'All right then,' she said after a while. 'I'll Chubb the front door. You go to see Sam first thing in the morning. I'll get things ready. I'm gonna call Natalie now.'

Mum hot-stepped to fetch her phone. I heard her babbling away in the kitchen. I gazed at my reflection in the bathroom mirror and then I went to my room. I sat on my bed. I bent over double.

Still chatting on her mobile, Mum was clattering about in her bedroom, opening wardrobe doors and drawers.

My phone buzzed. It was Elaine. 'Are you all right, Mo? You looked a bit out of it when we left you.'

'I'm OK,' I said.

'You sure? If you want, when Mum goes to her bed I can come around, keep you company. What d'you say?'

I desperately wanted her to come over.

'No, I'm all right.'

'It's only me and you now, Mo. Can't believe Naomi's gone for real. We gotta stay tight. We've gotta stay together.'

I didn't have the heart to tell her I was fleeing too.

'I know,' I replied.

'Look after yourself, sistren. I'll check on you in the morning.'

'OK, thanks. Bye.'

I killed the call. I leaked tears again. *I've lost Naomi. I'm losing Sam. And I'm gonna lose Elaine too. Oh God! I don't deserve this.* I picked up my photo album, curled up on my bed and leafed through the pages.

29

Goodbye

I didn't know what time I fell asleep but when I woke my photo album was still in my hands. I spotted a suitcase standing beside my wardrobe. My chest of drawers was emptied. The curtains were pulled. Sunlight flooded my room. Guilt churned around in my belly. I climbed out of bed and made for the kitchen. Mum was wheeling her suitcase along the hallway; she parked it close to the front door.

'You're up, Mo! Natalie's gonna take us in for a week or until we sort ourselves out. She'll be here around half past ten. Is that all right with you?'

'I suppose so,' I replied. 'I need a drink.'

'D'you want breakfast, Mo? I can fry a couple of eggs?'

'No, it's all right.'

I found a carton of orange juice in the fridge. I poured myself a glass. I checked the time on the radio – 7.45 a.m.

I didn't bother lathering myself in the shower. Instead, I stood still, allowing the water to bounce off me. I closed my eyes. Twenty centimetres long. Two brass screws in the handle. White to instant red.

I brushed my hair for twenty minutes. I gazed into the mirror. I put a comb through it. Still wasn't satisfied. I pulled on my new cream sweater and light blue jeans. I wore the same trainers as last night – I hadn't bleached away Sean O'Shea's blood.

Mum stood by the front door. She had a lopsided smile where her mouth was curled, but her eyes betrayed her dread. 'Remember, Mo, Natalie will be here around ten-thirty. Give Sam my love. I'm gonna pop in and see Lorna if she's home. I'll give her my spare set of keys but I won't tell her we're going away. Is that all right with you?'

'I suppose so,' I replied.

She opened the front door for me, a mixture of panic and love on her face. I said my goodbye and headed down the stairwell with Mum watching me like a presidential body-guard. I avoided the seventh step.

It took me five minutes to reach the bus stop. My phone sang. It was Elaine. I couldn't answer it. I fought back the tears. I couldn't stop the primal *'Aaaarrrrgggghhh,'* that burst from my mouth. I closed my eyes and tried to get my breathing on point. Then I checked the mobile that Manjaro had given me. Shit! I was supposed to fling it away. It had two messages from Early B. I opened the first one.

Sorry to tell you. Folly Ranks has passed. His name will be written large. RIP!

I checked the second text.

Sean O'Shea's light is out. Hit the pillows and keep a low profile. Throw away this phone.

The bus arrived. There were seats available. I decided to stand. I felt all eyes were locking on me. *Murderer!*

I jumped off at Crongton General. I came to a decision. I knew what I had to do. I hot-stepped along the corridors, holding the tears off. I made it to the intensive care unit. Lorna was in the waiting room, talking to a doctor. I approached her. Tears drowned her eyes but she was smiling.

'Thank you,' she said to the doctor.

She turned around to face me. She struggled to find words. She opened her arms and I accepted her embrace. 'God is good,' she said finally. 'He does listen!'

She let me go.

'They called me just over an hour ago,' she said. 'He's out of his coma! They tell me he should make a full recovery.'

Lorna wiped my tears away. 'Go and see him,' she urged. 'He knows you've been here every day. Go on. Go and see him!'

I entered Sam's room. The tubes were gone. The bleeps had quit. His head was bandaged. The skin around his eyes had darkened. I sat down beside him and tapped him on his shoulder. He opened his eyes. He tried to smile.

'Mo,' he said weakly.

'Sam.'

'I've been out of it for the longest time,' he said. 'Everything is stiff. It pains me to move.'

'What d'you expect?' I said. 'You've been lazing in that bed for weeks.'

Sam's eyes locked on my own for a long minute. 'Mum told me,' his voice dropped. 'Mum told me you've been coming to see me every day since I've been in here.'

I nodded.

'I appreciate that to the max,' he said. 'I need nuff physio to get my muscles on point again but when I get out of here I'm gonna ...'

His face curled into that delicious smile of his. 'I'm gonna whup your ass at b-ball. See if I don't! You know I've been letting you win.'

'In your dreams,' I replied.

I closed my eyes. Curved. Twenty centimetres long. Two brass screws in the black handle.

'Would you wait for me, Sam?'

'What d'you mean, Mo? Wait for what?'

'Don't worry about what,' I said. 'Answer the question! Would you wait for me?'

Sam gazed at me, his face morphed into a question mark. 'Of course,' he said. 'It's not even debateable.'

'You promise?' I insisted.

He looked at me hard again. 'What's this about, Mo?'

'Do you *promise*?'

'Yes ... yes I do. You've always been there for me, Mo.'

'Soul blood?'

'Soul blood,' he repeated.

I placed my hands around his jaws and kissed him gently on the mouth. His lips were dry. The skin around his nostrils looked sore. I pecked him on both cheeks. My lips lingered. The wispy hairs of his trainee moustache tickled my cheeks.

'I've gotta step,' I said.

'Mo?'

'Remember your promise,' I said. 'Soul blood.'

I stood up and left his room. I couldn't turn around.

'Mo?'

I didn't stop to say goodbye to Lorna. By the time I hit the lift I'd doubled up in pain. I managed to compose myself at the bus stop. I caught the 159 to central Crongton. I parked at the back, holding my head within my hands. I closed my eyes. Someone next to me mentioned it might rain today. Another replied it might brighten up later on. Sean O'Shea would never feel rain again. And the sun's warm rays would no more bless Folly Ranks.

I threw the phone that Manjaro had given me in the Crongton stream. I marched along the High Street. I bounced up the steps of the police station. I pushed through the swing doors. A female fed was scribbling something down behind a shoulder-high counter. I approached her. She looked up. I uploaded a long breath and locked my gaze in the spot between her eyebrows. She had pretty violet eyes. Her mouth curled up as she half-smiled to greet me. I exhaled.

'I think I killed somebody last night ...' I said. 'I didn't mean to.'

If any of the issues in this book have affected you, you might find some of the following organisations helpful.

ChildLine
ChildLine is the free helpline for young people in the UK. You can call, email or chat online to them confidentially about any problem you might have.

Confidential helpline: 0800 1111
Website: http://www.childline.org.uk/

Gangsline
Gangsline is a non-profit organisation established in 2007 to provide help and support to young men and women involved in gang culture.

Confidential helpline: 0800 032 9538
Website: https://www.gangsline.com

The Mix
The Mix aims to find young people aged thirteen to twenty-five the best help whatever the problem. They offer online articles and videos, plus telephone and email helplines, peer-to-peer and counselling services.

Confidential helpline: 0808 808 4994
Website: http://www.themix.org.uk/

NSPCC

Whether you're thinking about joining a gang, are already involved or want to leave, you can call the NSPCC's 24-hour helpline anonymously or find out more information on their website.

Confidential helpline: 0808 800 5000
Website: http://www.nspcc.org.uk/preventing-abuse/
keeping-children-safe/staying-safe-away-from-home/
gangs-young-people/

Safe

Run by the Metropolitan Police, Safe is a website that provides information and advice on many different aspects of life, specifically for young people, including gangs and group violence and knife and gun crime.

Website: http://www.safe.met.police.uk/

Young Minds

Young Minds offers offer information to young people and children about mental health and emotional wellbeing.

Website: http://www.youngminds.org.uk/
for_children_young_people

ACKNOWLEDGEMENTS

Nuff gratitude and thanks to my editor supreme, Sarah Castleton – you always pose the right questions and extract the very best out of me. A big Crongton roar to the Atom team behind me, Olivia, Stephanie, Sam, James and everyone else at Little, Brown. Take another bow Ms Laura Susijn, my agent – thanks for everything. Special mention to Clara Susijn, the first reader of *Straight Outta Crongton* (I hope you get top ratings at school for this).

Crongton fist bumps to Irenosen Okojie who unwittingly tossed me the seed that led to the flowering of Mo Baker – thanks for all your encouragement and making me believe I can get inside a fifteen-year-old girl's head. Crongton high fives to so many who have offered their unwavering support over the years: Courttia Newland, Yvvette Edwards, Sandra Agard, Sunny Singh, Yvonne Archer, Ethosheia Hylton, Nadifa Mohammed, Malorie Blackman, Devon Thomas, Paul Gilroy, Rosie Canning, Vanessa Walters, Tim O'Dell, Lemn Sissay, Patricia Cumper, Alan Gibbons, Patrice Lawrence, Deborah Badoo, Tony Bradman, Maggie Norris, Words of Colour, The Hackney Christmas Dinner crew, The Big House project, Lambeth College and schools up and down the country who have welcomed me with nuff fanfare, mint teas and custard creams into their staff rooms and assembly halls. Special shoulder bumps to the judges of the *Guardian* Children's Fiction Prize 2016, David Almond, SF Said & Kate Saunders. I am eternally grateful – you made my mother sooooo proud.

A big mention to all you librarians out there – we children's and YA authors couldn't survive or be initially inspired without you. Last but not least a massive Crongton salute to all you readers out there. Thank you very much. More from Crongton ends coming soon . . .